Schrödinger's cat has far more than nine lives, and far fewer. All of us are unknowing cats, alive and dead at once, and of all the might-have-beens in between, we record only one.

Yoon Ha Lee, *Conservation of Shadows*

In fact, the mere act of opening the box will determine the state of the cat, although in this case there were three determinate states the cat could be in: these being Alive, Dead, and Bloody Furious.

Terry Pratchett, *Lords and Ladies*

Chapter	CONTENTS	Page
1	2045	1
2	Ryker	8
3	Scott	13
4	Bullets	16
5	Deductions	21
6	McGuire's dream	27
7	Jace's nightmare	32
8	Dancing in the dark	36
9	The dark side	41
10	A dark night in future London	47
11	The wrong question	53
12	The answer to the right question	58
13	Back to the future	66
14	Kayla	76
15	Traces	84
16	Loot	88
17	Careless	92
18	Escape	99
19	Time tourism	105
20	A blank page	113
21	A nice little earner	120
22	Section 27 Clause 8	124

Chapter	Page
23 A brief history of time travel	130
24 Floss's new flat	138
25 Mutual charm offensive	145
26 A night at the opera	155
27 Exploring London	163
28 A walk in the park	168
29 An idea and an inference	173
30 Mini-break in 2015	178
31 The mad scheme	185
32 Missing person	192
33 Gone fishing	200
34 Back to the past	208
35 Time is, time was, time is past	219
36 The answer?	224
37 Reunion	229
38 Confrontation	237
39 Quinn gets a present, Floss and Jace get a pizza	245
40 Expect the unexpected	253
41 Parting and meeting	256
42 The meaning of life	263
43 Floss's team	270

CHAPTER 1

2045

It's hard to arrest a man who owns a time travel device; if he sees you coming he can press a couple of buttons and be sometime else. For this reason, Jace had been in favour of a honey trap. Kayla could have picked him up, no problem; one wide-eyed gaze from her violet eyes, a flutter of dark lashes, and McGuire would have followed her anywhere, tongue hanging out. But at the briefing in the deserted IEMA headquarters that Saturday evening, as they sat round Quinn's desk in a pool of light, Quinn overruled this.

"He's dangerous. If he smells a rat Kayla would be vulnerable."

"She can handle him," Jace said. "The guy's a stick insect. A child could push him over with one finger."

"Thank you," said Kayla.

"Let alone Kayla with her superb combat skills," he added, too late. She gave him a look.

Quinn shook his head decisively. "We'll do this by the book. A raid at first light, surprise him while he's asleep. You and me at the front, Kayla and the others round the back in case he runs for it." He turned to Kayla. "Bring Scott."

"Is that a good idea? He's had no experience."

"He won't get experience sitting in the office. I'll keep an eye on him. We'll meet here tomorrow at zero five hundred hours."

Kayla emailed Scott, then Quinn got to his feet. The meeting was over. In the lift Jace put his arm around Kayla's waist. "Stay at my place tonight."

"Hmm. Not sure you deserve it."

"I'm thinking of you! It's nearer for tomorrow."

"I suppose that's true . . ."

Jace pressed her against the elevator wall and kissed her, drinking in her perfume, feeling the muscles beneath delectable curves. He murmured, "Why don't we get married?"

She gave him a slow smile. "Now that's a novel idea. Never been asked that before. I'll give it some thought."

The lift doors parted and they walked hand in hand through the warm spring night towards Jace's flat.

In the pale Sunday light of a May dawn, Jace, Quinn and Scott stood outside the derelict warehouse, dressed in dark trousers and hoodies. The day was colder than it looked.

Though he must have been on a dozen IEMA raids by now, Jace still got the adrenaline rush, the sensation of being extra alive, every sound, sight and smell heightened. Going by Scott's trembling hands, bright eyes and flushed face, their new recruit evidently felt the same. Jace's doubts about him resurfaced. Not that he wasn't intelligent. He was. He was also enthusiastic – if anything, too enthusiastic. Scott was young, had only been on the team three weeks, and tended to be impulsive. To Jace's mind, he should be with Kayla, not here at the sharp end where he was likely to get in the way. Still, at least he wasn't lumbered with him.

Quinn nodded to Jace. Silently they moved in opposite directions, hugging the wall in case McGuire glanced out of one of the huge windows. He had no reason to expect them, but most likely he'd have the TiTrav on his wrist and they weren't taking chances. Funny that Quinn thought him dangerous; had told them to shoot if necessary. Jace was the only one of the team to have encountered McGuire before, and he didn't think the man clever enough to be dangerous – he was a loser, a drifter, a jackal hovering round others' prey, easily scared. He wondered how someone as useless as him had managed to get hold of a TiTrav in the first place. They'd only been on the open market for six days in 2032 before the World Government passed a hasty bill to outlaw their sale, possession and use. No one knew how many illicit TiTravs were still in circulation, but the number probably wasn't in double figures.

Jace picked his way over fallen masonry and scrubby plants till he reached the small door within the big one and slipped inside, careful to avoid crunching the broken plaster that littered the floor. He waited for his eyesight to adjust so he could check for tripwires, though he couldn't imagine McGuire setting traps. Pale shafts of sunlight from high windows traversed a vast dim space dotted with pillars. He couldn't see Kayla and Farouk, but they'd be there, concealed in the shadows at the back. Above him was a low mezzanine, reached by spiral staircases at either end.

Quinn, followed by Scott, appeared beside the far staircase. Quinn got out his weapon and lifted his thumb to signal Go. They began to climb the stairs, stealthily, making no sound.

Jace slowed as his head levelled with the mezzanine's dusty floorboards. Staying at the side, he gradually moved upwards until he could see the long narrow space bordered by a scabby white wall on the left, a metal railing on the right. Sunshine streamed through the window, illuminating a sleeping bag curled like a grub on a mattress on the floor. Someone was inside the sleeping bag. At the top of the second staircase, two faces appeared. Jace frowned. He had assumed Scott would be left at the bottom of the staircase. They moved slowly towards each other, closing in on the mattress. The floorboards creaked beneath their feet and they stopped. Quinn nodded.

Jace switched on his vidcam and shouted, "McGuire! On your feet! Hands in the air where I can see them."

The sleeping bag writhed and a pale face appeared, topped with chaotic hair. Hands emerged, then shoulders and torso clad in a thick over-sized sweater. McGuire wriggled his scrawny limbs out of the sleeping bag, eyes on Jace, hands above his head. The baggy sleeves slipped a little. Not seeing a TiTrav on either of his wrists, Jace relaxed, put his gun away and got out flexicuffs. Hardly worth cuffing this pathetic figure, but Quinn had said to do things by the book.

McGuire made an effort to sound affronted. "What d'you want me for?"

"Peter William McGuire, acting as an officer of the International Event Modification Authority I am arresting you on suspicion of committing timecrime and being in illegal possession of a TiTrav. You will be given the opportunity to contact a lawyer in due course. You do not have to answer our questions. Everything you do and say is being filmed and may be used as evidence against you."

"I haven't done anything! I'm innocent! You've got no proof."

"Then you have nothing to worry about. After a few unproductive but cordial hours with the time team at IEMA you can go back to bed. I don't expect you've much else on this morning – urgent appointments, people to see, things like that? Nah. I'll buy you breakfast." He lifted the cuffs. "Turn around."

Grudgingly, McGuire turned. He saw Quinn and Scott for the first time, and it was as if an electric shock went through his body. Before Jace could react, he had leaped for the railing and vaulted over. As they all rushed to the rail, they heard the thump when he landed. For a moment, seeing McGuire motionless in a heap on the floor, Jace thought he was dead. Then McGuire jumped to his feet and ran.

Quinn said, "Jace, after him."

As Jace sprinted for the spiral stairs, a sound made him swivel. Quinn and Scott both had their guns out. He yelled, "Don't shoot! He's not got it!" but his voice was obliterated by gunfire. Jace raced to the foot of the stairs.

Alone in the middle of the wide space McGuire lay face down on the gritty boards like a pile of old rags, as ruined as the building. Jace ran to him and turned his limp bony frame over. Faded blue eyes stared unblinking at the ceiling. One bullet had hit his right arm below the elbow in textbook style, the other gone straight through his heart. Jace pulled up McGuire's left sleeve. As he'd thought, no TiTrav. He tried his right wrist, then his pockets; a packet of grey-market legal highs, a dataphone, a couple of thousand pound notes. Nothing of importance. No weapon. His death had been a stupid, unnecessary mishap. He got slowly to his feet as the others gathered round. Scott's face was drained of colour and he was shaking.

Jace said to Quinn, "Why did you shoot? Didn't you see his wrists were bare?"

"No. You were closer than we were. You should have told us."

"I thought you knew! You saw me put my gun away because I didn't need it. I was talking to the guy!"

"He's dead. This discussion is irrelevant. Get the body collected and taken to the pathologist. Tell him I want the autopsy done straight away." As Jace got out his phone, Quinn turned to Scott. "Don't take it to heart. These things happen. It's hard to shoot a moving target accurately in the heat of the moment. And McGuire's no great loss to humanity." Scott stared dumbly at him. Quinn put a hand on his arm and said, his voice sympathetic, "I take full responsibility for bringing you on this mission. You have nothing to answer for." He turned to the others, who looked shaken and sombre. "Now find the TiTrav. We know he had one. It has to be here."

McGuire's death cast a pall over the day. The atmosphere was subdued, lacking the usual light-hearted jokes and banter. As the light faded that evening, Quinn gathered his team together. They had carried out an inch by inch search of the entire warehouse with barely a break. After this proved fruitless they had scanned the building and surrounding area with metal detectors. The TiTrav hadn't been found. Everyone was getting tired and tetchy, except Scott who was tired and silent. Quinn looked round the group.

"Theories?"

Scott stared at his boots. Farouk rubbed his hands over his grimy face, making it grimier. "Are we sure he even had it to begin with?"

"The alert came from his house."

Kayla said, "Yes, but it didn't *have* to be him flicking the switch. We made the assumption his landlady was telling the truth. Perhaps she wasn't. Perhaps there was someone else in the house."

"She seemed okay to me," Jace said. "Why would she lie?"

"Covering up for someone?"

"I suppose it's possible . . ."

Farouk said, "Here's another idea: he could have hidden it somewhere we can't get at, like buried six feet down where the detectors won't reach."

Jace shook his head. "Can't see McGuire doing that. Too much work. And the ground's not disturbed."

"He could have hidden it somewhere else entirely."

Kayla said, "I think his instinct would have been to keep it close. Maybe he sold it on. We could check out places he might do that."

Jace was already scrolling through the contacts list on McGuire's dataphone. He looked up. "I might have guessed.

Ryker. This could be the time we pin something on the slippery bastard."

CHAPTER 2

Ryker

The team made a brief stop at a pizza restaurant to refuel, with the exception of Scott, whom they dropped off at his home. While they ate, Quinn filled out, filed and printed a search warrant; not the first for Ryker's premises. They'd pulled him in a couple of times too, but had failed to get anywhere on either occasion. Officially, the man remained as clean as a whistle.

Ryker's workshop was under a railway arch south of the river. In contravention of the terms of his commercial lease he lived there too, so was likely to be in, though it was now 8.45 on a Sunday evening. When they emerged on to the pavement the pod they had ordered waited for them, glowing in the dark, blue light on to show it was picking up. They stepped inside, Jace told it the name of a street round the corner from Ryker's and the pod glided off. Rain spattered against its curved glass windows; Jace stared out, yawning. It had been a long discouraging day, and wasn't over yet.

As they neared their destination the streets got less like anywhere you'd want to live; rundown, neglected and looking their worst in the rain and the streetlights' harsh glare. The pod let them out in a main road with mean brick buildings on either side, ripe for redevelopment. They followed the pavement under a railway bridge, and turned right into an unlit dead end lined with Victorian railway arches, each housing a small business. Only one had light shining through high up windows in the bricked-in arch; above the door bell a cracked plastic plate offered:

RYKER
Robotics Engineer
BEWARE OF THE DOG

Quinn pressed the bell push. Immediately a frenzied barking started up the other side of the door. Jace pounded the wooden panels, making as much noise as the dog, playing the role of hard cop. "Open up, Ryker, or we'll break the fucking door down."

Kayla murmured, "There's nothing quite like a charm offensive to win friends and influence people."

Jace grinned at her as the grating sound of heavy bolts being moved replaced the barking. The door opened and Ryker stood on the threshold, lean, scruffy and hostile, a big German Shepherd beside him. Muffled shots sounded from a film playing on the computer in front of an upholstered swivel chair; on the desk stood three bottles of beer and a half-eaten carton of fast food, the accoutrements of his interrupted cosy evening.

Quinn handed him the search warrant. Ryker read it sourly, then stood aside to let them in. Though things being worked on lay about, the place was organized, with no extraneous clutter. More workshop than home, the workbenches, a small forge, lathes, a pillar drill and a milling machine occupied most of the area. The computer desk was at the back, and bed and kitchen units fitted in where they could round the edges of the space, jostled by racks and shelves. The benches were littered with tools and electronic bits and pieces. Damp and crusted lime discoloured the brick-built arch of the ceiling.

Quinn sat in the one comfortable chair as if it were his, switched off the computer's sound, and helped himself to a chip. Like Jace, Quinn was over six foot, but a little heavier, his neck nearly as wide as his close-cropped head. This might have given him an air of menace, but for the intelligence and humour in his eyes. He swivelled gently to and fro, watched by everyone in the room. Jace wondered how he managed to exude authority so effortlessly.

Finally Quinn said pleasantly, "We arrested a friend of yours today, Mr Ryker. Peter McGuire. Have you seen him lately?"

Ryker's eyes were stony. "As it happens, he dropped by yesterday. What of it?"

"Why did he come to see you?"

Ryker shrugged. "He was in the area. We had a bit of a chat."

"What about?"

"This and that."

"Did he have a TiTrav with him?"

"If he did, I didn't see it."

"Our information suggests he may have left one here with you, maybe for repair."

Ryker said piously, "Repairing a TiTrav would be timecrime. Unless it was for you lot, obviously, when I'd be pleased to help, and do keep me in mind should you have the need. Otherwise I wouldn't touch it. I'm strictly legit."

There was a pause. "If I hit him," Jace suggested to Quinn, "he might get a bit more cooperative. Shall I?"

"No need for that," Quinn said, getting to his feet. "Mr Ryker, would you open that safe for me?"

Ryker's safe was so old it opened with a key. Inside were a dozen dataphones and a small bundle of bank notes. Quinn counted them before putting them back and letting Ryker shut the safe.

"Most honest citizens don't have a use for cash," Quinn remarked. He turned to his team. "Search him. Then take the place apart. Remember we could be looking for a dismantled TiTrav."

The search that followed went on into the small hours, and Jace's conviction right from the start that they were wasting their time didn't make it any more fun. Not that he believed in Ryker's innocence; he didn't. But the man's demeanour was the giveaway. Ryker wasn't anxious. He sat impassively throughout and watched them, waiting for them to finish and go. The dog watched them too. So did Quinn, between bouts of trawling through the computer; but while he watched he wandered around, picking things up and putting them down again.

Jace took photographs while Farouk summoned the van with the equipment. When it arrived, they unloaded ladders and a platform, put on vinyl gloves and systematically examined every inch of the ceiling, looking for a concealed hiding place behind a loose brick. Grit fell in their eyes as they worked and the dust made them sneeze. Finding nothing, they moved on to the machines and workbenches.

There was only one small piece of excitement all evening. Jace was testing hand power tools on one of the benches to make sure the TiTrav wasn't hidden in any of the casings when Farouk, on his knees behind the kitchen units, jumped up and used an expression that had not been heard to pass his lips before.

Jace said, "Fuck me, that's a first. I thought swearing was haram?"

"He got it from you," Kayla said. "You're a terrible influence. Are you okay, Farouk?"

Farouk kicked the cabinet. His foot went straight through the flimsy panel. "A bastard mousetrap got my fingers!"

Quinn looked up from the computer screen and told him to calm down. Ryker cracked his only smile of the evening, which drew Quinn's attention to him.

"I'm finding a surprising number of TiTrav resources in your files. Technical stuff, service software, updates, diagrams, coding . . . I doubt our own technicians have as much. I'm wondering why anyone without a TiTrav would need this."

"It's interesting," Ryker said. "It's my hobby."

They applied stickers as they went, a different colour for each operative, so that nowhere would be missed or gone over twice. These were left in situ. By the time they'd exhausted every possible hiding place – and many impossible ones – it looked as if a hurricane en route from a giant's wedding had spread confetti through the workshop. The team communicated in monosyllables, working mechanically, longing to get home. Two unproductive searches in one day was two too many. When they ran out of places to search, they stood in a disconsolate group, tacitly admitting defeat.

"We're done here," said Quinn.

"Happy now?" said Ryker, standing up. "I suppose there's no chance of an apology for time wasted and nuisance caused. If you lot will bugger off I'll tidy up and go to bed."

"Mr Ryker, on behalf of IEMA I apologize," said Quinn. "Once again you emerge without a stain on your character. Few people have been so frequently subjected to repeated scrutiny and found to be blameless. I can only congratulate you on your record and hope you retain it."

They were halfway to the door when Quinn turned. "Perhaps I should tell you, as you were his friend, that Peter McGuire resisted arrest this morning. So we shot him. Dead. Goodnight."

CHAPTER 3

Scott

The elevator reached the tenth floor and Jace opened the door to his rented studio flat, three hundred square feet and a balcony in Hoxton. Fleetingly, he considered having a shower, then decided in favour of immediate sleep. He pressed the button to lower the bed out of the wall and took off his jacket.

The doorbell rang.

Cursing, he walked to the entry phone. Scott's face filled the screen.

"What is it?"

"Can I come up and talk to you?"

"At this hour? What about? Can't it wait till morning?"

"I'd really rather talk to you now, if you don't mind."

Jace pressed the lock release, then went to the kitchen area and put the kettle on. He heard the clunk of the lift doors and went to let Scott in.

"Coffee?"

"No thanks. I've been in the bar over the road all evening waiting for you to come back." He smiled nervously. "Too much coffee."

"Take a seat." Scott sat on the edge of the sofa. The kettle boiled and Jace made himself coffee. He put it on the table in front of the sofa, then got out the bottle of brandy and a couple of glasses.

"Shoot. Brandy?"

"Oh, thanks, yes please. Did you find anything at Ryker's?"

"Not a solitary time travelling sausage."

There was a lengthy pause. Scott sipped his brandy. Jace glanced at the clock. *Jesus, 3.10.* "Look, it's been a long day, so if you could get to the point . . ."

Scott jumped. "Sorry, yes. Okay. I don't know if you know this, but my mother married an American so I lived in the States for a while." Jace shook his head. "I went to college there. My stepdad was a pistol shooter, very keen. I did a lot of shooting with him. I think he hoped I'd take it up professionally. He'd won the World Speed Shooting Championship in 2035, and he reckoned I was good enough to follow in his footsteps. I didn't want to take it that seriously, I had other priorities, but I did a lot of practice." Scott finished his brandy in one gulp and met Jace's eyes. "Which means that when I shoot a man who's sixty feet away intending to hit him in the lower arm, then that's where I hit him."

There was a pause. Jace said, "So you're saying Quinn killed McGuire?"

"I know I didn't."

"What do you want me to do about it?"

Scott flushed. He looked down, then up again. "Nothing, I guess. If I'm honest I just don't like everybody thinking it was my bad aim that killed a man, when it wasn't."

"Well, now I know it too."

"Really? You believe me?"

"Maybe."

Scott frowned, hesitated and said, "Analysis of the bullets

would prove whose gun fired which shot."

"Right. They won't do that as a matter of course. You'd need authorization."

"Who from?"

"Ah well. Quinn."

Scott's face fell. Jace said, "Probably not the best idea, three weeks into a new job, to try to prove your boss got something wrong. Won't improve your promotion prospects. I'll have a think about it, but maybe don't mention it to anyone else for now. It might be best to let it go. Quinn's made it clear he'll ensure you don't get into any trouble over it."

After Scott had left, Jace walked to the window and stared out at the city lights, wide awake again, analysing, balancing probabilities. Scott had clearly believed what he said; but on the whole, Jace was inclined to think him mistaken. He might be as good a shot as he claimed, but he had been nervous and excited, and had never fired at a human being before.

There was another reason the team had all believed Scott's shot to be the fatal one. Quinn was good with a pistol, too; seven years before, he'd been part of the British Olympic shooting team in Detroit, and won gold.

CHAPTER 4

Bullets

When Jace arrived for the meeting on Monday morning, only Kayla had got there before him. Quinn, sitting at his computer, glanced up and smiled. "You're early too."

He returned his attention to the screen, and Jace sat at the round table with Kayla to wait for the others, trying not to yawn after the short night. Quinn's office was cool; he had a weakness for elaborate clothes – the jacket he wore was black damask, with a high collar, and rows of silver buttons – but he liked his furnishings plain. The only decoration in his office consisted of contrasting textures of marble, glass, slate and steel. A clutter of transparent plastic on one end of the big desk added an incongruous note. Always inquisitive, Jace got up again to see what it was.

Individually packed in tamper-evident bags were McGuire's possessions that had been taken from his body. As well as the items from his pockets Jace had already seen, there was the microchip from his arm, two small bar-coded bags containing cartridges, and two similar bags each containing a bullet. The labels read:

IEMA Pathology Department1/2
NAME: Peter William McGuire

DATE OF DEATH: 14th May 2045
ITEM: bullet
LOCATION: lower arm
NOTES:

IEMA Pathology Department 2/2
NAME: Peter William McGuire
DATE OF DEATH: 14th May 2045
ITEM: bullet
LOCATION: heart
NOTES: 2/2 bullets, cause of death

"His effects should have gone straight to Records," Quinn said, seeing Jace pick over the bags. "I doubt he had family. The taxpayer will be funding his funeral." He removed the dataphone, put everything else back into a larger bag and moved it to the top of a cabinet.

While he was doing this the door opened and Scott and Farouk walked in together. Quinn joined his team at the table, switched on the vidcam and opened the meeting.

"As you all know – with the possible exception of Scott – McGuire's TiTrav is the first we've had wind of in the UK for nearly six months. I don't need to tell you the potential consequences of having one of these things on the loose. Our absolute priority is to find it, and we need to do that within the next few days. Everyone in IEMA has their eye on us. If we fail, the Americans will send a team, and there is no way I am going to have that happen while I am running this department. So, let's have your ideas."

Kayla said, "McGuire may have had no family – and I'll be checking that – but he must have had associates besides Ryker. He got his drugs from someone, for one thing –"

She was cut short by a knock on the door. Quinn looked up in irritation as the door opened and a young woman entered.

"Mr Quinn, I'm sorry to interrupt, but Sir Douglas would like you to come to his office immediately."

Sir Douglas Calhoun was IEMA UK's chief executive. Quinn got to his feet and looked round the table. "We'll finish this later, by which time I'd like you to have come up with some leads." He ripped McGuire's dataphone out of its plastic bag and handed it to Jace. "You can start by checking out every contact on here." He followed the young woman out of the room.

The others stayed in the office for a few minutes, discussing possibilities, then got up to go.

"If only McGuire hadn't got himself shot. A man like that, he'd have told us anything we wanted to know if we only surrounded him and frowned a bit," Farouk said tactlessly. "Would have saved us a lot of work."

Scott stirred but said nothing.

Jace said, "At least it's not one of the early TiTravs. If someone's got it we'll know the minute they turn it on. Which makes it pretty useless, really."

There was another knock on the door and a man's head appeared. He looked around. "Mr Quinn not here?" He pointed to the bag of evidence. "Do you know if he's finished with those yet so I can take them down to Records?"

"Yes, take them," said Jace.

The rest of the day they spent attempting to trace McGuire's contacts. It turned out he did have one living relative, a daughter. She was seventeen, and her name was Saffron McGuire. It seemed a surname was all he had given her; her parents had not been together for long, and never married. Her mother had brought her up alone. Jace sent Kayla to see Saffron, with the idea she might find a female cop more sympathetic. She'd just lost her father, after all, even if they'd had little contact.

Kayla returned an hour or so later. Jace looked up from his online search, which was not going well. The only promising lead from McGuire's dataphone turned out to have been in prison for the past six months. "How did you get on?"

Kayla dumped her handbag on Jace's desk and pulled up a chair. "I didn't see her. She locked herself in her bedroom and wouldn't come out."

"Did she say anything through the door?"

"Yes. 'Fuck off'."

"Ah. What about her mother?"

"She was quite friendly. She's got a boyfriend who lives in the flat. They've been together for five years."

"Did she say anything useful?"

"No. She was happy to chat, she made me a cup of tea, but she hasn't seen McGuire for years. Said she should never have got involved with him, he was always a waster, but she was just a teenager and didn't know any better. He was good-looking, apparently, when he was young. She wasn't surprised he'd come to a sticky end. Nor particularly upset, either."

"Did you ask about the TiTrav?"

"Yes, and she tut-tutted and said he never had any sense."

"D'you think by any remote chance he might have given it to his daughter to hide?"

"Gwen – that's the mother – said Saffron hadn't seen him since her birthday three weeks before."

"As far as she knows. It's a pity you didn't get to talk to the girl."

"I really doubt she'd have it. Even McGuire wouldn't be irresponsible enough to involve his child in timecrime, surely."

"True. I have a feeling we won't find it. I reckon it's just a matter of time till we're all trying through gritted teeth to be very polite and welcoming to our American counterparts."

Before leaving the building, Jace went down to Records to collect McGuire's two thousand pounds. He had downloaded all the data from McGuire's phone, and intended to deliver it and the money to the daughter on his way home. Of course, these items could just as well be handed over with the meagre belongings from his rented room, once the team had finished with them, but Jace had an ulterior motive. He'd need to log her chip to acknowledge receipt, and he couldn't do that through a door. Maybe face to face she'd find it harder to refuse to talk.

The man in Records peeled open the big plastic bag and tipped the contents on the counter. "Just the money, sir?"

"Yes . . ." Jace picked it up. That left four bags. He frowned – surely there had been more than this when he last saw them? He rifled through them: drugs, chip, cartridge 1/2, cartridge 2/2.

"Is this everything?"

"That's what I collected this morning from Mr Quinn's office, sir."

Jace hesitated, said, "Thanks," and turned to go.

The two tamper-proof bags containing the bullets that had been removed from McGuire's body were missing.

CHAPTER 5

Deductions

Outside Records Jace thumbed Quinn's number into his phone, and reached his voicemail. This was not a surprise. Quinn did not like being at the beck and call of a dataphone, and frequently turned it off. Jace didn't leave a message. He ordered a pod and went to call on Saffron McGuire.

Saffron and her mother lived in a tower block in Haggerston dating from the 1960s. The flats, originally built for allocation to council tenants rather than selection by buyers on the open market, lacked any sort of visual appeal. They were surrounded by muddy grass bordered by metal barriers redolent of a prison. He rang the bell and told Saffron's mother who he was; the release clicked. The lift ground its way upwards in slow motion. Jace deliberately hadn't rung to say he was coming, and he hoped Saffron wasn't descending in one lift as he rose at a stately pace in the other. He reached the seventeenth floor and a plump woman in her thirties with a pleasant smile opened the door. Jace explained his errand and Gwen asked him in. He followed her into the living room, where a man watching television looked up briefly, then back to the screen.

The flat seemed huge, compared to his own – though with low ceilings and badly-proportioned windows, and of course no built-in robotics.

"I don't know if she'll talk to you," Gwen said, apologetically. "She was quite rude to the lady who came this morning. Teenagers, what can you do? Of course, you have to make allowances, she's upset over what happened to Peter – her dad. Would you like a cup of tea?"

"That's very kind, but no thanks. Would you tell Saffron I have her father's phone for her? I'll need to log her chip before I hand it over."

Gwen went back into the hall and called through a closed door. "Saffy?" Jace moved a little so he could see her. "There's a gentleman from IEMA wants to talk to you." A brief muffled response came through the door, which Jace couldn't make out because of the noise of the television. "He's got your father's phone, if you'll come out."

After a moment or two the door opened and Saffron emerged, a small whirlwind of colour and fury. Jace's eyebrows went up. In a world where women's fashion dealt in understatement and elegance, Saffron's appearance was arresting, to say the least. Her hair was a mixture of blonde, red, pink and black, her eyes were black-rimmed in a pale face, and there was a stud through her lower lip. She wore a black string vest and a multi-coloured full skirt, teamed with black tights full of holes, and heavy boots that laced up to the knee. Her eyes narrowed as she glared up at him.

"My name is Jace Carnady, Miss McGuire. I'm sorry about your loss."

"No you're not. You're just saying that. Give me his phone."

"I'd like to have a quick word with you first, if you don't mind."

"I do mind. I've got nothing to say to any of you time police scum."

"Saffy!"

"It's all right," Jace said. He didn't blame the girl. But for his team's errors her father would be alive. If he'd only told Quinn the man was unarmed and not wearing a TiTrav instead of assuming he knew, or if Scott and Quinn had both hit his arm like they should have done, he wouldn't be here. She hated the lot of them, and she was right to do so. This had been a wasted journey.

He got out his dataphone and brought up the reader. Saffron turned so her upper arm faced him. She had a circle tattooed round the faint dimple that indicated the site of the chip, decorated with skulls and roses, with a scroll saying FREEDOM DIED HERE and an arrow pointing at the circle. With a beep, the reader identified her and Jace put his phone away. He got out McGuire's phone and the two thousand pounds and gave them to the girl. She started towards her bedroom, then turned and came back, right up to Jace, staring into his eyes. Her face was pretty, he realized, in spite of her expression of contempt; heart-shaped, with big eyes and full lips. She was so close he could see that beneath the black makeup, her eyes were swollen; bloodshot too.

"Actually, on second thoughts, I have got something to say to you. My dad was a good man. Maybe not always on the right side of the law, but he did his best with what life doled out to him, which wasn't much." Tears came into her eyes and she blinked them away furiously. "When I got older he started to talk to me properly, tell me stuff he didn't tell anyone else. About his life and everything. He used to wait for me outside school and we'd go to a café or the park." Jace was aware of Gwen stiffening beside him. She hadn't known about this. "And according to him, there's a bigger villain inside bleeding IEMA than you'll ever find outside of it. You're all a load of wankers."

Jace said, "If you have any information –" but Saffron had already spun on her heel and headed for the bedroom. She slammed the door behind her.

Jace was back in the derelict warehouse, except it was darker and smaller and partly his flat. He stood alone on the mezzanine looking down over the railing to where Quinn stood in a pool of light with Scott. At any moment, a bad, a terrible thing was going to happen. As Jace thought, *I have to do something*, he woke, heart pumping fast.

"Light."

He sat up. The clock told him it was a quarter to five. For a moment he didn't move. He breathed deeply, feeling disturbed. His subconscious was trying to get some message through to his conscious brain. Something wasn't right about McGuire's death and the missing TiTrav. He got out of bed, sat at his computer and dictated notes in an attempt to make sense of what he knew. He started with the obvious:

- Unless there is some simple explanation, like they've been sent to the lab without the Records man knowing, the bullets from McGuire's body have gone missing.
- Either Quinn or Scott killed McGuire.
- Possibility a) Scott killed McGuire, even though he is certain he didn't. My opinion yesterday was that he did kill him by mistake.
- Possibility b) Quinn killed McGuire, but thinks Scott did.
- Possibility c) Quinn killed McGuire accidentally, but is too vain to admit it and prefers to blame Scott.
- Possibility d) Quinn deliberately killed McGuire, and offloaded the blame on to Scott. That is why he insisted on Scott coming along on the raid and kept him close, even though Scott is so inexperienced that he was more likely to be a liability than any help. And there is no way to prove whose bullet was the fatal one, since they have gone missing. (Unless of course they turn up again. See first point.)

- Saffron said that her father had told her there was somebody at IEMA who was corrupt.

Jace reread Possibility d) uneasily. Taken together with the first and last points it seemed horribly plausible; it fitted every fact bar one; the fact that he'd worked with, liked and respected Quinn for three years, and couldn't believe he would commit premeditated murder. He knew him too well; he'd been to his house in Fulham, met his wife and children. Also, this theory opened up yet more unanswered questions. He carried on dictating, watching the words patter on to the screen.

- Why would Quinn want McGuire dead?
- Why did McGuire panic when he saw Quinn (and Scott)? Panic to the point of jumping over a railing, knowing it was a ten foot drop on to concrete? He hadn't been worried by my arresting him, he was sullen and resigned. Why would two more time cops make such a difference? Time cops he didn't know. Or perhaps he did . . . Did he recognize Quinn (or Scott)? If so, where from?
- What happened to the TiTrav? There definitely was a TiTrav, because the alert told us someone in McGuire's lodgings had switched one on for two minutes and forty-three seconds before turning it off again. Was there another person present, the real owner of the TiTrav, who had now vamoosed? But that landlady . . . she was so indignant at the idea of anyone in her house committing timecrime and, as she put it, jeopardizing everyone's future. Selfish and irresponsible, she'd called it. She wasn't lying.

So, if McGuire *had* had the TiTrav on Thursday, where the hell was it now? Ryker hadn't got it. Of course, Farouk could have been right, and McGuire had hidden it somewhere else, in which case it might well never turn up. But he went to see Ryker, so maybe it had already been sold on through Ryker before

IEMA got there. If that was the case, he could dismiss Possibility d) and his nascent suspicions of Quinn – and he really wanted to do that. Jace was happy with his job, and his boss, and with Kayla. He was happy with his life, just as it was. He did not want to rock the boat.

Jace got up from the desk, had a quick shower, didn't bother shaving, dressed and got a pod back to Ryker's.

CHAPTER 6

McGuire's dream

A grey dawn was breaking as Jace reached Ryker's railway arch once more. The place looked even more decrepit by daylight. He rang the bell, and with a sense of déjà vu amplified by lack of sleep, waited for the dog's ferocious barking. After thirty seconds he pushed the bell again. The dog stopped barking.

"What d'you want?" Ryker's voice.

"I'd like a word."

"What about?"

"About something I don't want to shout through a door."

Once more the bolts scraped back and Ryker stood unfriendly on the threshold, dressed in a grey vest and tracksuit bottoms, rumpled with sleep. He looked at Jace without enthusiasm, then craned to see beyond him as if he had expected more people. "Forgotten something? Thought of somewhere you didn't search? Got a new lead?"

"None of those. Can I come in?"

"Let's see your warrant."

"I haven't got one. This isn't strictly IEMA business."

Ryker thought about this, then jerked his head and Jace followed him inside. They both sat, looking at each other. The dog curled up, his head on Ryker's feet, eyes on Jace. Jace said, "This is off the record. Anything you tell me won't go any further than this room."

"Oh yes. What d'you think I'm going to tell you?"

"I know McGuire had a TiTrav. He brought it with him when he came to see you last Thursday."

"That's your version of events. Not mine."

Jace continued, "He didn't have it on him when he died. You haven't got it. So who has?"

Ryker looked at him in disbelief. "You came back here on your own, thinking I'd tell you what I didn't tell your boss two days ago? How does that work? You're wasting your time, mate."

Jace faced the fact that he wasn't going to get anything out of Ryker without giving an explanation in exchange. But sharing his suspicions about Quinn – particularly when he could be entirely mistaken – with a man like Ryker was not a sensible idea. He sat for a moment, not saying anything. He shouldn't have come. What had made him think Ryker would help? He was here because he couldn't think of any other avenue to explore. This was another wasted journey.

Ryker was studying him, head a little on one side. Suddenly his eyes narrowed, and an incredulous half smile appeared on his face. "You think one of your lot has got it." He stared at Jace. "Well, fuck me pink and call me a radish. That's what you're doing back here on your own."

Only the extreme disquiet which had brought Jace there made him say, reluctantly, "It's true . . . I do have a suspicion that . . . one of my colleagues in the department . . . may have the TiTrav. If I'm right, then what McGuire told you may help me find out who it is." Ryker eyed him, assessing him, saying nothing. "If I'm right, then that's why McGuire's dead."

After a pause, Ryker said, "Did you know he had a daughter? Saffron. She's seventeen."

"Yes."

"He wasn't much of a parent, left home when she was little, but he kept in touch. She'll miss him."

"I know. I'm sorry."

"Turn out your pockets."

Jace put his dataphone on the desk. That was all he had with him. Ryker took it over to the safe and put it inside, then picked something up from a shelf. "First thing I did Sunday morning after you'd gone, checked you hadn't left a bug behind. Stand up."

Jace stood, and Ryker ran the scanner carefully over him, both sides. Satisfied Jace wasn't wearing a concealed listening device, he turned it off and sat back in his chair. "If you do find who it is, I'm not saying this in court, okay? I'll deny telling you anything."

"Understood."

"Okay, then." He said nothing for a minute. Jace waited. Then Ryker began to talk.

"Pete came here Friday all hyped up, and showed me a TiTrav. He wanted to get shot of it fast, and he wanted fifty million for it. He said the buyer had to arrange for the money to look like he'd come into it lawfully, so he could explain where it came from if anyone got curious. He'd thought it all out. I told him, as it happens I know someone who'd pay that and arrange it to look kosher, but he could get more if he gave me time to contact a few likely customers and get them into a bidding war. But he didn't want to wait. He saw himself buying a nice house outside of London where Saffy could come and stay, and buying her her own little flat here. Setting her up, maybe paying for university too if she fancied it. He wouldn't have had much change from fifty million after doing that, with property the price it is, but that's really all he wanted. He was excited about it, about changing his life and Saffy's, and wanted to do it fast." Ryker got up. "I need a cup of tea. Want some?"

"Thanks."

Ryker went over to the kitchen. The kitchen unit whose side Farouk had kicked in was now back against the wall, hardboard nailed neatly over the hole. Jace glanced round the room. The stickers that were reachable had gone, but a scattering at the top of the arched ceiling remained. Everything else had been put back the way it had been when they arrived. This must have taken Ryker hours. For the first time Jace understood that a visit from his team caused quite a lot of inconvenience to the person visited, even if no arrest followed.

Ryker returned with two mugs of tea, pushed one towards Jace and continued with his story. "Pete went to turn it on to show me it worked, but I stopped him. He didn't know they come with a tracker. He said he'd already turned it on for a couple of minutes. I told him not to go back home, IEMA would be looking for him right now. Poor bugger, he went white as a sheet. I took the tracker out for him –"

"It's not possible to remove the tracker."

Ryker shrugged. "That's what your engineers think. And I unlocked it and put in a new password. I said he could leave the TiTrav with me, but he didn't want to. I said I'd put the deal through as quick as I could, and try to get him a bit more money to cover the identity change he was going to need. I told him I had a contact who could set him up with a chip, no problem, but he wasn't happy. He was afraid they'd watch Saffy to get to him. It spoiled his plan."

"So was that the last time you saw him?"

"Yes. Not the last time I heard from him, though. He rang me a few hours later, told me the deal was off, he'd had to give the TiTrav to a man who'd put the frighteners on him, threatened to hack his arm off and take it if he didn't. I said, couldn't you have bargained with him, got at least something out of it for yourself, and he said no. That was the end of his dream for him and Saffy. The one time he got lucky, that was how it ended, poor sod." Ryker drained his tea and put the mug down.

"Then you shot him."

"I didn't shoot him."

"One of you lot did."

"Who was the man who took the TiTrav?"

"Can't tell you that. Pete didn't know him."

"Did he say what he looked like? His age? Anything?"

"No."

"Where did McGuire get the TiTrav?"

"No idea."

"Who was your buyer?"

Ryker gave him a hard look. "You don't need to know that. I've told you what you came here for. Now nail the bastard."

CHAPTER 7

Jace's nightmare

Shit. The more Jace thought about it, the more uncertain he became about what to do next. His observations, and the unsubstantiated assertions – he couldn't call them facts – he'd collected from Saffron and Ryker seemed to point to Quinn's guilt. But it was all circumstantial, and Ryker was hardly a reliable witness – plus he'd refuse to give evidence.

So what should he do? His instinct was to have it out with Quinn, because the idea that he had stolen a TiTrav and committed murder to conceal it was simply preposterous. Quinn had been something of a role model for Jace. He had a formidable intellect and charisma in spades, dominating any company he was in with his presence and wit. He carried off the latest Regency-influenced fashions he favoured with aplomb, and ran his department with an amiable manner and absolute authority.

Probably the man was innocent, and, after laughing at Jace's gullibility, would be able to offer some perfectly reasonable explanation. But if he *was* gamekeeper turned poacher, the stakes were stratospheric, and a suspicious Jace would be a problem to be neutralized. Like McGuire . . .

Another option: Jace could put the matter into the hands of

one of Quinn's superiors at IEMA. Quinn headed the department, so it would have to be someone outside it. Two problems; he didn't know any of the higher management personally, so wasn't sure whom to approach. And to convince them he would need to tell them Ryker's story, and he had told Ryker he wouldn't do that. Timecrime carried a mandatory minimum sentence of fifteen years. If he was vague about his source – pretend a stranger had contacted him anonymously out of the blue – the allegations would carry even less weight. Plus these people, like him, had known, liked and worked with Quinn for years. They'd appointed him, for goodness' sake. They were going to find it as difficult as Jace did to believe he was corrupt.

He picked up his phone to tell Kayla his suspicions and ask her advice, then changed his mind. The knowledge might endanger her. He decided to leave it for the moment; go in to work as normal, keep his eyes open, and wait for a solution to come to him. Perhaps he should put off doing anything until the Americans arrived, which they would within days if the TiTrav was not found. He could tell them his suspicions in confidence, knowing they would not be predisposed in Quinn's favour.

The day passed slowly, the investigation proceeding without results. Jace didn't mention the missing bullets. He found it difficult to concentrate. He was staring into space wondering how long it would be before the Americans arrived, when Quinn walked past him on his way to the door. Without breaking step he murmured,

"I'm choosing to believe that behind that blank exterior, a hundred billion neurons are firing to some purpose."

Jace started guiltily and got back to scanning the list of phone calls McGuire had made. Working backwards, he had reached November of the year before. He wasn't going to find anything. He was frowning at the list trying to focus, mind elsewhere, when a hand touched his shoulder.

"What's the matter?" Kayla, looking at him shrewdly.

"Nothing. Lack of sleep. Lack of weekend."

"Are you sure that's all? You look . . . kind of preoccupied. That's not like you."

"I'm fine. Just a bit tired."

Kayla checked to see that Quinn wasn't around, and pulled up a chair next to Jace. She ran a finger down his face and spoke softly. "How about I come and cook you something nice this evening? You won't have to do a thing. Then an early night . . ."

She'd already noticed his preoccupation; he imagined her that evening, delicately, almost imperceptibly probing until she guessed what the problem was. Kayla was smart. He said, "Maybe later in the week? I'm too knackered to enjoy it tonight."

She raised her eyebrows. "That'd be a first. Okay, don't tell me. I'll work out what's eating you for myself."

So that evening after an unproductive day Jace went home alone, poured himself a whiskey and lay back on the sofa, weary and anxious, mind going round like a hamster on a wheel. His eyes closed . . .

He was back in the derelict warehouse, on the dark mezzanine looking down. Quinn and Scott stood in a pool of light. Again, the overwhelming feeling of dread, of something frightful about to happen. As he watched, Quinn pulled out his gun and fired. Scott collapsed into a heap on the concrete then disappeared. Quinn turned and looked up at Jace. The gun lifted.

Jace woke, sweating, heart pounding. *Christ*. He swung his legs off the sofa and glanced at the time. Nearly seven o'clock. Beyond the balcony daylight still shone on his view of London rooftops. What was his subconscious trying to tell him now? That Scott was in danger? Why should he be?

Suddenly it came to him. Suppose the TiTrav never turned

up, which it wouldn't if Quinn had it. The department would not write it off, or even leave it on the books as an unsolved case the way the police did. Tracking it down would remain an absolute priority, because eliminating illegal time travel was what they did, their raison d'être. The American team would arrive and start examining everything all over again in minute detail, going back to first principles. The longer the hunt went on, the wider the net would be cast and the wilder the theories that would be considered – including the possibility that someone corrupt in the department had got hold of it.

If, however, Scott disappeared and the TiTrav never surfaced, there would be a strong supposition that he had obtained it from McGuire, 'accidentally' killed him to cover up, and fled. His expertise with a pistol would add credibility to this hypothesis. He was new in the team, too new for anyone to have got to know what he was like. He was the ideal fall guy.

Jace got up, buckled his gun belt, and headed for the flats where they had dropped off Scott the Sunday before.

CHAPTER 8

Dancing in the dark

Scott lived in a raffish part of East London, where high density housing had been built in the 2020s to cope with London's ever-increasing population, and the inexorable rise of house prices. These chic blocks soared improbably among seedy little shops and street markets. The flats only cost between four and five million to buy, or around two thousand a week to rent, had sleek kitchen units and bathrooms and every robotic convenience. They were even smaller than Jace's.

Jace approached the entrance, pushed past a man suggesting he visit the lap dancing bar next door, and stared at a daunting battalion of numbered bells. He'd just have to keep trying until he chanced on the right one. Assuming Scott was in. He heard the hum of a pod pulling up behind him and swivelled as its passenger got out. With a shock, Jace recognized Quinn. He put his hand on his gun, stood beside the door and waited.

Quinn saw him and walked up to him. "Jace! What are you doing here?"

Jace didn't smile in return. "I might ask you the same."

"I'm here to see Scott."

"Why? What for?"

"You haven't answered my question yet."

"By an amazing coincidence, I'm calling on Scott, too."

Quinn nodded slowly. "So you've been making the same deductions I have. I might have guessed. But you should have come to me, not acted alone. This could be dangerous."

"What are you talking about?"

"Ah." Quinn's eyebrows went up. "I thought I was talking about the same thing you were. Okay. Let me make myself clearer. It occurred to me that Scott may have killed McGuire deliberately. You wouldn't know this, but he shot pistols competitively in the States, so it's pretty unlikely he killed him by accident."

Jace felt winded. He hadn't considered Scott as a suspect, though now Quinn suggested it, he saw the facts could indeed be read that way. It was conceivable the purpose of Scott's visit to him had been to cast suspicion elsewhere; a pre-emptive strike. Now Jace was face to face with his boss, the theories that had seemed so indisputable lost their force. Quinn, besides being hugely able, was solid; an authority figure, part of the establishment. Unlike Ryker. He was still talking.

"If that's the case, he may well have McGuire's TiTrav – that could have been his motive for murder. So I've come here to put this to him, see what he says, and if necessary, arrest him. As you're here, I'd appreciate your coming with me, just in case he tries anything."

Jace's brain flipped between two possible realities as if trying to make sense of a trompe l'oeil. While he was doing this, the man from the strip club who had accosted him before sidled up.

"Gentlemen, why not have your discussion in comfort over a drink while watching lovely ladies? No entry fee before eight thirty."

Jace shook his head impatiently. "No thanks."

"Why not?" said Quinn. "I can see you've got something on your mind. Let's have a quiet chat and you can tell me what it is."

They went down narrow steps to the sound of loud music,

which throbbed louder as they reached a dim red basement with tables dotted around a small stage. Curtained booths lined the walls. The place smelled of damp and alcohol, perfume and sweat. There was a scattering of customers, outnumbered three-to-one at that hour by scantily clad women working in the bar in various capacities. On the stage a pole dancer performed her act, lit by colour-changing spotlights. Quinn chose a table away from the stage, and after quick consideration of a list handed him by a micro-skirted waitress, ordered two Flatliners.

"What's a Flatliner?"

Quinn said, "No idea. We'll find out. Go with the flow."

Two women approached purposefully and Quinn dismissed them with polite reluctance, saying their delightful presence might prove distracting to a discussion of business matters. The drinks arrived in squat glasses; amber liquid shading to brown, with ice, a twist of peel, and an unidentifiable sprig of greenery. The absurdity of the situation suddenly struck Jace; the provocatively pouting dancer, the clichéd surroundings he'd only experienced before vicariously in movies, the names of the drinks, his surely mistaken melodramatic suspicions of his boss . . . He relaxed and began to laugh.

"*Quiet* chat, did you say?" he said, leaning in to be heard above the noise. He raised his glass. "Cheers." He sipped and grimaced. "Bloody hell. I'm guessing meths and paint stripper, with . . . let me see, the merest dash of shoe polish?"

"The first sip is the worst, no doubt. You may find it grows on you."

Another young woman joined them, sitting in one of the two unoccupied chairs and swaying forward to promote her assets. She had long hair, a shapely figure barely contained in a fringed bra and g-string, and might have been pretty under heavy makeup as traditional in its way as a geisha's. "Would you like a private dance, guys? I'll do both of you for the price of one."

Jace said, "Thanks, but no thanks." Unable not to, he watched as she walked away, then looked around the bar, fascinated by the weirdness of the place and the men who chose to come here. Those not enjoying one-on-one attention were staring at the pole dancer, who appeared to be reaching the climax of her act, spinning round the pole as the music got more deafening. "That's actually really impressive. Especially done in five inch heels."

"Jace, focus. We're here to talk." He dragged his gaze back to Quinn, who said, "You seemed a bit . . . strange when you saw me outside Scott's. What's up?"

Jace pulled himself together. The place was distracting. He looked Quinn in the eyes, trying to read him, though subtly things had shifted; now he was more worried by what his boss would think of him for having such crazy suspicions than anything else. True, given the data, *crazy* was a bit strong. It had all made sense, in its own way.

Yet another lap dancer sashayed up to their table to try her luck, smiling seductively. She leaned forward and purred, "I don't suppose either of you gents would like to buy me a drink?"

"We're gay," Quinn told her. "And in love."

"No problem, boys. I'm here if you change your mind."

The girl left and he turned to Jace, expression amused and quizzical, eyebrows raised. "Well? Why were you visiting Scott?"

Jace said reluctantly, his voice flat, "I couldn't help considering the possibility that you might have killed McGuire on purpose, after you took the TiTrav off him. Then blamed Scott. Because he was new in the department. Then I was worried you might get rid of him so people would assume he'd taken off with the TiTrav, then no one would suspect you. You'd be able to disappear the bullets, too, so no one could prove he wasn't McGuire's killer." He could hear, as if listening to someone else say it, how far-fetched the whole thing sounded; like the summary of a thriller's plot, ridiculous, sensational. He sat back, feeling a fool, waiting for Quinn's reaction, though his overriding emotion was relief that he'd been wrong.

Quinn said nothing for a moment then started to shake with laughter, gazing at Jace. Apparently Jace's solemn face made the joke funnier. Quinn thumped him on the shoulder, unable to get a word out. Jace couldn't help laughing a little too. He remembered he'd thought Quinn would laugh if told his conjectures.

Quinn's hilarity died down enough for him to speak. "So, once you'd warned Scott about me, what were you planning to do next?"

Jace's face felt hot. "I hadn't decided," he muttered. He drained his drink so he didn't have to look at Quinn.

Quinn stood, smiling. "Let's go and see Scott. You shall judge between us."

They headed for the exit, Quinn waving amiably at the row of girls as they walked past them and up the stairs. Jace's legs felt tired and his head ached. Having a nap in the daytime was never a good idea. That vile drink hadn't helped, either. He should have had the sense to leave it.

A couple were entering Scott's building as they neared the door, and they followed them into the lobby. The couple peeled off to the left, and Quinn pushed the button for the elevator. It arrived and they got in. The doors slid shut. Jace yawned uncontrollably.

"Sorry," he said. "I didn't get much sleep last night."

Quinn was watching him oddly, like he was waiting for something. Jace could hardly keep his eyes open. He swayed and had to grab the hand rail for support. Suddenly he understood. *Oh shit.* He fumbled for his gun with slow fingers, but Quinn already had his out, pointing at Jace.

CHAPTER 9

The dark side

Jace smelled wool and became aware that he was lying on a rug or carpet. The memory of Quinn's perfidy flooded his mind, and he concentrated on appearing to be unconscious while he assessed his situation. The room was warm and quiet, the hum of traffic just audible. Cautiously, he flexed his muscles, and discovered he couldn't move freely. His hands were fastened behind him with the plastic cuffs the department used. His feet were tied too. The shoulder he lay on was numb from his awkward position, his head throbbed and he felt queasy. Hot panic surged through him. Quinn was going to kill him instead of Scott. One scapegoat was as good as another.

"You're awake." Quinn's voice.

Jace opened his eyes. They were in a smallish modern living room elegantly decorated in blues and greys. Quinn sat on a sofa a few feet from him, drink in hand, relaxed. He had taken off his jacket, and looked so normal that part of Jace's mind could not quite believe this was happening. It was, though; Quinn, his boss, had drugged him and tied him up. He could think of nothing there was any point in saying. He cursed himself for his stupidity and lack of judgment.

"I'm sorry about this, Jace. I'd far rather it was Scott lying where you are – not that he would be, because I wouldn't want to talk to him first." Quinn lifted the cuff of his Darcy shirt, revealing the silver TiTrav on his left wrist. "You guessed right, in every respect. Remarkable. You're a credit to the department – and my judgment in hiring you. But you have a failing. You didn't trust your own conclusions enough, and you trusted me too much."

Jace was damned if he was going to ask what Quinn had planned for him. He'd find out all too soon. "Why did you do it?"

"I've been waiting for an opportunity to get my hands on a TiTrav for some time. I imagined I'd be able to borrow one of the department's, but the security on them is ridiculously tight, even for me." He added with interest, "Don't tell me you've never fantasized about being able to travel in time?"

Jace had. As a teenager he'd been obsessed with the idea ever since reading about the early experiments, which back then no one thought would have a practical application. If he was honest, one of the main, if undeclared, reasons he'd applied to join IEMA was the hope he might get the chance to time travel. Senior officers did make regular (strictly controlled) forays into the future, to monitor climate change, population trends and similar data. Quinn had. Jace was not high enough up the ladder to be eligible yet. "Of course I have. But it's banned for a reason. Because it's so easy to screw up the future."

"Is that what you think?" Quinn laughed wryly. "I'll tell you something classified, since you are not in a position to be anything but discreet. You don't know what this planet is like in a hundred and fifty years' time. The top brass at IEMA and the World Government do. So, as it happens, do I, because I've been to the future – for legitimate research purposes – and seen it. From about 2065, people stop breeding. Everyone becomes infertile because of an extremely virulent contraceptive virus, and we don't know how to stop it happening. Gradually, as people fail to reproduce themselves, our civilization grinds to a halt. By

2170, humanity is extinct. The last person has died and plants and animals have the planet to themselves. And nobody's managed to find out what to do to prevent it, though my God they've certainly tried. I've tried – and will go on trying – myself. So talk of the danger of time travel is a little beside the point. It's not possible to make the future worse than it's already going to be. In fact, lots of random time travel might be a good thing, might accidentally send us in a different direction from the future we're currently heading for. Because right now, we're all doomed."

Facing as he was his own personal extinction, Jace couldn't get very worked up about humanity's. He said wearily, "Did you put this point to IEMA executives?"

"No, because I intend to keep my job."

"So you're saying it's okay to have this illegal TiTrav because you're going to use it to avert the annihilation of the human race?"

He'd made Quinn laugh again. "Er, no, though thank you for crediting me with such altruism. That justification had not occurred to me, largely because I don't feel the need to justify myself. True, I *am* trying to find the solution, because I like a challenge. It's a fascinating conundrum, like Fermat's Last Theorem."

"It was three hundred and fifty-eight years before Andrew Wiles solved that little puzzle."

"How many people know that? Jace, if I have to kill you I'm going to miss you. We have a greater incentive – Fermat's Theorem was hardly a life or death matter. That aside, it's my personal aspirations I'll mainly be using time travel for, and they're quite modest and more easily achieved. I intend to become obscenely rich and have a great deal of fun, in the knowledge that things won't get really depressing for quite some time, and when they do, I will relocate to the past. Some time with antibiotics, so the recent past. London in the 1980s would probably suit me."

Jace's brain felt as if he'd got it back after it had been borrowed for use as a football, which hindered coherent thought. He didn't feel up to sustaining his share of the conversation, and couldn't imagine why Quinn wanted to explain his viewpoint – which was what he seemed to be doing. Jace took the line of least resistance, and lay inert, listening to the silence. The effect of whatever Quinn had spiked his drink with would wear off in time – if he lived long enough.

"You're wondering why I'm saying all this to you," Quinn remarked with disconcerting accuracy. "I like you, Jace. I regard you as a friend. I don't want to get rid of you unless I have to. I'm going to be very, very cautious with how I use this thing at first, because I have no intention of getting caught. But in a year or so, when the scandal of Scott's disappearance is forgotten, I shall be more adventurous." There was relish in his voice. "Think of all the places and events there are to visit in history. Who wouldn't want to see gladiators fight in the Colosseum, cruise on the Titanic, watch the first production of Hamlet at the Globe, visit the brothels of Pompeii . . ."

"You murdered a man so you can be a *time tourist?* Jesus wept." Jace closed his eyes to shut Quinn out. He wanted to be at home, in his own bed, and safe.

"Is that so strange? I've got everything else I want. Jace. *Jace*, look at me."

"You want me to look at you, you'll have to untie me. I'm getting a crick in my neck."

"I'm not going to untie you. Yet. I'm going to make you an offer." Jace opened his eyes. "Some of the places I'll be visiting will be dangerous. I wouldn't mind having someone to watch my back. You'd be ideal; you're tough and you're bright and we work well together."

A tiny flicker of hope sparked in Jace's chest. His mind went into overdrive. There was no way he would agree to become Quinn's time-travelling minder, even to save his own life. Perhaps he'd have considered the offer, if Quinn hadn't killed McGuire deliberately to cover up his own misdeeds . . . but he had. That was heinous, unforgivable. He remembered Saffron's face, her pain and anger. And now he intended to kill Scott. The man was unhinged. But if Jace pretended to agree, so Quinn untied him, and he played along for a bit, he could pick his moment – which would have to be before anything happened to Scott – and jump him or surreptitiously phone Kayla for help . . .

He said, "So what you're doing is building an alternative department? Your own personal team on the dark side? Why would I want to join?"

"The dark side?" Quinn's eyebrows went up. He intoned, in a passable imitation of Darth Vader, "You are beaten, it is useless to resist. There is no escape. Don't make me destroy you, when together we can bring order to the galaxy. Join me, it is your destiny." In his normal voice he added, "If money interests you, it's easy to make when you have access to time travel. I'd be accommodating, if we were partners. Of course, you'd have to abandon a few scruples, and get used to the idea that you'd be doing exactly what your day job is meant to prevent. But then, I've explained why your job is entirely futile. For my part, I'd need to be convinced I can rely on you, that you weren't just agreeing to this in order to get out of the predicament you're in so you can report me to my superiors."

"I don't see how I can convince you of that."

"Luckily, I do. I was planning to maroon Scott two hundred years in the future, leave him to survive as best he could." Quinn paused for a moment. "But I'll know I can trust you if you kill him first. It might even be a mercy to Scott. And to make sure you don't double-cross me, you'll do it with your bare hands while I cover you both with a gun."

With the sudden rush of adrenaline coursing through his veins Jace found he was able to twist himself into a sitting position. From this vantage point he stared at Quinn with rage and disgust. He didn't consciously decide what to say; the words spilled out on their own.

"I used to respect you, Quinn. Admire you. Like you. Not any more. Turns out you're a contemptible, lying, two-faced scumbag who doesn't give a shit for anyone except himself. I've met some lowlifes in my job, God knows, but the lowest and meanest of them is a hundred times better than you. You murdered McGuire and now you want to drag me down to your level by making me murder Scott. I'd rather die. Go fuck yourself."

Quinn's face changed. That got home, Jace thought.

"You'd rather die . . . I can arrange that for you."

Without warning, he left the sofa and smashed his fist into the side of Jace's head, knocking him face down on to the floor. Jace's desperate bucking and kicking made it take a little longer, but within a few minutes Quinn had used a third restraint to fasten the plastic cuffs binding Jace's hands and feet together behind his back.

A moment later Jace felt his wrist being grasped. He twisted to look over his shoulder, blinking blood out of his eyes. Quinn had hold of him with his left hand, and was pressing the two buttons on the TiTrav.

CHAPTER 10

A dark night in future London

Monday, 4th September 2180

The world went black and spun. When Jace had imagined taking his first time trip, it had not been like this; in his daydreams he hadn't been hogtied, powerless, with death on the agenda. An unquantifiable amount of time passed, then his body smashed to the ground as Quinn let go of him. He smelled wet earth. Autumn leaves and ragged grass pressed damply against his face. A cool breeze blew. Lifting his head as much as he was able, he saw a tangled mass of saplings and creepers smothering mossy gravestones, gilded by the amber light of a setting sun. He guessed where he was. Quinn had brought him to the future, after the end of mankind.

Jace waited to find out his fate, heart thumping. Quinn either intended to put a bullet in his brain, or to abandon him in the future as he had planned to abandon Scott. If the latter then maybe, if he was fast, he could hit out the moment his hands were free and overpower him.

Quinn walked into Jace's view, and stood quietly looking down at him. His face was cold; bereft of its normal humour, it looked like a stranger's. He didn't reach for his gun. Instead he pushed up his left sleeve, and tapped at the TiTrav's screen.

Jace's heart sank. He said urgently, "You can't leave me like this! Cut me free before you go."

Quinn paused. "I'm surprised you ask me that," he said. "As you pointed out, I don't give a shit for anyone except myself. You are here by your own choice. You've got a week to ten days to think about that, while you die of dehydration."

He pressed the buttons and disappeared. Primeval dismay and terror gripped Jace, one human alone on the planet, a tiny speck of life soon to be snuffed out. The air seemed to grow darker and heavier, pressing in on him. The sigh of the wind in the trees emphasized the silence of a dead city. He made a monumental effort to pull himself together, summoning anger and pride to help him.

I am not going to panic. That bastard is not going to get the better of me. First, I have to work out how to get free. Think.

Quinn had secured him with three of the zip-tie flexicuffs they used in the department. Jace was very familiar with their construction; they were made from two tough plastic strips that passed through a single roller-lock retention block. They could be cut easily enough with wire cutters, or released by slipping a pin between the block and the serrated side of the strap, or melted with a flame. That was why the time police always cuffed people's hands behind their backs, with the lock the other side from the captive's thumbs.

Jace did not carry a lighter or pins, and his penknife was out of reach in his pocket. The position he was tied in restricted most movement, and was acutely uncomfortable. He tried twisting his wrists in opposite directions to put tension on the plastic, then wrenching his hands away from each other in the hope of bursting the catch. This achieved nothing except painful wrists.

He needed something solid and rough he could rub the plastic against until it wore away, and he needed to do it now before darkness fell and while he was still relatively fresh, before he got too weak from thirst, hunger, and cold. The nearest headstone was ten or twelve feet away. *Right.* Jace transferred his weight from knees to hips, then moved his shoulders and repeated the action, jack-knifing his body towards the stone. It was slow going, and painful in a multitude of different ways. The thin plastic cut into his wrists and ankles, and he ached all over. He had to steamroller over small branches in his path, his jacket buttons catching and dragging, impeding his progress.

Halfway to the stone he stopped for a rest. His back was killing him. Perhaps Quinn would feel remorse when his anger had died and return, if only to put him out of his misery with a bullet. On reflection, insulting him had been stupid and self-indulgent. He should have stuck to his original plan to play along, hoping for an opportunity to turn the tables before it got to the point where he was supposed to kill Scott. He and Scott together just might, with a lot of luck, have overpowered an armed Quinn, and he'd thrown away that chance. Almost any scenario he could think of would be better than this.

If Quinn came back, he wanted to be untied, waiting for him, ready. He imagined punching him in the face, beating him up. The savage satisfaction of this thought made him set off with renewed zeal towards the stone slab in the deepening twilight. The white scuts of rabbits gleamed in the light of a full moon as they moved about close by; they seemed to know he was not in a position to pose a threat. The grass was alive with small black slugs inches from his nose, and it was getting difficult to see them. However, slugs were the least of his worries. He tried to ignore the pain: he could do this. He remembered his Krav Maga instructor tapping the side of his skull and saying, "It's all in here. Believe you can do it, and you can."

Time was hard to judge, but Jace reckoned it took him about twenty minutes to reach the gravestone. Brambles lapping its base scratched his face and caught at his clothes. He had to rock himself over on to his other side and shuffle backwards, feeling with his fingers to line up the plastic holding his wrists and ankles together with the edge of the slab. He pulled off strands of ivy and bramble, then got hold of the spare wrist band to keep it out of the way as much as possible. At least Quinn hadn't threaded both of them through, which would have given him twice the work.

He paused for a breather, gathering his strength, then moved his hands up and down the few inches they would go, fretting the taut strap against the corner of the stone. He had hoped to do it fast enough for friction to melt the plastic, which would have been quick, but he couldn't. He'd just have to wear it away.

His arms were quickly screaming at him to rest, and every now and then the stone caught his knuckles and scraped skin off. It was difficult to exert much pressure, but the worst thing was that he couldn't judge his progress – could neither see nor feel if the stone was having any effect at all on the plastic. His mouth was dry, his stomach empty, he hurt all over. He told himself it could have been worse; Quinn could have used metal handcuffs, and he'd have had zero hope of getting them off.

Doggedly, Jace counted out loud; twenty rubs, pause, relax, three breaths and start again. He tried moving his feet for a bit to give his arms a rest, but this was more difficult to control and he went back to lifting his arms sideways, up and down, up and down.

The air was cold and the sky had grown so dark Jace could see very little. The rabbits had gone. Some creature moved in the undergrowth, a cat, a rat or a fox. Then unmistakably, he heard the howl of a wolf not far off, and redoubled his efforts, now counting under his breath. Lying trussed on the ground while a pack of wolves ripped him to pieces was not something he wished to experience.

The hours passed. Once or twice he nodded off, until the pain in his limbs woke him. When the night was darkest and the agony seemed too much to bear, tears ran down his face and death seemed inviting. Death not being an immediate option, he summoned the dregs of his resolution and carried on with the repetitive movement, trying to visualize the plastic as practically worn through, about to give way . . . he'd be a fool to give up when he was so nearly there.

It was almost an anticlimax when it finally happened. Jace's legs began to straighten behind him on their own, became painful in a new and different and very welcome way. Gradually he extended his body, flexing his spine, letting his sore muscles relax.

He rolled on to his back and sat up against the gravestone, knees bent, so he could work on the band on his right wrist. This position was immeasurably more comfortable, and he could move his arms a greater distance and apply more force. As the cuff gave way and his hands separated, he noticed the darkness was less absolute, and shapes were becoming distinct once more. Birds tweeted in a desultory autumnal way. It was dawn. It had taken him all night to get this far.

His wrists were sore and bloody where the bands had cut into them, his knuckles raw. He wiped his face on his sleeve to try to remove the slugs' slime. He felt in his pockets for his penknife to release his feet, but the moment he found his phone had gone, he realized Quinn must have searched him while he was unconscious. In the corner of an inner pocket his fingers closed on something Quinn had missed; hard and triangular like a plectrum, it was a locator he'd borrowed from Kayla weeks ago and forgotten about. Jace smiled a grim smile to himself. If a time traveller approached within a mile radius, the locator would give him a minute's notice, beeping louder the nearer it got to the location where the traveller would time in. He put it carefully away again, and used a slim metal tag on a zip to slide into the roller-lock and remove the cuffs from his feet and the remaining wrist band.

Jace stretched and looked about him; exhausted, chilled to the bone, and feeling as if he'd been on the rack. What would be happening back in his own time? Nothing yet; it would be around six in the morning there as well as here. But later . . . he imagined life going on without him, his colleagues discussing his unexplained absence, ringing his dataphone. As the hours passed, Quinn's initial pretended concern would turn to reluctant drawing of conclusions: the obvious, neat solution to the mystery of the vanishing TiTrav and the missing operative.

Would Kayla accept this story, or not believe it of him and do some investigating on her own? That would be dangerous for her. He desperately longed to be back in his own time, sorting things out, exposing Quinn. Frustration and misery gripped him. This would not do; if he was going to survive, and he was, he had work to do – he needed to get his stiff limbs moving, explore, discover where he was, look for shelter, tools and food.

The tops of tall buildings were visible above the trees. He headed towards them, to look for a knife.

CHAPTER 11

The wrong question

Thursday, 23rd July 2015

"Florence?"

Floss swivelled, house keys poised by the lock, her other hand holding her bike steady. Nobody had called her Florence since her school days. Screwing up her eyes against the sun, she saw a tall solidly built man with stubble-short hair standing on the pavement. She could have sworn the street was empty a moment before. Though it was a warm evening, he wore a padded jacket and heavy boots.

He came up the steps towards her. "Florence Dryden?"

"Yes, what is it?"

His hand reached out and grabbed her arm, jerking her away from the bicycle. For an astonished second she looked into cold blue eyes, then the world went dark, inky black, and her stomach felt as if she was simultaneously plummeting in a lift and spinning on a fairground ride. Time passed, long enough for her to wonder if he had hit her over the head – was this what being knocked out felt like? Or maybe this was what death felt like. Terror assailed her while she battled with acute nausea, then she felt solid ground beneath her feet and could see again. Someone barrelled past her, knocking her out of the stranger's grasp and on to all fours. Floss vomited convulsively on rough wet grass, eyes watering, damp soaking through the knees of her jeans while a steady rain fell on her back and seeped through her tee shirt. Behind her she heard thuds and grunts. As soon as she could, her stomach emptier than it had ever been before, weak as a kitten, she struggled upright and turned.

She wasn't in Islington any more. Ancient gravestones covered in moss and ivy leaned drunkenly towards each other, and tree saplings sprouted through ragged grass. Where was she? And how had she got here, and why was the light all wrong; grey when it should be amber? Perhaps she had been unconscious for hours. She shivered, her clothes offering no protection against the cold rain, and that was wrong too in July.

Nearby two men were fighting savagely, the man who'd brought her here and another who looked like a tramp. The man slammed the tramp into a headstone and reached under his jacket. The tramp punched him, kneed him in the stomach and knocked his arm away fast and hard, and whatever the man had hold of spun out of his hand. They crashed to the ground grappling, the man's hand groping about for what he had dropped. It had to be a weapon. Floss leaped forward, saw something black nestling in the wet grass and grabbed just as his fingers touched it.

Though different from those she had seen in films and on television, this was unmistakably a gun, small and made to fit the contours of a hand, with silver knobs and sliders on one side. Floss had never held a gun before. It felt heavy for its size, and warm. She didn't know what to do – should she call out, try to stop them fighting? Who were they, anyway?

The tramp seemed to be winning. His arm went round the other man's neck, straining, and they both became still for several seconds. Then the tramp got to his feet and walked towards Floss, limping a little.

He was broad-shouldered and lean, and his clothes – vaguely piratical with fraying braid and a few surviving gold buttons – were worn and discoloured with grease and grime. Lank dark hair curled below his shoulders, and his beard came to his chest. His eyes were bright and impossible to read in a face dark with dirt. He looked her over, breathing hard.

Floss held out the gun in both hands like she'd seen in the movies, finger on the trigger, pointing at him. "Don't come any closer!"

He took a step towards her.

"I'll fire!"

"No, you won't." His voice was low, with a rough, husky edge to it, as if he hadn't used it for a while.

"I will! Stop there!"

He took another pace forward. Floss aimed the gun at the sky and squeezed the trigger. Nothing happened. The man stepped up to her and took the gun out of her hands and put it in his pocket.

"You didn't take the safety off. You'd better come back to the house."

He turned to the other man, grabbed the back of his collar and began to drag him along the ground. Something about the way his head lolled seemed wrong.

"Is he . . . all right?"

He gave a curt laugh. "No. He stopped being all right when I broke his neck."

Appalled, Floss watched him walk away, the body trailing after him, then got out her mobile, feeling sick again, shaking with shock and cold. No signal. She hastened off in the opposite direction from the one the man was taking, stumbling over the rough ground. Above the trees, their leaves just beginning to change colour, she could make out the tops of tall buildings. People there would help, take her in and let her use their phone.

Footsteps made her turn. He'd dropped the body to come after her. "Don't wander off, you'll get lost. There's wolves out there. And the odd lion."

Floss stared at him in disbelief. "*Wolves and lions?* Where is this?"

"London. Bunhill Fields. Near Silicon Roundabout."

Relief flooded Floss. That was practically home ground. She recognized the old graveyard now, though the last time she'd been there two or three years ago it had been better maintained. They'd really let it go since then. All she had to do was escape from this homicidal maniac. Who now had a gun. Edging away, she attempted a polite smile. "Thank you. Now I know where I am I'll be off."

He shrugged. "Suit yourself." He pointed to a small square brick building overgrown with ivy. "That's where I live, over there, if you need me."

He started to move away. Relieved but cautious, Floss managed another insincere smile and turned decisively to go.

"But you asked the wrong question," the man said over his shoulder.

Pretending not to hear, Floss picked her way towards the safety of City Road. At the gates she paused. They were solid rust, with barely perceptible scraps of black and gold paint clinging here and there. And beyond the gates . . .

The surface of the road was broken up into great zigzag cracks, with grass and small trees growing through the tarmac, and in places an invading carpet of ivy. The only noise was the wind in the trees and the patter of rain. Buildings across the street looked normal at first glance. Look again, and you could see the broken window panes, the encroaching creepers, the damp spreading down the walls from sagging gutters full of weeds. Floss climbed up the gate, hanging on to the stone pilaster, and craned in both directions. The front wall of one house had collapsed into a heap of bricks, exposing the rooms like an opened dolls' house. A lamppost lay at an angle across the road. Further away was a pile of fallen scaffolding, next to an area of water like a small lake. Everywhere was going back to nature; no lights, no traffic, no humans. The place smelled like the countryside, not like a city. In the distance skyscrapers appeared intact, until you noticed black specks spattered over their smooth façades, indicating missing panes of glass. A movement caught her eye – at the other side of the pond a wild boar trotted towards the water, surrounded by a troop of striped piglets.

Perhaps this was all just a very, very vivid dream, and she was actually lying in a hospital bed, badly injured and unconscious with morphine dripping into her veins. This struck her as a more inviting prospect than the alternative, that this was real. She shut her eyes tight for a few seconds, and opened them again fast when something ran over her hand.

Floss shook off the spider and put one leg over the gate. Then she stopped, remembering what the man had said about wolves and lions. It no longer seemed quite so improbable. Perhaps he had simply been telling the truth. His eyes had looked sane. Maybe she should go back and ask him what was going on. On the other hand, she'd just watched him kill a man. An idea came to her, an irrational idea she was unable to resist. Floss clambered down the far side of the gate and warily headed towards Old Street Roundabout.

She was going to go home.

CHAPTER 12

The answer to the right question

Finding her route to Islington wasn't too hard; the roads were still recognizable, even though their surfaces were breaking up and well on their way to becoming linear forests. Floss only got lost once, in an area with new unfamiliar buildings. She kept a wary eye out for carnivores, but didn't see anything larger than a fox trotting along the pavement. Cats stared at her but wouldn't come near. A small herd of deer had taken possession of Shoreditch Park, which had changed very little. Floss remembered reading that tree seedlings won't grow where deer browse.

On the way, she climbed twenty flights of stairs in one of the more robust-looking skyscrapers, and from there she could see that the desolation spread to the misty horizon. No light, no fires, no movement, no aeroplanes. The view had a strange beauty, with trees flourishing in all the spaces between the buildings. There were more tall office blocks than she remembered. The city looked to have been abandoned for a long, long time. Something catastrophic had happened here, and Floss couldn't work out what. Nothing seemed to add up.

It wasn't until she got to her street, a Victorian terrace facing a main road and backing on to the railway, that she fully acknowledged the futility of her journey. Doggedly, she worked out which was number eleven, and stood gazing at the house where her tiny attic studio had been. Most of its stucco had fallen off, and buddleia stems thrust out of the windows. The remaining portion of roof sagged, and a sycamore grew through what had once been her flat. She stood, staring, heart pounding, more alone than she'd ever been in her life. The longer she looked, the more panicky she became.

Floss walked up the steps to the front door, part of her hoping a miracle would happen if she stood on the spot she'd been transported from. The door's wood was warped and paintless, with only two panels in place. She pushed the edge, and what was left disintegrated and creaked wearily to the floor in a puff of dust. Inside was worse than outside. Fallen masonry, plaster and timber covered the floors, and furniture rotted where it stood, legs giving way, fabric frail and split with age, splotched with bird droppings. Books decayed on their shelves. In the rooms open to the sky, nettles flourished waist high, and birds, ants and spiders had moved in.

Floss wept.

The sky grew darker, and eventually hunger and cold drove her back the way she had come. There was nowhere else to go.

When Floss climbed back over Bunhill Fields' gate and headed towards the man's house it was 8.45 by her watch, and dark. The clouds had cleared and a huge moon shone above the trees. She'd been gone two and a half hours.

The yellow glow of candlelight glinted through the few non-boarded up panes. Floss approached cautiously, picking her way between stacked junk surrounding the building. A pipe sticking out from a galvanized water tank caught her shin painfully, tearing her jeans and drawing blood. She tiptoed to the window and peered in, grasping the tang of the knife she'd found in a ruined kitchen. Its handle had decayed to dust, the steel's surface was brown and pitted, but she had spent half an hour whetting the edge on a wall to a ragged sharpness. Floss was not under the illusion that this would even the odds should the tramp attack her, but she was a believer in doing what you could.

The man was sitting at a table, eating by the light of an elaborate seven branch candelabra, reading a book. Like everywhere else she had seen, the room was derelict, but it had been swept clean, and flames flickered in a square stove whose pipe went vertically through the roof. Beside the stove, wood was stacked to the ceiling. The room's bareness and lack of personal possessions gave the place a curiously medieval atmosphere like a monk's cell, dedicated to contemplation. A plank supported on bricks held an orderly row of rusty tools, several knives all bigger than hers, some convex lenses, a row of church candles and a dead rabbit. Strings of onions hung from hooks. A narrow metal bedstead with a sagging mattress, yellowed duvet and grubby blankets stood in one corner, with a pile of books on the floor next to it. Drips plopped from the ceiling into a metal bucket.

The man looked up and saw her. She jumped backwards, feeling foolish. The door opened and he stood silhouetted on the threshold.

"Thought you'd be back. You look freezing. Come in."

She followed him inside, cautiously, not sure what to expect. The air seemed warm compared to outside and smelled of damp plaster and wood smoke. He fetched a padded jacket from the bed and handed it to her. It was clean, nearly new. Only after she'd gratefully put the jacket on did she realize where it came from, and wondered what he had done with the corpse. On the table was a small pile of items, the contents of someone's pockets; a penknife, a bunch of keys, a neat electronic gadget she couldn't identify, a man's metal cuff. She took off a sandal and rubbed her chilly toes, keeping a wary eye on the man who was doing something by the stove. He came back with a steaming dish in his hand which he pushed towards her.

Floss's mouth watered. "What is it?"

"Rabbit stew."

The stew wasn't bad; a bit smoky and consisting mostly of rabbit meat and onions, but she spooned it up eagerly. He poured wine into a smeary glass for her. It was so smooth and delicious, she reached for the bottle to view its label: Château Mouton Rothschild 2011. Food and drink made her feel more able to cope with the situation, whatever it was. She smiled nervously at the man, raising her glass.

"Cheers. I ought to introduce myself. I'm Floss. Floss Dryden." She nearly held out her hand, but thought better of it. His were no doubt filthy. And he was a killer. "Who are you?"

"Jace Carnady."

She decided it would be best not to ask him straight away why he had killed her abductor. Or how he'd seemed to be waiting for him. Instead she asked the question that had been vaguely niggling her all the time she'd been exploring. "You know earlier, when you said I asked the wrong question? What did you mean?"

"You asked where this is. You should have asked when."

"Why when?"

"This is the future. Not sure which year, Quinn didn't tell me. Some time after 2170."

A pause while Floss considered this information, sipping her wine and eyeing him uncertainly. He topped up her glass, waiting for her reaction, expression sardonic.

"That's crazy," she finally said, her tone less convinced than her words. "You're asking me to believe I've time travelled to the future?"

"Nope." He shrugged. "Your opinion is your own concern. I really don't care what you believe."

"But there's no such thing as time travel!"

"Where do you think you are, then? Does it look like your own time? When was that, anyway?"

"2015." An eerie howl in the distance made Floss glance towards the window. Other howls answered it. That was either a pack of wolves, or . . . something else that made a noise exactly like a pack of wolves.

Jace said, "Don't worry, they can't get over the railings. One reason I stayed here."

"Okay. Assuming this is the future, how did I get here, and why?"

"Ansel Quinn – that man – brought you. Why, I don't know. My guess is to get you out of the way."

"Out of the way of what, exactly?"

"How should I know? But I can get you back home. Most likely."

"Can you really?" In spite of her revulsion towards a murderer, Floss couldn't suppress her relief and gratitude. "That would be awesome!" She pictured Chris sitting in the bar, wondering what had happened to her friend, who was usually so reliable; trying to reach her on her mobile; in the end giving up and leaving. This vignette was small and distant, as if she was looking through the wrong end of a telescope. The ruined room was much more real.

"In theory I should be able to get you back to the same minute you left. First we have to go to wherever Quinn left from."

"Why?"

Jace picked up the cuff from the pile on the table. It was stylish, made from matt silvery metal, and turned out to have a touch screen and buttons and a tiny ice-blue light that pulsed every few seconds. Near the top of the screen the metal was dented and scratched. Jace turned it in his hands, strong capable hands ingrained with dirt, the nails black-rimmed. "This is how Quinn got you here. You set the time and place, and the TiTrav does all the rest. Press these two buttons at the same time, and off you go. Anyone you're holding on to goes with you. It seems to be working okay, though it got a bit battered in the fight. Only problem is, he's used the limiter. It won't go anywhere except the location and time he set."

"Where's that?"

"I can't tell where the co-ordinates are. The time's 25th March 2050, 7.15 pm."

"Is 2050 your own time?"

"I suppose it is now. I left in 2045, and I've been here five years."

"So time travel is a thing people do – will do – did do in 2045?" Time travel really messed with your tenses.

"No. The government had it locked down. Time travel to the past's hardly ever sanctioned. It's just too risky. The minimum penalty for unauthorized travel to the past is fifteen years, no remission. Part of my job was tracing illegal time travel."

Floss considered this insight into the future, while simultaneously modifying her assessment of Jace Carnady. He was more intelligent than she'd thought, though still a killer, unpredictable and violent. Short on social niceties, too. Though she needed him, she wouldn't be sorry to see the last of him.

"Can't you take the limiter off?"

"I haven't got the code, and I don't want to try to get in in case I stop it working. Then we'd both be stuck here. There's a man I know who should be able to do it, if he's still around . . ."

"Is that illegal?"

Jace nodded. "And I doubt I have citizen status any more. So, d'you want to come?"

However dodgy, criminal and uncertain his plan, whatever her abhorrence of him, this was her only chance. She said, "I don't want to stay here."

"We'll leave when you've finished eating . . . actually, you're probably wasting your time eating, you'll just throw it up again." Jace swiped and tapped the screen, saying absently, "When you do get back, you might want to be careful, in case they send someone else after you."

At that moment, Floss didn't care. She just longed to be away from here, back in her proper life, even if Jace Carnady was right and she would be at risk. She wouldn't mind having to be careful. She put down her spoon.

He glanced at her unfinished plate. "Are you done?"

Floss nodded. She'd lost enthusiasm for the meal after what Jace had said about her throwing it up.

"Then let's go." He took off his jacket and undid the buckle of his leather belt, threaded the belt through the cuff and fastened it again.

"Why not put it on your wrist? Aren't you supposed to wear it?"

"It's locked. I don't have the code."

"So how did you get it off Quinn, then?" Pause, while Floss realized how he had got it off Quinn, and imagined him doing it. "Oh."

He seemed to find her revulsion faintly amusing. "At least he was dead. There are some nasty stories from the early days, when more of these were kicking around." Jace put on his jacket and stashed the pile on the table into various pockets. He added a rusty tobacco tin from the shelf, then did a visual check of the room, apparently not finding anything else he needed to take with him. "Hold on to me. Grab my belt."

He put his arm around her waist. Floss tried not to breathe in the rank stench of his clothes and body.

"I hope he set off from his apartment," he muttered. "We don't want to materialize into an office full of people wanting to know where Quinn is."

CHAPTER 13

Back to the future

Friday, 25th March 2050

Jace's plan, should they appear in the Event Modification Authority's offices, had been simple; use Quinn's gun to threaten the eight or so people likely to be present before they could raise the alarm, then run away. He could see there were various problems with this. Serious problems, problems that would likely result in sudden death. So it was a relief when they arrived instead in a luxury penthouse which had to belong to Quinn. Its floor-to-ceiling windows gave a panoramic vista of City of London skyscrapers, their lights sparkling in the night.

While the girl was spewing macerated rabbit in red wine on to the marble floor (displaying a pleasing rear view in old-fashioned tight jeans) he did a quick tour of the place to make sure it was empty, then sat at the desk. Luckily, given Jace did not know the password, Quinn had left the computer on, expecting to return immediately. "Food. French bread and cheddar. Diary."

"Does it ever get better?" Floss gasped, gazing up at him, her eyes huge in a white face. She was a looker, no doubt about it, even doubled up heaving her guts out.

"Probably. There are pills you can take." He turned back to the screen. Quinn had an appointment that evening with a woman called Jinghua. Jace went to his mail and after a bit of research cancelled it, fastidiously pastiching Quinn's writing style: *Sweetheart, something's come up. We're going to have to reschedule . . .* Five years ago the man had been married and living in a Fulham mews; apparently he was now playing the field. Or had been. The bread and cheese arrived and he took a bite. *God, that's good.* He looked up to see Floss about to clean the floor with a cloth she must have found in the kitchen.

"Vacwash." The machine hummed into the room, homing in on the mess, nudging Floss out of the way. She perched on the sofa arm and watched as the floor became pristine once more. The vacwash sprayed an ocean perfume and put itself away in the kitchen visible through an archway off the living room.

"What do we do next?" she said.

"Nothing until I've had a shower. Make yourself at home. If you want food or anything, tell the computer. Don't answer the door."

The shower was fantastic, his first for five years. There had been no running water where he came from, unless you counted the rain. In summer he used to dip in the canal while fishing. No soap, though, or shampoo. He smiled with pure pleasure at the hot water running down his back as the shower went through the leisurely cycle he had selected.

When he'd finished he found scissors and trimmed his beard, then used Quinn's shaver set to stubble. Jace hadn't liked his bearded backwoodsman look, but for anyone living rough the style had its advantages; it was effort-free and kept your neck warm.

He walked naked through the bedroom and into the vast

walk-in wardrobe. Who needed this many clothes? Quinn had been his height, luckily, and had lost some weight in the last five years, so they were much the same size. His taste wasn't quite Jace's, but everything was expensive, stylish and nearly new. He'd clearly done as he intended, and become obscenely rich. Bastard. Jace chose britches, a shirt and a gilet, and put them on.

He picked up his pile of old clothes. He had not realized, while wearing them year after year, day and night, just how much they stank. After taking them to the chute, he went into the living room, carrying his own boots since Quinn's were a size too small. He had wondered if a bit of polish would make them pass, but now that he took a good look at them, he could see they were beyond redemption.

The girl was sitting feet up on the sofa eating the last slice of a pizza and drinking champagne, vintage music pounding, a light display pulsing. As he walked in she swung her feet to the floor, gave him a startled look, and told the computer to put on the main lights and stop the music.

In the sudden silence she said, "Is that what people are wearing these days?"

He glanced down. "Yes. Why? This is maybe a bit fancier than I'd choose . . ." He handed her a comb and the scissors while she stared at his altered appearance. "I need you to cut my hair."

"I'll give it a go." She swallowed the last mouthful of pizza. "After that we'll go and see your friend and get me home? How short do you want it?"

"Just shorter. I'm going to catch up with stuff first, find out what's going on. All my information's five years out of date."

"Can't you do that after?"

"No."

He pulled out a dining chair and sat in front of a long

mirror. Floss combed and snipped carefully, studying the result in the mirror as she worked. He was amused to note his transformation from squalor to respectability had made her less wary of him, more relaxed. Amazing what soap, water and new clothes could do. She started to speak, stopped, paused, started again. "That man. Why did you kill him?"

"I needed his TiTrav. His time travel device."

"You didn't have to kill him. You had him overpowered. You could have just left him there."

"Yeah, I could. That's what he did to me. Left me to die. After he'd handcuffed my wrists and ankles, then tied them together."

Jace would never forget that night. When dawn came and he finally got free, he'd realized he had another mountain to climb just to survive. It had taken him three days to trap his first rabbit, two weeks to make fire. Ravenous, disgusted, he'd had to eat the meat slimy and raw. The cold at night had made sleep impossible except in snatches interspersed with jumping about to warm up.

"Why did he leave you to die?"

"Because I found out he was a crook. He'd killed a man, too."

"Who is – was he?"

"We worked together. He was my boss."

"When we arrived, you seemed to be waiting for him. You were right there, you jumped him straight away."

Jace almost smiled. "Ah well, he didn't search me carefully enough. He missed a locator in my pocket. Careless, that. I'd borrowed it for the job I was working on." From Kayla. His heart beat faster at the thought of seeing her again. "He didn't know I'd got one. I'd forgotten myself."

"What's a –"

"They give an alert when someone is about to time in. I

waited five years for that little beep to go off. Wore it round my neck."

Jace thought for a minute, listening to the crisp sound the scissors made. They'd been close as brothers; he knew how Quinn's mind worked. He had stayed in Bunhill Fields in the belief Quinn would begin to wish he had killed him outright; would start to obsess that Jace was not dead, would, in the end, return to check and set his mind at rest. Gradually as the weeks and months passed, this conviction faded; Jace had expected to die alone in that future London. The adrenaline rush when the locator had finally sounded, the almost unbearable revival of hope, the fear he'd somehow cock up the chance to get away . . .

"What if people come looking for him here? Perhaps we shouldn't be hanging around."

"I won't stay longer than I have to. I need to get this sorted out. I'm assuming there's a warrant out for me. We should be okay for a day or two."

She didn't say anything for a while, but concentrated on cutting his hair. She wasn't doing a bad job. "You're not a hairdresser, are you?"

She laughed. "No. I used to cut my boyfriend's hair at uni."

When she'd finished Jace sat down again at the computer screen. Floss wandered around until she found Quinn's Kindle and scrolled through the contents. His selection of novels not being to her liking, with Jace's help she downloaded one of her choice and immersed herself in it on the sofa.

Jace ordered three different pairs of boots his size using Quinn's Amazon account, figuring that one pair at least should fit him. As an afterthought, he added some motion sickness patches to his order. This done, he searched for *Wanted Criminals UK*, and on the Crimestoppers site selected *London* and *Timecrime*. The first image on the page was his, rotating slowly to show him from all angles. He'd expected this, but that didn't make it any more welcome. He rated the full five stars, and maximum reward for information leading to a conviction. Beneath the photo it said:

NAME: Jason CARNADY
NICKNAME: Jace
CRIME TYPE: Timecrime
DATE: 2045
CARNADY is wanted on suspicion of theft of a TiTrav and illegal time travel.
SEX: Male
AGE: 34
HEIGHT:
185 cm (approx 6' 1")
BUILD: Muscular
HAIR COLOUR: Dark

This was what he'd expected – no point dwelling on it. He went to the kitchen and found a knife, sharpened it to a razor edge, washed it twice and poured brandy over it. He took off his shirt, wiped brandy over his upper arm, and sat in front of the mirror again. Microchips were not inserted far under the skin – you needed one all the time when paying for things and identifying yourself, so there were few reasons anyone would want to remove them. Pity it was his right arm, and he was right-handed.

Fuck, that hurt. Blood ran down his arm. He gulped some brandy straight from the bottle, then slid the point of the knife into the cut he had made.

"What are you doing?" Floss was staring at him in horror, book forgotten in her hand.

"Cutting out my chip."

"I can't believe people are *microchipped* in 2045, like dogs." She got up and came over to take a look.

"Once America got them, it was just a matter of time till we did."

"The civil liberties people are okay with that, are they?"

"It got passed on the nod when New Alliance got its massive majority in '33. Voters' main worry back then was timecrime screwing up the future, not personal freedom. They probably still should be worrying, but they don't know that. And there's the convenience – a chip and a dataphone and you're set." He got back to work, then drew in his breath sharply. *Hell's teeth*. He couldn't see properly what he was doing, that was the problem.

"D'you want help with that?" she asked, uncertainly. He handed her the knife. "What am I looking for? How big is it?"

"About the size and shape of a grain of rice."

"Okay."

He clenched his teeth while she poked delicately around in the bloody hole he had created. Though outwardly calm, she bit her lip and apologized each time he involuntarily flinched. After what seemed like a long time she said, relief in her voice, "Is this it?"

He took the tiny cylinder from her. "Yes. Thanks."

She cleaned the wound for him and applied a plaster, then went back to her book. Jace put on his shirt and looked around the room. He picked up a small bronze of a reclining woman, placed his chip on the marble floor, and smashed it. After throwing the fragments over the terrace wall, he returned to the computer.

He did a quick sprint around the internet, picking up on the major stuff he'd missed in the past five years; less than he'd imagined. A general election (the same lot won), terrorist attacks, celebrity scandals, minor wars in far-off places. Most things remained much the same; the big news item he was looking for was not there. Something though was niggling him: why had Quinn abducted Floss? Was it IEMA business or private enterprise? Both seemed equally unlikely. He looked her up. Nothing at all, and this struck him as peculiar, particularly since privacy rules had been a lot more lax thirty years before. You'd expect to find *something*, if only an archive Facebook page.

Finally he started poking around in Quinn's digital life, tracing the sites he had used, the people he had contacted. Quinn had been promoted, had been running the whole of IEMA Intelligence. Kayla's name cropped up. He let out a laughing gasp – she'd got the job that used to be his own, then taken over Quinn's. Predictable, once he thought about it – she'd had the potential right from when she joined.

He searched for emails from her to Quinn. They filled two pages. As he read them in chronological order his face set. These were work emails, starting with routine queries as she adjusted to her promotion; crisp and business-like emails from a woman getting on top of her job. But the sign-offs ... intimate, witty, delightful. He remembered when he had been the recipient of emails like that from Kayla, the effect they'd had on him.

Quinn's appointment diary: search *Kayla*.

From mid-2046, the entry *7.30 am Kayla's flat* cropped up most weeks, always on a weekday. By the end of 2047, he was taking her to the Ritz, the Opera and Hoxton Studio. He must have left his wife by then and could see her openly; had evenings and weekends free, and was out to impress. That's when he'd got himself fit, no doubt. 2049, and they went less frequently to the classy venues; she was coming to his apartment.

Jace tried to calm his breathing. He thought of all the nights he'd lain fully dressed under the thin duvet, hungry, too cold to sleep. He'd warmed himself at thoughts of Kayla, remembering her, imagining what she was doing, thinking she'd be missing him. She had waited a year or so, it seemed. What had he expected, that she'd wait five years for him?

He felt he could forgive her anyone but Quinn. He told himself he was not being reasonable. On the heavy side five years ago, his hair cut short to camouflage male-pattern baldness, Quinn hadn't been handsome, but women hadn't seemed to mind. They liked the intelligence and humour in his eyes, the directness of his gaze, the way he focused his attention on them; and he was unquestionably an alpha male. Kayla hadn't known what the man was really like any more than he had; also doubtless hadn't known that his diary was scattered with other girls' names, Jinghua being the latest of a long line. Kayla was the only woman who'd lasted more than a couple of months – but then she was exceptional. Jace had started proposing when they'd only been going out for nine weeks. Kayla, not yet ready to settle down, used to tease him about it.

He got out Quinn's dataphone and scrolled through the messages till he got to: *Q, where are you? Call me. K.*

With an effort, he went back to non-Kayla emails, trying to work out what Quinn had been up to. After a while he got absorbed in this task. Then he did some different research, on luxury items for the man who has everything. He had completely forgotten Floss's presence. When he finally thought of her and looked around she was sound asleep, curled up on the sofa clutching her book. Clearly the day had got to her. The computer told him it was 12.13 am. He decided to leave Ryker till the morning, make an early start. His boots should have arrived by then. He fetched a blanket from one of the bedrooms and dropped it over the girl. She didn't stir.

He got into Quinn's ridiculously opulent king-size bed and lay for a while thinking, trying not to imagine Kayla lying where he lay now. He stared into the dark at the intermittent lights of passing aeroplanes; welcome confirmation he was back from the future, however much trouble awaited him here.

He regretted killing Quinn. It had let him off too easily. He should have been left there alone, without even a box of matches. Getting progressively weaker on a diet of nettles and blackberries, while he taught himself by trial and error how to catch rabbits and hunt deer and make fire and do without, scavenging for the few useful things time had not destroyed.

For year after year.

Gradually despairing of rescue.

Defeat and anger eating into his soul.

There was a clunk as the drone delivered his boots to the package bay. He listened to the whirr of its rotor blades fading into the night.

Jace turned on his left side, closed his eyes and slept like the dead.

CHAPTER 14

Kayla

Floss woke to an early spring morning, and took a few seconds to work out where – and when – she was. She'd never slept in her clothes before. No sign of Jace; for a moment she panicked, since he represented her only hope of returning to her own time. She walked softly round the vast apartment, decided he was probably asleep in the room behind the closed door, but didn't like to look in and check. So she locked herself in one of the bathrooms and had a shower, which apart from a settings selection – she went for Manual – was reassuringly like 2015 showers. The towels were thick and soft, and she found a hair dryer in the bedroom.

She dressed, asked the computer for breakfast (its idea of breakfast, or possibly Quinn's, turned out to be hot croissants and coffee), sat at the computer and checked its browsing history. She had to adjust to using a sensitive area on the desk to control it, and at first her fingers kept reaching for the non-existent mouse. Also the computer seemed to be responding to her eye movements, which both helped and confused. The interface was super-fast, different of course from what she was used to, but intuitive and she quickly adapted.

She was curious to find what Jace had been so engrossed in the evening before. Floss liked to have all the facts, and felt at a disadvantage in her current state of ignorance. She was not going to make the mistake of trusting Jace when she knew so little about him. It was possible he had not told her the truth, or not all of it. She paused for several minutes at his Crimestoppers page, skipped over the world news and extravagant gifts for men (he was thinking of compensating for his years with nothing, perhaps) to focus on Jace's associates and Quinn's social life. Curiosity satisfied, conjectures made and confirmed, she cleared her own and Jace's browsing data and turned to Google Street View. It now showed real time by default, and had sound. Floss leaned forward, fascinated, watching blurred-out people walking around like ghosts. There was not nearly so much traffic, though lots of bikes. With a few exceptions, most cars came in three sizes and were all rather similar, with adverts on the sides and blue or green lights on top.

Jace appeared in the doorway, nodding at her. The jacket he wore casually unbuttoned was military dress uniform meets pirate; braid, buttons, high collar; outrageously becoming. He didn't seem at all self-conscious wearing what was to Floss's mind fancy dress. Men's fashions had certainly changed in thirty years. He crossed to a hatch in the wall, got out a cardboard box and took it to the sofa to open.

"Catch." He chucked a small packet at her, which turned out to be travel sickness patches, and started trying on high boots with straps and buckles. He walked experimentally round the room and over to the computer. "What are you looking at?"

"Google Street View. I want to see what my old flat looks like."

She'd found it now. The house had gone up in the world; railings guarded the basement area instead of the old brick wall, the door was mulberry red, the stucco immaculate, the windows authentic replicas of the Victorian originals. Her tiny attic studio had been replaced by a roof extension with huge panes of glass and a narrow balcony with bay trees at either end. She clicked on Past Views and gazed nostalgically at the flat in 2015 when it was run down, affordable and hers.

Jace ordered coffee, egg, bacon and fried bread, and tried the second pair of boots while the kitchen prepared his meal.

"Why did you buy three pairs of boots?"

He said deadpan, "Because I'm not the one paying for them."

Floss thought again how much better he looked without the beard and grime. Now revealed, his face was interesting; uncompromising planes and angles, direct dark eyes that gave nothing away. As he was there she might as well get him to supply information unavailable on the internet.

"You know London in the future? Where did all the people go?"

"No one's supposed to know they're gone. It was classified when Quinn told me, and I've checked and the public still don't know. But since you've seen it for yourself . . . just don't tell anyone, okay?" Floss nodded. "A contraceptive virus wiped them out."

Floss stared at him silently, dumbfounded. This could not be a coincidence. In the end she said in a strained voice, "How do you know it was that?"

"Quinn worked for IEMA like me." He pronounced it EEMA. "International Event Modification Authority, the Intelligence Department. They made forays into the future at specific intervals, to see how stuff like global warming was developing, and check for any avoidable threats we hadn't seen coming. Epidemics, meteorites, riots."

"I thought time travel was hardly ever allowed?"

"Trips to the past, yes, it's just too risky, but the future's safer. Even that's strictly regulated, every trip vetted and recorded. Anyway, Quinn told me before he dumped me in the future that in a hundred and fifty years' time humans are extinct because of a rogue virus. What they hadn't worked out five years ago – and I'm assuming still haven't, since you and Quinn showed up there – is which button to push to prevent it happening."

Floss gazed out of the window, wondering whether to keep quiet or tell him. He was almost a complete stranger, ruthless, and likely to be untrustworthy . . . still, he was in danger from IEMA too, plus she owed him; had it not been for Jace she might right now be stuck in future London with wolves, the odd lion, and very little else. She made up her mind.

"I think I know why Quinn grabbed me. You see, I'm a research scientist . . ."

Now Jace was staring at her. "You don't look like a research scientist."

"Ah." Floss's eyes narrowed. "So what in your opinion do research scientists look like? Older, perhaps, plainer, *maler?*"

"Okay, you got me on older and plainer, but in 2050 jobs are gender-neutral. Not like in your day. No one burns bras any more, no need to."

"*Bra burning?* That was back in the 1960s! Like, more than twenty years before I was born! Anyway, it was a myth. Never happened. Don't they teach history any more?"

He rolled his eyes. "Can we get on? Fine, so you're a research scientist. I am neither surprised nor impressed. I accept this as normal. Continue."

Floss gave him a quelling look and continued. "I'm a research scientist, a very good one too, working on species-specific contraception contained in a genetically engineered virus. We're looking to develop a safe way of dealing with invasive non-native species."

"Like cane toads in Australia?"

"Yes, though we're working with mammals not amphibians. Imagine if you could eradicate all the rabbits in Australia, what huge benefits there'd be to the environment. And it's humane, unlike other methods of control."

"It's been done, about fifteen, twenty years ago. Worked like a charm. No more Aussie rabbits. Still got the cane toads, though."

She frowned. "I don't see how it could have mutated to affect humans. The virus escaping from one continent to another was our main concern. You wouldn't want to get rid of rabbits in Europe, for instance, where they belong. Spontaneous cross-species mutation seemed impossible. But if it *did* mutate – well, we were working to make it as potent and contagious as possible. There'd be no stopping it."

"Perhaps someone thought of adapting it as a human contraceptive."

Floss shook her head. "There'd be far too much risk. Virtually impossible to make it safe enough. Companies would be incredibly wary of taking it on. They'd never get a license for use. No, it can't be that. Look, all this time stuff is confusing me, but maybe whatever set it off hasn't happened yet."

"That's possible."

There was a thoughtful pause. Floss said, "I don't understand why Quinn took me to future London. Was that normal procedure, whenever IEMA reckoned it had located the catalyst for an undesirable outcome?"

"No. Theoretically, you'd be compulsorily resettled in our time, given compensation, somewhere to live and helped to find a job. Lifting someone from the past is exceptional. I don't know about the last five years, but before that it's only happened once before, in the States. I've no idea what Quinn was up to."

At that moment there was the click of a lock releasing. They both looked towards the sound, and the gun appeared in Jace's hand, smooth as a conjuring trick. The door opened and a woman walked in. She was tall, plainly dressed in a superbly cut grey trouser suit, with a soft camel coat draped casually over her shoulders and an air of unassailable confidence. Floss knew instantly who she was. *Can those violet eyes really be natural?*

Jace got slowly to his feet, staring at her, putting the gun away. Kayla's eyes widened.

"Jace!" She ran across the room, just as if she'd been waiting five years for this moment. Their arms went round each other. Floss walked slowly to the door and closed it, feeling somewhat de trop. By the time she turned back, they were standing a little apart, eyes locked together.

Jace said, "Well. Hi."

"What happened to you?"

"Bad stuff. Good stuff. Life."

Kayla gazed at him, shaking her head. "Same old Jace. You look terrific. Ansel's jacket suits you. You know there's a warrant out for your arrest?"

"Yeah." He gave her a slow smile Floss hadn't seen before. "Are you going to arrest me, then?"

"I ought to. What are you doing here?"

"Lying low."

"Where's Ansel?"

"I don't know. He wasn't here when I woke up." This lie cheered Floss, for reasons she did not analyse. *Ha. Doesn't seem like he trusts her any more than I do.*

A tiny line appeared between Kayla's eyebrows. "He was expecting me. It's not like him not to be here. I hope nothing's happened . . ."

Kayla sat on the sofa and checked her phone, at the same

time undoing her jacket to reveal a lowish-cut top. Jace settled on the sofa arm, still gazing at her. Floss, having become invisible, perched on the chair across the room by the computer and watched them.

Kayla put her phone away. "It's so lovely to see you again, Jace, after all this time. Where on earth have you been? Did you steal the TiTrav?"

"I was unavoidably detained, and no, I did not steal the TiTrav."

"Ansel said you didn't! He said there was no way it could be you, and that's what I thought too. But all the evidence pointed in your direction, you'd vanished without trace, so had the TiTrav . . . In the end he accepted it."

"And so did you."

"Not at first, but after a year, when you hadn't come back, it seemed . . . You still haven't told me where you were. Tell me what happened, what's going on."

Just perceptibly, Jace's face had hardened during this exchange, and now he stood, his expression non-committal. "I don't think that would be a good idea right now, either for you or me. And we have to go. Catch up with you later."

Floss took the hint and got to her feet again.

Kayla's eyes flicked in her direction, and back to Jace. She gave him an intimate smile. "Hmm . . . Just for you, Jace, I'll pretend I arrived after you left. Perhaps Ansel will be more forthcoming when he gets back."

Jace picked up a leather bag from beside the sofa and walked towards the door. Floss grabbed her ill-gotten jacket and followed, giving a little friendly wave when she reached the threshold, hoping to annoy. Jace closed the door behind them.

They walked to the lift, whose doors sighed open immediately. Jace said, "Ground," and the lift doors closed. He took a deep breath, and got out Quinn's phone to order a pod.

Floss noticed his hands were shaking.

"Will she tell anyone she's seen us?"

"She'll want to talk to Quinn first." He was about to pocket the phone, then he looked again, and brought up an email. His mouth straightened as he read it.

"Are we going to see your friend now?"

He finished with the phone and gave her a sideways look. "Once I've got some money."

CHAPTER 15

Traces

The moment the door closed behind Jace, Kayla emailed Quinn.

Q, I've just met Jace in your apartment. He says you went out early. Is this true? What should I do? I'm worried about you. K.

She waited for a few moments as if hoping for an immediate response, then slid open the terrace door, walked to the balustrade and looked over. Below, she saw Jace and that oddly dressed girl walk across the pavement as a pod pulled over. They got inside and it set off towards Silicon Roundabout. Kayla shivered in the chilly March air. Back in the apartment, she paced about, thinking furiously, repeatedly checking her phone. Something was not right. She hadn't pressed Jace for answers because it had been clear from his demeanour he was not going to give any. If that tiresome girl hadn't been with him, she could have persuaded him to talk. If only Ansel would ring. She tried his number again. He did not pick up.

This was not that unusual; Ansel refused to be tied to his phone, and frequently went offline. But he was consistently punctual and reliable. He had arranged to meet her here, and if held up he would have let her know. Unless something had happened to him . . .

Kayla went to his bedroom, more to keep herself occupied while she waited than to look for clues. Two pairs of new boots in boxes lay on the floor. Something else was different in there, and it took her a minute to work out what. The Jiajing dragon jar that stood on the table by the window was missing. She opened the right-hand bedside drawer, which was divided into sections to hold watches, dark glasses, cufflinks and cravat pins. There were fewer items than she remembered. Ansel had a weakness for expensive watches and owned several. None were in the drawer.

Why had Jace been wearing Ansel's clothes? What was in the bag he'd taken with him? And why was he so evasive about where he'd been? Alarm seized her. Sitting on the edge of the bed, she got out her phone and connected and logged in to her IEMA computer. She went to Surveillance and retrieved Jace's details. For a moment she hesitated. As head of the Timecrime Department, she was able to initiate tracking on a suspect without requesting permission first, but the trace would remain on record. She would effectively be alerting the system to Jace's presence; betraying him, you could say. But he was a wanted man; if he was innocent he had nothing to fear. It was her duty. And considered from a personal viewpoint, Jace belonged to her past. Quinn was her present and, she hoped, her future. She wanted to marry him. She had never taken Jace seriously as a long-term prospect, fond though she'd been of him.

Kayla initiated tracking, starting at 9.30 that morning. Nothing for a moment; then instead of lines of times, coordinates and addresses, the words NO DATA appeared on the screen. He'd taken out his chip, damning evidence of guilt. So why had he shown up again, in Quinn's apartment? And where was Quinn?

Seriously worried now, Kayla considered possible courses of action. She could have Jace arrested and questioned – except how would they find him? He must be using that girl's chip and dataphone to pay for the pod, and Kayla had no way of discovering her identity, so no way of finding out where they were headed. If only Quinn were here. He would know what to do.

She could always put *his* details into Surveillance...

She remembered, after her promotion, Quinn demonstrating how to track a suspect by this system. They'd been lovers by then. He'd looked her in the eye afterwards, and said, "Don't ever put a trace on me, or I'll fire you." He'd said it lightly, but she'd known he meant it; if she used the department's tracking facility on Ansel, she'd lose both her job and him.

It took Kayla several minutes' hard thinking to make up her mind to go against Quinn's wishes. She did not make the decision lightly – perhaps Jace's reappearance had, in some way she could not imagine, made it necessary for him to rush off with no time to let her know? If she got it wrong he would not forgive her. She pictured his displeasure, his face closing against her, his eyes becoming cold, the end of her hopes and plans.

But in the end she could bear the wait no longer. With trembling fingers she entered his details, starting the trace at 8 am that morning.

Within seconds lines of print appeared one by one on the screen.

0800: 51.527334, -0.088266 101 City Road EC1V 1JQ
0815: 51.527334, -0.088266 101 City Road EC1V 1JQ
0830: 51.527334, -0.088266 101 City Road EC1V 1JQ
0845: 51.527334, -0.088266 101 City Road EC1V 1JQ

He *had* been here this morning, then. That was reassuring. Jace had been telling her the truth. Where was Ansel now? Her eyes moved down the list.

0900: 51.527334, -0.088266 101 City Road EC1V 1JQ
0915: 51.527334, -0.088266 101 City Road EC1V 1JQ
0930: 51.527334, -0.088266 101 City Road EC1V 1JQ

But – she'd arrived at 9.30, and Ansel hadn't been here then. Kayla jumped to her feet and searched the bedroom, then ran from room to room, flinging open cupboards, looking under beds, checking anywhere big enough to hold a man. Quinn was not in the apartment. She sat down again, this time in the living room, and stared at the small screen.

0945: 51.523796, -0.087451 38 City Road EC1Y 1AU

Oh my God. Suddenly she understood. There was only one possible explanation of this: Jace had Ansel's chip and phone. She set the trace interval to ten seconds, and watched the location change, as the pod Jace and the girl were in steadily moved away from her into the heart of the City.

CHAPTER 16

Loot

From the spacious lobby they exited into what Floss realized, with a shock of recognition, was City Road. Here Jace stopped. A chilly wind blew and her toes felt icy; it was not ideal weather for sandals.

"What are we waiting for?"

"Our pod."

As he said this, one of the strange-looking cars, a small one, pulled in to the kerb beside them and its door slid open. They got in.

"Hey, a driverless car! That is so cool . . ."

Jace held Quinn's phone up to the screen and spoke to the car. "The nearest pawnshop."

A dulcet female voice said, "Thank you, Ansel Quinn. Do you mean pawn, P-A-W-N, or porn, P-O-R-N?"

"P-A-W-N."

"The closest pawnshop is Hershman and Sons Jewellers and Pawnbrokers, Copthall Avenue, zero point seven miles distance. Estimated time of arrival, 9.42 am. Your saved preference is the advertisement-free option. If this journey is approved, touch Yes on the screen. If not, touch No for other options."

Jace tapped Yes, and the car swivelled on the spot and

moved smoothly and silently into the traffic. The interior was different from any vehicle Floss had been in, with two comfortable seats and big curving windows. The screen now showed a satnav-type map with the car moving towards their destination. Above the screen, a notice told passengers not to leave the pod until the green light came on. Another said:

NO SMOKING

Automatic fixed penalty charge £1,000

If smoke is detected the pod will park and the doors will open

Jace got out Quinn's phone, looked at the caller ID, and put it away again. Floss took off one sandal at a time and rubbed some life back into her toes, watching the other pods weave courteously about the road, giving way to one another, pedestrians and cyclists. This must be cycling heaven.

"So no flying cars yet?" she said. Jace shook his head. "Bummer. Does anyone still use ordinary cars?"

"Motor club enthusiasts. There's not many places you're allowed to drive them these days. Petrol's pricey, too, so you have to be a fanatic or seriously rich. But the roads are much safer, almost no accidents at all. Difficult to believe in your day people accepted the carnage."

"Yes." Floss went quiet, staring out of the window, reluctant to discuss this topic. *Goodness, there was Bunhill Fields...* "We're passing your old home! Or future home, depending on the way you look at it..."

"Old home," said Jace, firmly.

The pod stopped beside Hershman & Sons' respectable blue and gold façade, and thanked them for travelling before letting them out and shimmering off. Inside the shop Jace headed for a cubicle and sat opposite the young assistant. He reached into his bag and one by one laid the contents on the counter, finally adding the bag itself.

First, two watches. "One Tag Heuer, and this is a Lange & Söhne." A bottle of brandy. "Domaine de Joÿ." Dark glasses. "These are Quantum Shades." A blue and white jar. "Ming. And the bag's Saint Laurent."

The young man stared for a moment at the haul, then excused himself to fetch Mr Hershman.

"You stole these from Quinn's flat?" Floss muttered out of the side of her mouth, disapprovingly.

"It's not as if he'll be needing them any more," said Jace. "And he owes me."

"Some might say he'd already paid."

"Suddenly he's your best friend?"

Floss's retort was stillborn as a middle-aged man took his colleague's place, wreathed in smiles. He examined each watch through a loupe, then moved on to the other items, taking his time, jotting notes on a pad. He gave Jace a shrewd look.

"Some very nice pieces here. I must congratulate you on your taste. The Lange & Söhne is a fine watch, very fine. I can offer you a total . . ." he scanned his list, totting it up, ". . . of two hundred and thirty-seven thousand pounds."

Floss was careful to keep her face expressionless. Jace said, with the confidence engendered by selling goods that had cost him absolutely nothing, "I'm thinking more along the lines of three hundred thousand."

There followed a few minutes' negotiation, with Mr Hershman endeavouring to conceal his excitement and Jace so laid back he was practically horizontal. In the end Jace agreed to sell the goods for £287,500. Asked for ID, he stood sideways by a device in the wall which flashed its approval.

"Bank transfer . . . or would you prefer cash?"

"Cash."

Mr Hershman disappeared for a minute, returning with neat bundles of used banknotes held together with rubber bands. Jace counted them, which took quite a time. Floss picked up a hundred-pound note and scrutinized it, fascinated. Though surprisingly similar to the fifty-pound notes of her own day, this bore an image that could only be a middle-aged and now crowned Prince William. Winston Churchill featured on the reverse with a World War II battle scene.

Mr Hershman had noticed her inspecting the note. "You won't find anything wrong," he said. "We checked them most carefully after we printed them."

Floss laughed politely at his small joke. Jace stashed the cash and his receipt in various pockets, summoned another pod and they set off south of the river to see Ryker. Something was niggling Floss.

"How did you give him an ID?"

"I gave him Quinn's."

"How?"

"I cut out his chip after I killed him. Taped it to my arm this morning."

CHAPTER 17

Careless

Floss stared out of the windows, trying to pick out places she knew. London was still its old self, continually changing yet remaining in essence the same; a riotous mix of architectural styles. Victorian gems, jewel-like parks and stunning new buildings mingled with dreary blocks of flats and Toytown closes left over from the last century. Most roofs were made from matt black panels. Jace told her they were solar panels, and compulsory. Windows at any rate had improved; if some were still uPVC, at least they were better designed. And the streets looked wider, more open; Floss puzzled over this then suddenly realized there were no lines of cars parked along the kerbs.

The people, too, looked different but the same. No one was more than a little overweight, for one thing; clearly science had solved the obesity epidemic. Fashion was eclectic, as in Floss's own time, but men were more flashily dressed than they had been for the past three hundred years – much more than the women. They were peacocks, wandering around looking like Jane Austen heroes, or cast members of *Pirates of the Caribbean*. Women's garments were plain; eclipse plumage, often elegant but definitely drab.

They reached a run of scabby unloved streets with litter and potholes. The pod turned into a cul de sac beside the railway and bumped over patched cobbles. On the left was a high fence, on the right a series of railway arches, each walled off with a ramshackle combination of bricks and mortar, windows and corrugated iron, no two alike. Between a bike repair shop and a boxing club was the only arch whose purpose was not obvious. Above the door RYKER was painted in letters so ragged they might have been graffiti.

Jace rang the bell. They heard a deep bark which got louder. The door opened and a man stood there, holding back by the collar a large German Shepherd who was straining to get at them. Ryker was lean and scruffy and wary, dressed in worn dun-coloured jacket and britches. A lower deck pirate, Floss thought instantly.

He looked Jace over. "What do you want?"

"Can we come in?"

"What for?"

"Private business."

"Give me your phones and walk through the scanner."

Jace handed him Quinn's phone, and Floss gave him hers. Ryker did a double take at the 2014 Samsung, and put them both away in a safe with gold scrolling and a brass handle that would have been an antique in Floss's time. They walked through the scanner, a sort of skeletal metal doorway, into a dim interior full of big machines and smelling of mice, lit here and there by naked bulbs. Work benches were littered with tools and electronic items in pieces. The floor was grimy concrete. In one corner stood a few salvaged kitchen units, in the other a door. A ladder led to a narrow platform made from scaffolding running along the back wall, on which stood a rumpled bed and a chest of drawers. The gold bits on Jace's jacket glinted where the light caught them. To Floss his get-up looked more outlandish than ever in those utilitarian and shabby surroundings.

Jace glanced around. "No one else here?"

"No." Ryker went to a workbench with four computer screens on it, pushed a decrepit typist's chair towards Floss with unexpected civility, and lifted coils of wire off another for Jace. He sat on the edge of the bench and waited. The dog curled up in his nearby basket with a sigh; still watching them, though. Floss held out her hand for him to sniff, and fondled his ears; he accepted this attention with reserve.

Jace said, "What would you charge to unlock a TiTrav, and unset the limiter?"

After a pause, Ryker said, "That's illegal."

"Don't let's have this again. Remember what you told me five years ago? It won't be the first illegal thing you've done."

Ryker's eyes were cool. "That was off the record. Just because I gave you a bit of information five years ago doesn't mean we're best mates. Back then, your lot had this whole place turned over for six hours, and you didn't find a thing. IEMA's got nothing on me."

"This isn't to do with IEMA. I'm simply offering you money to do a job."

"Timecrime. You could be setting me up."

Jace remained calm, but his patience was beginning to show. "I don't work for IEMA any more. There's a warrant out for my arrest. I'm putting myself in your hands, coming here. One phone call and you could claim the reward."

Ryker stiffened. "I got standards. I don't grass anyone up, even ex-time cops." He turned to Floss. "And who are you, if you don't mind me asking?"

"I'm from 2015. I want to get back there." Floss tried a smile. "It would be great if you could fix the TiTrav."

Ryker came to a decision and turned back to Jace. "Okay. Let's see what you've got."

Jace unbuckled the TiTrav from his belt and laid it on the bench. Ryker looked from it to Jace and his face broke into a sudden grin. "You weren't kidding when you said this wasn't IEMA business, were you?" He picked it up and examined it, running his fingers over the damaged case, tapping the screen. "If you want to sell, I know someone who'll pay whatever you want, and no questions asked."

"It's not for sale."

"Or he'd be interested in just borrowing it. For a fee." Jace shook his head. "If you change your mind . . ." Ryker fiddled around some more with the TiTrav, then his head lifted. "I seen this one before. It's the same one you were talking about last time I saw you, that Pete had stolen off him."

"I know."

"What you don't know is someone brought it back to me a few days later, to get the tracker taken off. I reckon it was the stinking bastard who killed Pete." The ghost of a smile crossed his face. "I didn't tell him I'd already taken it off."

"Who was that?"

Ryker sat back. "Now I'm not at all sure I should tell you that. I got paid well enough at the time – after a little discussion. His first idea was I should do it for free, and I had to put him right about that. Explain to him he had quite a bit to lose, same as me. But I also got told what to expect if I wasn't discreet. In detail. And I believed him." He paused. "But somehow I doubt you'd have got hold of this if the last owner was still alive. That's why it's locked. And probably why it's a bit knocked about."

"You're right. Quinn's dead."

Ryker showed no surprise at the name. "I knew you didn't nail him when he turned up here. So he shafted you instead?"

"You could say that. How much do you want?"

"Fifty thousand. In cash. Up front. And don't bother

haggling, that's my price, take it or leave it."

"You'll have to do it while I watch."

Jace felt in an inside pocket and handed him a bundle of fifty one thousand notes. Ryker went round the workbench and sat to count them. Jace followed and stood behind his chair to keep an eye on him. Not wanting to be left out, so did Floss. Ryker finished counting and put the money away.

The safe clunked shut and he turned, fixing a beady eye on Jace. "One thing. If you've got any fancy ideas about shooting me when I've finished and getting your cash back, remember you'll need me again if it starts playing up."

"I'm paying you to make it work. A TiTrav's not much good if it's unreliable."

Ryker shrugged. "This model's quality but it's getting on, there's updates it should have had over the last couple of years and I can't hack in to get them, IEMA upped their game in '47. Bound to be slower working out co-ordinates. Not a lot you can do about that, unless you want a visit from your old buddies." He settled at the workbench and connected the TiTrav to his computer. Rows of incomprehensible data appeared on the monitor. Ryker seemed comfortable with it, altering and adding bits of code. Five minutes later, the catch clicked and the two halves opened. He smiled with satisfaction.

After another ten minutes' work he said, "I'll have to take the back off. Something's not right." He reached for a screwdriver, unscrewed eight tiny screws and delicately removed a small curved panel set flush with the inside. "Oh dear oh dear. Now that was just careless." He gazed reproachfully at Jace. "You got blood in it."

"I was being careful. As careful as I could." Jace sounded defensive. "I didn't expect him to bleed as much as he did. He was dead."

"How bad is it?" Floss asked.

"Hard to say. It's only along the top here, came in through this crack in the casing. They're watertight unless you damage them." Ryker got out dental brushes, cotton buds, a box of tissues and a bottle of clear fluid, and set to gently removing Quinn's dried blood. This took some time. At last Ryker replaced the screws and went back to tinkering with the software.

"I've put in a new pass code: 123456, same number to open it and for access." He glanced at Jace. "You'll want to change that." He tapped and swiped the screen, intent, muttering to himself now and then. "I fixed it for Pete so even if it's switched on, ain't no one can trace it no matter what they got. I left the history cause that's quicker if you want to go back somewhere, but anyone looks, it's not there."

Jace nodded approvingly. "That's good."

"You put in xyz and up it comes. You can't change that code, but you won't need to."

He went quiet for a bit, concentrating. Floss gazed around idly, wondering what the other things on the bench were. She picked up something that looked like a robotic hand. Ryker told her to put it down.

Finally he sat back, his expression dubious. "I done the best I could. It should be good to go . . . you may find it plays up a bit. If it does, turn it off and on, reset it and try again. Basically it's all right. Won't let you down. I've unset the limiter. When you've got time, bring it back and I'll fix the case. D'you want to try it out?"

Jace took the TiTrav and said he'd go five minutes into the future. He snapped the cuff on to his wrist, set the time and location, pressed the two buttons simultaneously, and vanished.

Floss immediately started to worry that the device would malfunction and he wouldn't return, leaving her stranded in

2050, or that he planned to vamoose without her, leaving her stranded in 2050. She really didn't want to be stranded in 2050. Ryker offered Floss a coffee, and went over to the grotty kitchen to make it, rinsing a couple of mugs while the kettle boiled. She got out one of the motion sickness patches and stuck it on the inside of her elbow so she'd be prepared if Jace returned ready to take her back to 2015. Hope and fear tangled in her gut.

As Ryker put the mugs down on the bench, the doorbell sounded and the dog leaped up and bounded to the door, barking. Ryker peered at the image of the alleyway on the left-hand monitor. A woman stood outside the door, looking away, scanning the street. She turned.

Kayla.

CHAPTER 18

Escape

"I know her. She's Time Police." Ryker's face was grey. "He's set me up."

"I don't think he has. Why would he?" Floss wished Jace was back. Surely he should be back by now. How long had he been gone? "She must have followed us. Don't open the door. She can't know you're in."

Ryker moved the image around to scan the alley. Just Kayla. He brought up another image on the next screen, a brick wall, an overgrown path, a block of flats. No one visible. He relaxed fractionally. "Looks like she's on her own. She'll go away in the end."

Suddenly Jace was in the room.

Floss said in a low voice, "Kayla's outside."

"On her own?" Floss nodded. "I'll talk to her."

He moved towards the door. Floss caught at his arm. "D'you think that's a good idea? She's Time Police, she's Quinn's girlfriend, she followed us here."

Jace looked sharply at her. "How do you –"

Ryker jumped to his feet. "Shit!"

Floss ran back and looked from screen to screen. Both showed men carrying weapons, running into the alley, erupting through the bushes at the rear of the building, maybe six or seven in total. A loud bang made the dog go into a furious volley of barks. They were breaking the door down.

When they burst in, they'd notice the two warm coffee mugs, and know someone had just left. Floss took her mug to the sink, hastily tipped the coffee away and rinsed it.

"Floss! Leave that!" Jace said. "We need to go."

Floss ran and grabbed his belt. He scrolled down the TiTrav's screen, one eye on the entrance. Suddenly she said, "Our phones!"

Ryker opened the safe and handed them to Floss. She pocketed them. Jace's arm went round her. They could hear banging on the other side of the building now. Jace said with a hint of warning in his tone, "We weren't here, Ryker." He tapped hastily at the screen. Something burst through the top of the door, letting in the daylight. Another bang, then the door crashed to the floor.

Kayla shouted, "Freeze! Hands in the air!"

Jace pressed both buttons. Floss heard a last muted bang as the world went dark.

When the horrible whirling, stomach-churning sensation was over and her feet felt solid ground beneath them once more, Floss opened her eyes. Her immediate reaction was relief that she felt only mild nausea, with no urge to throw up. Then she realized where they were; not Islington in 2015. Back in bloody Bunhill Fields, in the deserted London of the future. The air was damp and a chill gust swirled autumn leaves on to unkempt grass. She let go of Jace's belt and tried not to wail.

"What are we doing *here?*"

"We had to get out fast. This was in the history and I knew what it was."

"My *flat* was in the history."

"It would have taken longer. I had to change the time

setting."

"Why on earth . . . ? If you hadn't done that you might have had time to choose my flat!"

Jace's voice was hoarse. He looked spent. "It's an IEMA rule. You don't go into the future or the past the same day someone else has."

"You don't work for IEMA any more!"

"It's a rule because it's dangerous." After a moment he added, "Okay . . . so the same day wouldn't matter . . . but we couldn't go the same minute. We'd have met Quinn."

Floss turned away so he wouldn't see the tears in her eyes, breathing deeply, trying to get a grip. She shouldn't be making a fuss; after all, this detour didn't matter. She said in a small voice, "I want to go home."

"No problem. I'll take you home." Jace leant back against a tombstone and focused on the screen. "23rd July 2015, 6.15 pm, London. This it?"

"Must be." *And it took him all of five seconds to find it.*

"I'll set it five minutes later."

"Make it one minute in case my bike gets stolen."

"Hold on." Floss gripped his belt and shut her eyes. He held her waist and pressed the two buttons. Nothing happened. She opened her eyes. Jace swore softly and pressed the buttons again. She noticed beads of sweat on his forehead, which was not reassuring. He turned the TiTrav off and waited ten seconds, pressed the reset, and turned it on again. Floss prayed. Nothing. Jace tried once more, leaving it off for longer. A light drizzle began to fall; the sky darkened. Nothing happened.

Bitter disappointment turned to impotent rage. The beastly thing wasn't going to work. Trembling with frustration and fear, she said on a rising note, "Suppose it never works again? We'll be stuck here forever! When we could have been in *my*

London – I could be back there now, in my flat! And it's *your stupid fault!* All you had to do was pick that instead of this. Haven't you spent enough time here already? I can't *believe* you did this!"

Jace didn't answer. He slumped against the headstone and shut his eyes. Floss let go of his belt and stared at him hopelessly. Her hand felt wet. She looked down and saw it was covered in blood. She gazed, horrified. "Jace! You're bleeding. Where are you hurt?"

"I don't know." His hand went to his side and he swayed. "She shot me."

Dear God. It was her fault. If only she hadn't thought of their phones at the last minute and delayed their getaway by those few seconds . . . if only they were in 2015, with hospitals and doctors a 999 call away. Floss held his wrist and pressed the two buttons, but the TiTrav was still not working.

She put his arm over her shoulder. First she had to get him out of the rain. "Can you make it to your house?" Jace leaned his weight on her, breathing heavily. They set off, stumbling over the rough grass, Floss trying to encourage him. "You're doing fine, keep going, nearly there . . ."

Without warning his legs gave way; unable to support his full weight, she lowered him to the ground. He groaned and his eyes closed. She undid his waistcoat. The shirt below was more scarlet than white. Pulling it up, she saw blood welling out of a hole in his side. *Oh God, he's going to die.* Desperately, she racked her brain for the little she knew of first aid. Keep him warm, stop the bleeding. She shrugged out of her coat and tucked it round him. She pulled off her sweater, folded it and pressed it against the bullet hole. There'd be an exit wound beneath him which she couldn't reach. The rain fell faster. She felt terribly, appallingly out of her depth. Jace's skin was pallid, his breathing ragged. His eyes opened briefly and closed again.

"Keep talking to me, Jace. You'll be okay." He had to be. She couldn't bear it if he wasn't.

"She meant to hit my arm. It was bright out there... darker inside, she couldn't see..." He fumbled with the TiTrav. After a moment it came off and he gave it to Floss. "I didn't change the password... 1234... 56. Ryker... said it might play up... basically all right..." His breath was coming in long rasping gasps. She didn't know what to do.

"Does it hurt?"

He gave her a wry smile.

She smiled tremulously back. "Stupid question. Can I get you anything? Water..."

"Don't go," he said. "Hold my hand."

She gripped his hand in hers. It felt cold. "I'm here."

"I'm sorry..." His dark eyes locked on hers, then his gaze drifted off. His eyes closed. The ragged breathing slowed and ceased.

"Jace!" Her eyes filled with tears and she began to sob. A great and terrible grief welled up inside her. "Jace..."

Floss knew he was dead, but dragged him to his house anyway, slipping and stumbling and weeping. She couldn't leave him out in the rain. When she had heaved him over the step and inside, she wasn't strong enough to lift him on to the bed, so she laid him on the floor and put the stained duvet over him and her sweater under his head. The wound wasn't bleeding any more. She sat beside him in the gathering dusk, hoping for a miracle; that his eyes would open and he'd be all right. She watched him, knowing this was not going to happen.

Her thoughts went to Ryker, who'd been seen by the Time Police in company with illegal time travellers. He faced a minimum fifteen years' jail. She thought of her mother, who wouldn't see her again or know what had happened to her if the TiTrav didn't work; and of herself, maybe destined to live out the rest of her life the way Jace had been when she first met him.

When it got too dark to distinguish Jace's features, she reached out and touched his face. His flesh felt unnaturally cold and stiff. Floss got up and sat at the table, staring out of the window at the blackness, listening to the rain beating on the roof.

CHAPTER 19

Time Tourism

Wednesday, 8th November, 2045

While the internal enquiry under Sir Richard Burbank rambled on, Quinn gave evidence along with the rest of his team and bided his time. Ryker was cross-examined but, predictably, failed to either provide any useful information or incriminate himself. Eventually Sir Richard concluded that all the evidence pointed to Carnady's guilt, and no further investigation would be made on this score. Though tracking down the miscreant and finding the device remained an IEMA priority, in the absence of any leads at all, gradually the dust settled over the sensational disappearance of Jace and the TiTrav.

Three months after the enquiry, Quinn began time travelling discreetly to his apartment in the near future, where he printed out lists of stocks and shares prices. Armed with this information, he was able to make unerring investments – along with minor failures to allay suspicion. But, satisfactory as he found his growing fortune, this was dull stuff. Soon, he judged, he could begin to experience at first hand the most intriguing periods of history.

His first choice was the Colosseum, to see the shows that

had held fifty thousand people in thrall. He would go the year it opened, 80 AD.

He planned the trip with care. To the surprise of his wife, he threw a fancy dress party, thus giving him the excuse he needed to obtain a Roman nobleman's costume. He hired one from the National Theatre, whose wardrobe mistress assured him the designer was renowned for getting every last historical detail correct. And indeed, the plain white wool toga looked authentic enough when he tried it on in his clandestine Clerkenwell pied-à-terre before taking it home. He turned this way and that in front of the mirror. It suited him. At the party Kayla, becomingly attired as Nell Gwyn, said he looked the epitome of gravitas, and offered him an orange.

Quinn's plan was to arrive at the Colosseum as people were going in, and blend unnoticed with the crowd. He knew that the classes were segregated, from nobles seated in the bottom two tiers nearest the action, to women and slaves right at the top. According to his research, entry was free but a ticket in the form of a clay disc was required. These tesserae had a seat number stamped on, and were distributed in advance. However, some things were a constant; where tickets existed, so did ticket touts. He took some carefully chosen items in a leather satchel to barter – disposable lighters, glass marbles, magnifying glasses, small jars of spices, pads of paper, pens and a few wind-up toys.

The trip started well. When he arrived just outside the building, at first he only had eyes for its magnificence. He could not help smiling with delight as he stood, eyes narrowed against the brilliant sunshine, and gazed upwards at a sight unseen for two thousand years. The white travertine stone cladding dazzled. Of course, he'd visited Rome in his own time and viewed the ancient ruins, but the Colosseum in its pristine state was something else. Huge, superb, embodying the might of Rome. Just for this, it had been worth the trouble of obtaining the TiTrav.

After a moment he looked about him. He was in an area lined with market stalls selling food, drinks and knick-knacks, all of which he could see clearly because of the total absence of milling crowds. Apart from the stallholders, beggars, a few bored soldiers a hundred yards away, and a dog scratching itself in the sun, the place was deserted. Thunderous roars from inside told him the show had already started.

Not a problem – he would reset the TiTrav to take him back half an hour. He had lifted his wrist to set the time when a feeling of being watched made him look up. The stallholders were staring at him and muttering in little groups. Perhaps they had noticed him materialize. Probably not the best idea to disappear while they watched; the last thing he wanted was to cause a stir, given that he planned on spending a few hours there. A man wearing a short belted woollen tunic detached himself from the huddle, approached and said something incomprehensible.

Quinn dropped his arm to his side and said, in his public school Latin, "Greetings. Can you tell me where I might purchase a ticket for the games?"

The man frowned and gabbled something else, a question.

Quinn said slowly and clearly, "I am a stranger here. Perhaps you can tell me how to obtain a ticket? I have valuable goods to barter."

More men had arrived, short sunburned men smelling of sweat and garlic and fish. They gathered around him, pointing at his sandals and toga and fingering the fabric – the seams fascinated them – making comments he did not understand. The TiTrav came in for some attention, too, and he tried to keep his left arm by his side so the screen was out of sight. One man held out a broad-brimmed hat he seemed to think Quinn should buy. They seemed amiable enough, just very interested.

Quinn felt a sudden urge to impress these simple folk. He delved in his bag, got out a disposable lighter, and flicked it on. The men all started back with murmurs of astonishment, then pressed closer. He handed the lighter to the first man.

"A gift from the future." He spoke in English, momentarily giving up on Latin. The man tried and failed to make the lighter work; Quinn demonstrated and handed it back. The man produced a flame, gave a gap-toothed grin, and raised his eyebrows, pointing to himself.

Quinn smiled benignly. Back to Latin. "Yes, the fire maker is yours, you may keep it."

The man bowed, and left quickly with his loot. The others, though, remained, looking expectant. Perhaps the gift had been a mistake. Quinn found himself hemmed in, unable to move. He said firmly, "It has been delightful meeting you all, but now you must excuse me." When this had no effect and they still stood there, plucking at his garments, he looked grave and said, "I really must go, I am missing the entertainment. Unless you are able to help me with the purchase of a ticket, please return to your stalls. I am sure you have work to do."

A red-bearded man seemed to take this amiss. He addressed the group, gesticulating as he did so. Quinn could only make out a couple of words, *nobile genere*, but the gist was unmistakable; the man was mocking the way he talked, his toga, his sandals. Now he was crudely mimicking Quinn: strutting around, speaking in a superior, patronizing way. His fellows grinned. The mood of the group changed subtly, became less friendly. One or two of them cast glances towards the soldiers.

Resolutely, Quinn turned on his heel, but they tagged along, surrounding him, jabbering in their incomprehensible patois. He stood still and crossed his hands then moved them apart decisively, miming *enough*, and walked with determination towards the nearest arch, hoping the men would lose interest. Someone inside the Colosseum would tell him where he could buy a ticket. However, the men stuck with him. They had time on their hands and nothing better to do.

From inside the amphitheatre the crowd was bellowing like a monstrous animal, baying for blood. It irked him to be missing the show. Stepping through the archway into cool shade, he found himself in a spacious corridor curving out of sight left and right. Ahead were steep stairs. It was deserted. His companions became bolder and rougher, jostling him and tugging at his bag. He realized that they were now out of view of the soldiers, and perhaps coming inside had been a mistake. He gripped his bag. Someone seized his left arm in strong fingers and turned his wrist to show the TiTrav's screen, poking at it like a chimp with a stolen dataphone, exclaiming at the changing display. This was too much and without thinking, he lashed out. Quinn had little experience of hitting people, but this time he got lucky – or unlucky. He felt the bone crunch as the punch connected with the man's nose. Blood poured out.

With that blow a line had been crossed.

For a moment all was still. No one was smiling any more. Then knives appeared in their hands like a jagged row of shark's teeth. For the first time in his successful and confident life, Quinn felt seriously frightened. Red-Beard pushed him hard against the wall with his hand, scowling. He hawked and spat, then thrust his knife at the top of Quinn's chest, stabbing through the cloth and lightly piercing his skin. He moved the knife lower and did it again, then again, staring into Quinn's eyes, hissing something unmistakably menacing, speaking slowly and emphasizing each syllable, so for the first time Quinn was able to distinguish some of the words – the rest he could guess. The pain was shocking.

He dropped the bag, fumbled for the TiTrav and pressed the two buttons.

The National Theatre did not refund his deposit on the toga. He had to be careful not to let his wife and Kayla see the cuts on his chest until they had healed. But that was the least of it; the experience gave him an unshakeable aversion for trips to the past.

In spite of this, he made a couple of further forays, neither of which re-ignited his enthusiasm. The Titanic had at first seemed rewarding. Its doomed splendour, the indefinable texture and flavour of a bygone age, enchanted him. He wandered around the vast first class areas, and mingled successfully with passengers in the Verandah Café. But after less than an hour a suspicious purser started to hound him and ask awkward questions in front of the people he'd been chatting to and, humiliated, he'd had to leave.

His trip to the grassy knoll to solve the classic riddle of who killed JFK proved a much worse experience – he was very nearly shot by a police officer.

Quinn was accustomed to power, to being in control of events. He had hated being out of his depth, pushed around, the butt of lesser men; these were not experiences he wished to repeat. Not on his own. Quinn was big and reasonably strong, but he was not a trained fighter. Jace would have been good in a situation like the one at the Colosseum – *had* been good in situations like that, when their work had taken them to rough areas. There was that time in Rotherhithe . . . No one pushed Quinn when Jace was around. Quinn felt his absence on the team. He missed him, and once his fury had faded even felt some guilt about leaving him to die – though not enough to go and rescue him. Pity Jace had been so holier-than-thou when offered an opportunity others would kill for. Literally.

There was another reason Quinn regretted leaving him hog-tied in an empty London. He could not be absolutely certain Jace was dead. At the time there had seemed no possibility he could escape. His subconscious mind thought otherwise. In Quinn's nightmares Jace was alive and vengeful, and Quinn would wake, sweating. And if anyone could get out of such a situation, it would be Jace. He was resourceful, tough. If he had survived, it was just conceivable he might encounter one of IEMA's expeditions to the future, with disastrous consequences. Quinn could not now understand why he hadn't shot him – yes, he'd lost his temper and wanted him to suffer, but if he'd shot him in the leg he'd still have died slowly, and with no hope of survival even if he managed to escape his bonds.

He told himself he was worrying about nothing. With an effort, Quinn stopped thinking about Jace, who was almost certainly dead, and returned to considering his options. He no longer wanted to be – what was it Jace had called him? A time tourist. Unthinkable to leave the TiTrav mouldering unused in its hiding place. So what to do with it?

Forget the past for now. The future existed, and could be visited; which did not mean that it was set and could not be altered. There was more to life than money. He had always kept a journal, adding to it whenever something interesting happened, but now he took care to make meticulous notes each day. Then every Thursday when he got home after work he travelled one week into the future, in his own flat, in order to consult the diary for the week ahead. As well as details of each day's events, he wrote suggestions in red; for example, *Do not let Farouk interview Reece, he's cocked it up. Get Kayla to do it.* Exceptionally, if data warranted it, he would check one month ahead.

This method of passing information from the future to the past prevented a host of small annoyances, and won him a reputation in the department for godlike prescience and the luck of the devil.

CHAPTER 20

A blank page

Wednesday, 23rd March 2050, 7.15 pm

How politicians loved the sound of their own voices. Only Quinn's frustration stopped him falling asleep. Maintaining a bland and attentive expression, he waited for Lord Clanranald to finish. This was the fourth time he had sat through this same speech. One by one the man made exactly the same points as last time and the time before and the time before that; Quinn's carefully calculated adjustments had made no difference at all to the outcome. Various countries' IEMA representatives slumped in their green leather seats, eyes on their notes, or gazed blankly at the vast dull oil paintings that adorned the panelling, not appreciating their own luck to only hear it once.

Thank Christ, Clanranald was getting to the familiar peroration, his measured cadences slowing down for emphasis.

"We must not play God with people's lives. Removing this young woman from her own time would be a gross infringement of her personal liberty. However great the catastrophe we are united in wishing to avert, the end must not be used to justify the means. Particularly when we have no way of being one hundred per cent certain that she is indeed the key factor in the calamity in prospect. And without that certainty, we cannot go forward. Mr Quinn, persuasively though he has spoken, has not produced the solid evidence we would need to take such serious action: action, I feel bound to add, that would not be without its own consequences."

He sat, removed his spectacles and polished them, grave and complacent, while a murmur of conversation began in the panelled room as the meeting broke up. Quinn's little group gathered their papers, stood and moved towards the door. Kayla gave him a sympathetic look.

"Bad luck. No one could have done more than you did."

"That pompous fool is the only one with the power to do anything." Quinn eyed him with loathing as he chatted to the American representative. "And he's too cautious to *want* to do anything – except talk, which he's proved he can do at inordinate length."

Outside the Palace of Westminster Quinn said goodbye to his colleagues and stepped into a pod. He knew Kayla had expected to come home with him, perhaps have dinner out first; but he was not in the mood to appreciate her tact and understanding. His exasperation would not let him relax. He had been so sure that this time he'd prevail, yet the outcome remained the same. Confident in his own analysis, he was certain Florence Dryden had been the catalyst for humanity's destruction: if she was only taken out of the equation, the contraceptive virus would fail and the future of the world be secure. His repeated failure to convince Lord Clanranald of this incensed him.

Back in his apartment he ordered filet mignon and a salad. He opened a bottle of Châteauneuf-du-Pape while the kitchen prepared his meal, and walked to the window glass in hand, sipping. After this latest meeting, he had to concede that no matter what approach he used, he would never carry Lord Clanranald with him. Sighing, he sat at his computer and wrote up the day's notes methodically in his diary.

Thursday, 17th March 2050

Quinn stood in his apartment, TiTrav on his wrist, setting the date and place; here, one week's time. As was his habit, he also set the return journey, back to where and when he was, using the limiter. Doing this meant that if anything untoward happened in the future, just by pressing two buttons he could be safely home.

Blackness, a spinning sensation, then his living room materialized around him. The light was different; rain dashed against the big windows. Quinn sat at his desk.

"Wake. Diary."

He read his future-written account of the meeting and Clanranald's obduracy. Though not given to dramatic gestures, he thumped his fist on the desk before leaving for his own time.

Returned to his living room he paced to and fro, itching to prove himself right and Clanranald wrong. A thought came to him: why not? No one would ever know. From the start, he had always been exceedingly careful; he was surely entitled to branch out now. He had laughed five years ago when Jace suggested he might be intending to use the thing for altruistic purposes. Strange if that turned out to be the case.

Averting humanity's extinction had proved to be more interesting than anything else on offer, probably because it was the only real challenge in his life. He excelled at his job – given with a little help from knowing in advance what would happen – and women had a regrettable tendency to fall into his hands like ripe plums before he'd got round to asking them. Even Kayla, who had objected to his married status – it had taken him less than three months to charm her out of her scruples and into his bed. He had enjoyed the three months' seduction almost more than her capitulation, remarkable woman though she was.

Florence Dryden. Now, that was a challenge worthy of his intellect. After five years of restraint, he faced overwhelming temptation to make a major intervention. A quick trip to pick her up, then – it came to him – drop her off where he'd left Jace. This would kill several birds with one stone. If London in 2185 was not depopulated, that would prove that he was right about Florence Dryden. He could safely leave her there in the future with no repercussions for himself in his own time. That he would get no credit for saving humanity did not trouble him. His own satisfaction would be enough.

If, on the other hand, London was still deserted five years after he had taken Jace there, he could reassure himself with the sight of Jace's shackled bones where he had left him. The idea grew on Quinn. He would go now, intercept Florence Dryden on her doorstep as she arrived home after work. Why wait? But first, he would check his journal. He pressed the buttons on the TiTrav to return to the 24th March. Blackness, turmoil, his living room on a rainy evening. Once more he turned to eight days from that day's date, Thursday 24th March. His impatient retailing of Clanranald's verdict was no longer there.

The page was blank.

Quinn stared, then clicked backwards through the journal. Every page since the entry he'd written the day before on Wednesday 16th March was equally empty. In five years, this had never happened, and it could only mean one thing; his future self had not been able to fill in the diary. Something major had occurred to prevent him, and it didn't take a genius to guess what that something was.

If he went this evening to pick up Florence Dryden to take her to future London, he would not return. He wondered what had/would have – tenses became confusing when you had the power to travel in time – happened. He might have met with some mishap, such as a ruined building collapsing on him, or a pack of lions eating him. This was not as fanciful as it sounded. With man, their only predator departed, big cats were thriving in future London. The final act of the last Regent's Park Zoo keeper, before he succumbed to old age, must have been to turn them loose.

Or just possibly his dreams were accurate, and Jace had escaped his bonds five years ago. Somehow he had managed to survive and was still there, eager for vengeance, waiting for Quinn to return.

That settled the matter. The trip was off.

Perhaps he had given up the attempt to persuade Clanranald too easily. He had thought he had tried everything... but had he thought hard enough, were there options he had missed? An inspiration came to him. What about Clanranald's wife? She lived in his country seat in Scotland, and seldom came to London. Quinn made up his mind to visit her, find out if she was charmable, and if so, enlist her help persuading her husband to Quinn's point of view. He brought up City Airport, and booked a flight to Edinburgh the next morning, then emailed Kayla to say he would be away from the office all Thursday.

That done, he visited the future for the third time that night and consulted his diary, a little apprehensively. All was well; the pages were no longer blank. It seemed Lady Clanranald, though surprised to see him, had been receptive. She had given him lunch and promised to do her best. He had got the impression she was a little lonely and welcomed having someone civilized to talk to, had taken a liking to him. Apparently she wrote historical fiction. He read on. His idea was going to work; at the Palace of Westminster meeting, Clanranald had decided that in these exceptional circumstances, with humanity facing the grave risk of total extinction, and considering the weight of evidence that her role in the disaster was key, if inadvertent, the removal of Florence Dryden from her own time would be warranted. Quinn was given the mandate he asked for.

Smiling with satisfaction, back in the present, Quinn went to Amazon and downloaded Lady Clanranald's latest book. He would read it on the plane. In his experience, any author who was not a best seller was invariably delighted when someone had read her work and praised it. She had earned – would earn – this extra effort on his part.

Quinn suddenly thought of something – he had nearly forgotten to confirm that Florence Dryden actually *was* the cause of humanity's demise. A fortnight ahead should be enough . . . once more he pressed the two buttons. For a second nothing happened; then a message he had never seen before appeared on the TiTrav's screen.

Hey! We have a problem. Something needs fixing before you go anytime. Seek out your local friendly TiTrav dealer.

What's that? You're visiting the Cretaceous Period, and a big mean T Rex is sizing you up for lunch?

DON'T PANIC!

Hit Reset, then press those two little buttons anyway. It'll probably be fine. If it's not fine, it'll be quick :o)

When – or if, but don't let's be negative – you get home, don't forget to fix your TiTrav so you can experience lots more fun times!

Quinn stared at this revoltingly chirpy communication with disbelief. In the five years he'd been time travelling, he'd never had a problem, and had come to take the TiTrav's reliability for granted. He glanced at his watch – 9.30 – and went to see Ryker.

CHAPTER 21

A nice little earner

Ryker had finished work for the day really, but he was reprogramming a drinks unit for his neighbour in the next arch, an unpaid job, so he'd rather get it done tonight. Something cold nudged his thigh. Curtis's big amber eyes were fixed on his owner's, trusting and expectant. In his mouth was the red ball, his hiding toy.

"Are you bored?" Ryker fondled his ears. "Okay." He took the ball. "Hide your eyes." Curtis went under the desk, lay down and shut his eyes. "No cheating, mind."

Holding the ball, Ryker wandered around the room a few times to throw the dog off the scent. Then he balanced it on a high rung of the ladder leading to the scaffold platform. He went back to the desk.

"Find it, Curtis!"

Curtis leaped up and began to search the workshop, tail wagging. Ryker watched as the dog sniffed round places he'd found it before, then places he hadn't. He paused and considered Ryker, as if trying to read his mind, and did another circuit. Then he put his forepaws on the ladder to the bed and spotted the ball out of reach. He started to climb the ladder carefully. He hadn't got far before his efforts dislodged the ball and it dropped to the floor. Ball in mouth, he came to be praised.

"You are a canine genius, Curtis."

The dog's attention left Ryker. His big ears pricked. Next moment he hurtled to the door, doing his Hound of the Baskervilles impression as the doorbell rang. Ryker clicked to bring up the outside camera on the monitor. He recognized the man in the alleyway and his face took on the aspect of one who has sucked a lemon. Without hurrying, he went to the door and opened it as the bell rang again, not troubling to conceal his dislike and suspicion.

"What d'you want?"

"Good evening to you too, Mr Ryker. I want to come in."

Ryker stood aside grudgingly and Quinn strolled into the room. He sat at the computer desk and released the TiTrav from his wrist.

"It's not working. I'm getting an error message."

Ryker took it and switched it on. He smiled as he read the message. Culcavy wrote that himself; you didn't get it on the more recent IEMA TiTravs. He connected the device to his computer. The screen filled with code. Ryker concentrated, ignoring Quinn. He saw instantly what the problem was; one of the galactic data files had failed to load. Really minor – if Quinn had turned it off and pressed the reset button, the problem would have resolved itself. Everything else was fine . . . he scrolled down the screen, brow furrowed, making Quinn wait. Ryker's mind went to Saffy; lately he had been worrying about her, slaving away in that bar for a pittance with no prospects or place of her own. Since Pete died he'd kept in touch with her, bought her a meal now and then and let her talk about her dad. Now it occurred to him that with access to Quinn's TiTrav, he could make Pete's plans for her a reality.

After five minutes he said, "Lucky you didn't try to use it like this. Your atoms would be scattered right across the Milky

Way. Have you dropped it recently?"

"No. What's wrong with it?"

"The galactic data files are screwed big time and will need to be reloaded, but that's the least of it. The particle analyser's on the blink – I might be able to fix that, but really you could do with a replacement, and they're hard to get hold of. You need a new battery. The chronologer looks dodgy, too, but I can't be sure without running some diagnostics, and that'll take time." He turned to look at Quinn. "You'll have to leave it with me. It's going to take a week, maybe two, to find or make the parts. I'll see what I can do."

Quinn looked hard at him through narrowed eyes, and Ryker felt suddenly afraid. Perhaps he'd overplayed his hand. It would be really bad if Quinn guessed he was lying. He concentrated on maintaining a neutral expression and not showing fear. Then he had a flash of inspiration.

"And it'll cost you," he added. "It's your own fault, you should have brought it to me for a regular service."

The distraction worked. "I think we can leave money out of this discussion," said Quinn. "If I were you, Mr Ryker, I'd make keeping me happy the main focus of your efforts. I might also, in your place, do what I could to avoid spending the next twenty years in jail, or meeting an early and disagreeable death. But of course, it's entirely up to you."

This was better. Quinn was not likely to fit him up or kill him, because he needed him to keep the TiTrav working, not just now but in the future. The threat was an empty one. On the other hand, there were still plenty of things Quinn *could* do to Ryker. He started listing them in his head and, with an effort, made himself stop.

"Like I said, I'll do my best. If I put off the jobs I've got and ask around, I might be able to locate a battery. That's the easy part. There's a lot of delicate work here, and it's got to be done

one hundred per cent accurate. No point doing a rush job if you don't want it to let you down. I'll see if I can do it by Saturday week."

"Make sure it's in full working order." Quinn got to his feet. "Because when I collect it at nine am Saturday the twenty-sixth, you'll be coming with me on a test trip."

After Quinn had left, Ryker made himself a cup of tea, hands shaking. It was all good, though; he'd put one over on Quinn, the bastard, plus he'd be able to rent out the TiTrav to Vadik Sokolov. And he'd told Quinn it needed regular servicing, so that might turn into a nice little earner.

Quite a few people had let Ryker know they were in the market for hiring a TiTrav, if the opportunity arose; but not all of them could be trusted to bring it back. Vadik was an honest villain, and Ryker trusted him.

CHAPTER 22

Section 27 Clause 8

Thursday, 23rd July 2015 ~ Monday, 21st March 2050

"Florence?"

Floss swivelled, house keys poised by the lock, her other hand holding her bike steady. Nobody had called her Florence since her school days. Screwing up her eyes against the sun, she saw a big tall man with stubble-short hair standing on the pavement. She could have sworn the street was empty a moment before. He was strangely dressed in a long jacket with decorative buttons, a high collar and snowy shirt, reminiscent of Regency costume.

He came up the steps towards her. "Florence Dryden?"

"Yes, what is it?"

"Florence Dryden, by the powers vested in me by the World Government, I am apprehending you under Section 27 Clause 8, the prevention of extraordinary danger to humankind. You will be given legal representation in due course should you wish it."

Floss could make no sense at all of this. "*What?* What are you talking about?"

His hand reached out and seized her arm, jerking her away from the bicycle. For an astonished second she looked into cold blue eyes, then the world went dark, inky black, and her stomach felt as if she was simultaneously plummeting in a lift and spinning on a fairground ride. Time passed, long enough for her to wonder if he had hit her over the head – was this what being knocked out felt like? Or maybe this was what death felt like. Terror assailed her while she battled with acute nausea, then she felt solid ground beneath her feet and could see again.

She was in a large conference room with leather chairs and sofas. A waiter and waitress stood to one side behind a long table covered in a white cloth, on which were arranged bottles, glasses and canapés. A small group of people stood around, but Floss could focus on nothing beyond the fact that she was going to be very sick. She bent forward, the man's arm still supporting her, and threw up spectacularly on to the black marble floor. There were murmurs of concern. One man fetched her a seat, and a woman went to get her a glass of water. Floss took a drink, then stared about her. Through the floor-to-ceiling glass windows on two sides she saw rain and darkness. Some sort of strange robotic vacuum cleaner hummed quietly across the room and cleaned the floor.

"Where am I?" she said without a trace of irony.

The man who had brought her here pulled up a chair and sat beside her. His voice was calm and authoritative. "Don't be alarmed, Miss Dryden. You are in London, in the year 2050. Thirty-five years after your own time. My name is Ansel Quinn."

Floss could have dealt with this better had she not felt so shaky and weak. She said, "You're telling me you've brought me to the future?" He nodded. "Why?"

There was a rap on the door, and a man looked in. "They're ready to leave now, Mr Quinn."

Quinn stood. "You'll excuse me. I'll be back shortly. Kayla

and the others will take care of you and answer any questions you have." He smiled and left the room.

"How are you feeling?" the woman called Kayla asked. Everyone else stood around, watching her.

"Confused. You're telling me time travel is a thing?"

"Yes. Though it's illegal, with a few exceptions. Even in your time, scientists thought it was theoretically possible. An exceptionally brilliant physicist called Ben Culcavy actually made it happen."

"What about . . . violating the law of causality?"

"In practice, events proved to be infinitely changeable – which is a whole different problem, admittedly."

Why was she even having this weird conversation? Floss said, "Assuming for the moment this is true, then what do you want with me?"

"I think I'd better leave that to Ansel – Mr Quinn – to explain. Can I get you anything?"

"No." As Floss began to feel better, the enormity of her situation struck her. "How come you think you have the right to snatch me from my own time? When are you going to take me back?"

"Really, it's best to wait –"

Floss got to her feet. "No, it's not best to wait! You owe me an explanation, now!"

A woman with a professionally patient smile stepped forward and said in a soothing voice, "Florence, I understand you must be feeling very disorientated and upset. I'm Jess, and I've been assigned as your counsellor, to assist you through this difficult transitional stage. This is my colleague, Dr Ademola, who is a psychiatrist. We are here to answer any questions you may have, and help you as you adjust to your new life. We can have a quiet talk together here for as long as you like when Mr Quinn returns, and then we'll show you where you'll be living."

Floss looked at her as if she was mad. "I don't want to talk to you and I don't need a counsellor or a psychiatrist. I don't need some total stranger to understand my feelings. I just need to go back to my own time!"

The door opened while she was speaking and Quinn walked in, his face set. The others turned to him. He looked around the group.

"Lord Clanranald and Sir Douglas won't be coming after all. There's been a change of plan. The reception has been cancelled. You can all go home. I'm taking Miss Dryden to dinner."

After a surprised moment, people exchanged glances and moved towards the door. At a glance from Quinn, the waiter and waitress began to remove the refreshments. Only Kayla, Jess and Dr Ademola remained.

He turned to them. "You can go too. I'll deal with this."

Jess said, "This is most irregular. I strongly feel that after such a traumatic experience Florence needs the professional guidance that only a trained –"

"What she needs is answers, and I can give her those." Jess started to speak and Quinn cut her off. "I'll call you if I need you." He stared at her. She stared back, her colour rising, then she turned and walked out, followed by Dr Ademola.

Kayla put a hand on Quinn's arm and said, "Would you like me to –"

"No."

She left the room, glancing over her shoulder as she went. Floss said, "What the hell is going on? I demand an explanation."

"You shall have one. When we're sitting down over a good meal. Come with me."

Floss followed him to a lobby, where they got into a lift. Two seconds later, they emerged into a ground floor foyer, and out to the street. Quinn led her to a strange vehicle the shape of a squashed sphere with adverts on the side and a blue light on top. Its door slid open. Quinn motioned her inside, got in beside her and held what looked like some sort of mobile phone up to the screen. "Federico in Lamb's Passage."

A dulcet female voice said, "Thank you, Ansel Quinn. The restaurant, Federico, is zero point nine miles distance. Estimated time of arrival, 7.36 pm. Your saved preference is the advertisement-free option. If this journey is approved, touch Yes on the screen. If not, touch No for other options."

Quinn tapped Yes, and the car swivelled on the spot and moved smoothly and silently into the traffic, which consisted of similar vehicles and bicycles. For Floss, the driverless car removed her lingering doubts that she had actually been taken to the future, that she was not the victim of some insanely elaborate hoax for a television programme. Quinn was tapping intently on his phone, brow furrowed. Floss glanced surreptitiously at him, trying to get his measure without him noticing. Tall and well built, with an air of confidence, he was clearly a powerful man in this world. She'd put his age at thirty-seven. His fancy clothes, now she could have a good look at them, were beautifully made. The crimson velvet waistcoat was embroidered, and his high boots with silver buckles down the side had the soft sheen of expensive leather. He looked natural in these over-the-top clothes. Floss tried to imagine him in a business suit.

London moved past the big curved windows of the car. She craned to make out buildings she knew in the dark. The streetlights didn't have the orange glare of sodium, but gave a much nicer soft white light. They passed tall trees and railings and something about them seemed to interest Quinn. He turned his head to stare. Floss followed his gaze and recognized the far side of Bunhill Fields, unchanged in thirty years. This part of London was practically home ground.

She sat back and marshalled her thoughts. Ansel Quinn probably represented her best chance of getting back to her own time, so there was everything to be said for not antagonizing him. No point throwing a hissy fit. Stay calm, and find out what was going on. First, she needed information, which Quinn had said he would provide.

The car stopped outside an Italian restaurant. The sultry voice announced, "You have arrived at your destination. Thank you for travelling. Enjoy your evening." The door nearest the kerb slid open. Quinn got out and she followed him into the restaurant.

CHAPTER 23

A brief history of time travel

The interior was darkly elegant, candles on the tables illuminating white tablecloths, and about half full. The maître d' approached, smiling warmly. "Mr Quinn, how nice to see you. Madame." He showed them to a table in the corner with a view of the room and handed them menus. While Floss was choosing, thinking how bizarre it was to be eating out thirty-five years in the future with a stranger, Quinn asked after the man's wife and daughter and ordered a bottle of wine, which came directly. While he was talking to the maître d' and the waiter, Floss studied him under her lashes. Though not good-looking, he was attractive, she decided. She had thought his eyes cold, but she had been wrong; they were warm, humorous and interested. He treated the restaurant staff like real people; she could see they liked him. Their order given, he settled back in his chair and turned his full attention to Floss.

"Florence – may I call you that?"

"If you like, but no one does. It's Floss."

"Floss, then. Call me Ansel. I owe you an apology. There's been a mammoth fuck up. We thought – IEMA thought –"

"Who's IEMA?"

"The International Event Modification Authority. Stupid name. It's an international body that deals with time travel, regulation, enforcement, forward planning, things like that. I'm head of IEMA Intelligence in the UK. We know, from trips to the future, that there is a problem heading our way. A big problem."

Floss thought instantly of an asteroid on a collision course with Earth. "What sort of problem?"

"I'm afraid I can't tell you the details. It's classified." Floss stirred, but Quinn hadn't finished. "We worked out that you were the unwitting catalyst that set off a chain of events ending in disaster."

Probably not an asteroid, then. I'm going to have a child who turns into a future Hitler-type person . . .

"But we got it wrong. Now we've taken you out of the equation, the results are still the same." Quinn rubbed his face and swept his hands over his short hair. For a moment he looked exhausted.

"Well, I can see that's frustrating. But I'm sure you'll work it out in the end. Just take me back to my own time, no harm done." A tremor in Floss's voice betrayed her nervousness. If it was that simple he wouldn't have brought her here to explain. She waited anxiously for his reply.

"I'm really, really sorry about this. I accept full responsibility. We can't take you back to your own time."

"Why not? You have a time machine." He didn't reply at once. Floss said, "You made a mistake, but you can put it right. I don't see why this should be a problem."

Quinn sighed. "Time travel is subject to rigid regulation. As it happens, you're the first person we've lifted out of the past in this country, because it's kind of a big deal. You would not believe the lengths I had to go to to get permission to do it in the first place. This sort of thing is controlled by an incredible number of rules. And one of them is, if you remove someone from the past, he or she has to stay in the future. No going back, because of the possible contamination that might occur."

Floss gave him a dangerous stare. "So you are saying you've abducted me from my own time for reasons that turned out to be spurious, you won't take me back, and you won't even tell me what this is all about? That's . . . completely unacceptable. There must be some kind of legal appeal I can make to get this reversed."

"I'm afraid not. If it was possible to appeal, I'd help you do it. This is a special case, under the jurisdiction of IEMA and the World Government."

"If my knowing about it is potentially disastrous, why didn't you inject me with a soporific while you brought me here? Then you could have taken me back without my knowing I'd gone anywhere."

"It doesn't work like that. With you unconscious, the future would be a quantum superposition. Like Schrödinger's cat. The future does not change, the cat is not dead or alive, until one opens the box. We opened the box, and here you are." He added softly, "I'm sorry."

Floss experienced a horrible sinking feeling. She recognized a brick wall when she saw one. Only desperation made her say, "I won't tell anyone I've been to the future. I'll be absolutely discreet. You can rely on me."

"I'm sure we can. Unfortunately, the rules governing this are inflexible. If there was anything I could do, believe me, I would do it."

"But my mother – she'll be –" Gripped by sudden anguish, Floss couldn't speak for several seconds. Her eyes filled with tears. "Me just disappearing, her not knowing what's happened to me, imagining the worst, waiting and hoping and dreading for the rest of her life – you can't do this to her. My father died when I was ten, she didn't remarry, I'm her only child."

Quinn looked his sympathy, but said nothing. Floss needed

to be alone to get control of herself. She got up and stumbled to the Ladies, tears spilling down her cheeks. Locked in the cubicle, she fought down misery and panic and made herself stop crying. After five minutes, she came out, washed her hands and stared in the mirror above the basin. Apart from the fear in her eyes, she looked normal. Though she felt like screaming and sobbing and smashing glass, she knew that would do no good. She said quietly to herself:

"Right. Get a grip. I can do this. I do not need to panic, because I am going to get back to my own time. I do not need to worry about Mum, because I will be returning to my own time, and she won't even know I have gone. I will do whatever it takes to achieve this. Including staying calm, and working out the best way to get my hands on one of their time travel devices. They exist, therefore it is possible to steal one. Fear and panic will hinder my doing this." Floss took a deep breath, and shut her eyes while she visualized cramming her fear and panic into a suitcase and turning a key in the lock. She tried an experimental smile. "I am now going to go and sit down and eat my dinner and be very nice to Ansel Quinn, because he is head of IEMA Intelligence and may be able to help me."

She left the Ladies and headed for the corner table. Quinn got to his feet and pulled out her chair for her, concerned and attentive. Floss sat and drank some wine, then looked into his eyes. Making a massive effort, she smiled.

"I have thirty-five years to catch up on. By the end of this meal I want you to have told me everything I don't know. Every single thing. This is your mission for the evening, should you choose to accept it."

She read two things from his smile; relief that she was not going to be difficult, and speculation that her company this evening might even be enjoyable.

He said, "I'd be delighted."

"So, why not start by telling me about time travel?"

"Your wish is my command. Ben Culcavy is the inventor of time travel and probably the most famous recluse in the world. He's a maverick with a hint of mystery about him. Also rich; at twenty-one he was orphaned and inherited the family fortune, which his father had made from computer games. Strifer Max and his companion spider, Mortuus? After your time, maybe."

The hors d'oeuvres arrived. During the break in the conversation, Floss considered Culcavy's possibilities. She made a mental note to look up where he lived. He'd be certain to have a time machine. If you'd invented the thing, you'd hang on to one however illegal it was. Maybe she could persuade him to take her back to her own time . . .

The waiter left and Quinn resumed. "Back in 2029 or thereabouts he did some breakthrough work moving primitive organisms through time. Single-cell organisms, and less than a second of time, but still, when he published his results there was a lot of excitement and respect in scientific circles. Then the Daily Mail got hold of the story and did an interview with him, in which he said humans would time travel within ten years. They took a photo which made him look like a walking cliché mad scientist. The piece caused general merriment and ridicule among his peers. So he went off and got on with it. Stopped writing papers, turned into a hermit. People forgot about him. On his own, he made the first TiTravs. The next thing anyone knew, he was selling them for ten million pounds each on the open market."

"That's incredible, doing something so fantastically complex alone in just a few years. I mean, you're not just moving in time, but in a constantly shifting galaxy, space too. How do you sort out the logistics of that? Then miniaturize it to wear on your wrist?"

"How indeed. Incredible is the word. Culcavy's first crude

model occupied an entire barn. It's been speculated that he used it to travel to the future and bring back the final refined version."

"Ah, I've read about this. A consistent causal loop. So that actually works, then?"

"Who knows?"

Floss said demurely, "I assumed you would, Mr Quinn."

"Ansel. I hate to break it to you, but I do not know everything. Just . . . almost everything. How is your bruschetta?"

"Delicious, thank you. What happened next? How did time travel become illegal?"

"Culcavy sold some TiTravs – no more than a few dozen, probably, to rich men who had everything. He had offers for the technology, from airlines who wanted to use it to transport passengers, and from Amazon. Culcavy was in discussion with Jeff Bezos, who was dead keen and prepared to pay any amount of money. He wanted it so Amazon could make deliveries within seconds of the customer ordering. Then, six days after the first device went on sale, the World Government outlawed time travel, made it a crime carrying a minimum sentence of fifteen years."

"That seems a bit draconian."

"It's dangerous, random time travel to the past, because of the potential to affect the present and the future. With unrestricted time travel, chronology would cease to exist. The result would be mayhem, a constantly fluctuating present. You couldn't walk down the road without things changing around you."

"I can see that, but fifteen years . . ."

"Once the new law had been passed, the WG – the World Government – tried to track down the TiTravs that had already been sold. That wasn't made any easier by the fact that

Culcavy hadn't kept records and wasn't being particularly cooperative. We're still trying to locate a few rogue TiTravs we're certain are out there."

Aha. If illicit TiTravs exist, then maybe I could get hold of one...

Floss did not want Quinn to notice her interest in this subject and guess the reason. He was not a fool; though he was relaxed, and she could tell he was enjoying her company, this did not mean his brain was switched off. She did not underestimate him. Time to change the subject.

"Driverless cars – when did they take over? They'd only just been thought of in my time."

"Pods, we call them. TFL – Transport for London – started a fleet, and they became so popular that private cars turned into an indulgence for the very rich. In the end there were so few left it was possible to ban them from cities without public outrage."

As the meal progressed, they covered robotics, politics, film, television and literature. Quinn proved an amusing and well-informed companion. By the time they reached the coffee stage, they were getting on really well. Floss felt almost – almost but not quite – as if she was there by choice. But every now and then a black lurch of panic assailed her; a bit like eating a picnic with a friend on a sunny cliff top, and sporadically recalling that your feet dangle over a sixty-foot drop. *I am going to get back to my own time.*

She sipped her Armagnac. "Fashions. What you're wearing is – would have been – fancy dress in my time. When did men become peacocks?"

Quinn glanced down at his clothes. "I've never thought about it. It happened gradually, I think... actors and rock stars started a trend, and it spread. These things go in cycles. Men were drab for more than a century."

"You're nearly done. Tell me what I should be wearing. From what I observe it's not skinny jeans."

Quinn smiled. "Is that what they're called? They may be vintage, but on you they look charming."

"I bet you say that to all the women you abduct from the past."

"I've told you, you are unique. As for telling you what to wear, women's fashion is not my area of expertise. But, and this is something I have never said before, even to my wife when I had one, I will take you clothes shopping tomorrow. You can buy a whole new wardrobe, courtesy of IEMA. This is part of the process of settling you in."

Playing along as if reconciled to her fate, Floss said, "What are the other parts of the process? Where will I live?"

"IEMA has provided you with a flat. It's small, but will belong to you, and it's fully kitted out. I'll take you there tonight."

This was a relief. She had been afraid they'd keep her in a detention centre or prison. "Thank you. And what about getting a job?"

"That's Jess's department."

Floss said with a lack of enthusiasm she did not trouble to hide, "Will she be coming shopping with us tomorrow?"

Quinn smiled. "Not if you don't want her to."

CHAPTER 24

Floss's new flat

Quinn paid the bill, thanked Giovanni and summoned a pod which pulled in to the kerb as they left the restaurant. Quinn put his hand for a moment on Floss's slender waist to guide her towards it, with a surprising feeling of well-being. An evening he had expected to be tiresome had turned out to be the most enjoyable he'd had for months. Floss was good company, and pretty too: actually, *pretty* did not do her justice, was hardly the *mot juste*. Beautiful, distinguished even, with that bone structure and those intelligent eyes. Beside her, Kayla's familiar beauty seemed insipid. And she had a remarkably attractive voice, melodious and distinct . . . Thank God she hadn't made the scene she was entirely entitled to make.

This had been a bad day for Quinn. Admittedly with a little help from the TiTrav, he had won himself a reputation for infallibility over the last five years. Now he had publicly and with maximum effort proved himself cataclysmically wrong. Single-handedly, he had persuaded IEMA to make its first major intervention in the past by permanently removing Florence Dryden – Floss. He had staked his reputation; then those who had fought him every inch of the way turned out to have been right all along. They would never let him forget that. He remembered the moment he and Voss had returned from the trip to the future with the bad news that nothing had changed. Lord Clanranald and Sir Douglas Calhoun, who had intended to be part of the reception to celebrate averting humanity's demise, left immediately in order to distance themselves from the affair. The responsibility, they made clear, would be Quinn's alone.

And worse, the debacle had been completely avoidable. He had been so elated at finally winning his point, and so cocksure of the results that he had taken a risk. He should have found some excuse to delay picking up the girl, waited for Ryker to mend the TiTrav, and checked the outcome first.

As the pod moved off Quinn saw Kayla had texted him: *Q, I hope your evening is now over and wasn't too grim. K.* Kayla would have preferred the abductee from the past to be male, he knew, or older, or plainer. She took pains not to appear proprietorial and pretended she was as relaxed about their relationship as he was, but he saw through her play-acting. Sometimes she just couldn't help herself. He knew she wanted to move into his apartment, marry him, have his children, the whole bloody caboodle. She hadn't felt like that about Jace. A quotation from Thucydides came into his head; *It is a general rule of human nature that people despise those who treat them well, and look up to those who make no concessions.* Without replying he turned off the phone and pocketed it.

Floss said, "Can I see?"

He got his phone out again and handed it to her. He watched her study its sleek lines, and move her fingers over the screen. Her hands were competent, Elizabethan slim and pale.

"That is so cool. Why are they called dataphones?"

Quinn said, straight-faced, "They were originally designed and used exclusively for organizing one's social life."

"Really?"

"No. I'll get you your own tomorrow once you've got a chip. You can't function without one."

"A chip?" Floss's face screwed up. "You're telling me I have to be *microchipped?* Like a . . . *pet?*"

"Correct," he replied. "Life here is not possible without a chip and a phone. Only vagrants and outlaws don't have a chip. Together, they replace ID cards, credit cards, cash and a lot of security stuff. Book a ticket to a theatre and you can walk straight in. Their reader will recognize your chip and know you've paid."

"Does that mean terrorism is a thing of the past?"

He smiled at her naïvety. "No; foiling terrorism was one of the benefits politicians promised that nobody in his right mind believed would actually happen. Terrorists have no difficulty removing their chips and acquiring fake ones."

The pod passed his building in City Road, and a few minutes later pulled in to the brand new high rise where Floss would live. He showed her how to use the temporary card that would let her in until she had her chip and phone. The elevator whizzed them up to the forty-second floor and a long white corridor. Quinn opened the door labelled 633 and said, "Light."

It wasn't too bad; small, of course, not more than two hundred square feet, but with nine-foot ceilings and stylishly fitted out with every modern amenity. He looked at Floss to see what she thought of her new home. She walked to the big picture window leading on to a Juliet balcony and gazed out at the night view of London. Something seemed to strike her. She moved to one side and put her face at an angle to the glass, then turned to him.

"It's not real!"

He joined her. "You're right, I hadn't realized. It's a virtual window." He doubted they would have had them in her day, so he explained. "It livestreams the view from a camera on the outside of the building. Makes interior apartments less claustrophobic."

Her face was appalled. "People here live in flats with no windows?"

"It'll have adjustable air conditioning."

"Oh God, I can hear it." Indeed, there was a very slight background hum.

"Look on this as a temporary measure. If you still hate it once you've settled in, I'll see what I can do to get you moved. I think you'll find the area convenient. I live only five minutes away, in City Road." He showed her around. "Bathroom through here. You should find everything you need in the cupboards. This is the kitchen, fully robotic so just ask for what you want. Wardrobe and drawers here . . ." He gestured to a desk, chair, screen and keyboard. "This is your computer." At the flick of a switch on the wall a double bed slowly lowered itself, ready made up, a folded pair of white pyjamas lying on the duvet. "Bed."

"Thank you."

She looked young and lost standing there in her quaint old-fashioned clothes. Even while enjoying their tête-à-tête, Quinn had been aware at the back of his mind of her fortitude in the face of what must seem a disastrous change in her life. She made him feel oddly protective; he wanted to comfort her, get her out of here and back to his spacious apartment with real windows. Take her to bed and make love to her gently until she forgot her troubles and fell asleep in his arms.

He got out the temporary phone he had brought for her, keyed in his number and address and handed it to her. "Call me at any time, if you need me. I can be round here in minutes."

"Thank you," she said again.

"I'll collect you tomorrow morning at nine." He hesitated, and said quietly, "Being the entirely selfish person I am, I cannot regret the strange circumstances that enabled me to meet you." He half smiled, and left her alone in the tiny flat.

Back home, Quinn had a shower and brooded on a less agreeable topic, his loss of face. It occurred to him that he had the ability to fix this. Once Ryker had repaired the TiTrav, he could travel back in time and warn his former self that he'd got it wrong about the cause of depopulation. Leave Miss Dryden in her own time.

Two objections: one, he had never done this before, and was not sure how it worked. If he went back and did something to change the future, presumably he would return to an altered future where he had not obtained permission to remove Floss; but supposing his action inadvertently changed something else in an undesirable way? To take an extreme example, if he had died in the new future, it would not be possible to return and resume his life. The further back in time one went, the greater the risk of unintended consequences. Ten minutes, an hour would be unlikely to cause problems; a fortnight was a different matter. Ryker might well know the answer, but Quinn did not want to ask him. It would show weakness. Bad enough that he depended on the man to keep the thing working.

The other objection was that, having met Floss, he was unwilling to write her out of his life. She was the most interesting woman he'd met since Kayla five or six years ago; she was his treat, his reward, though for what he did not specify. Quinn was used to getting what he wanted; he was not good at forgoing possible pleasure. He decided to let things be.

As soon as she was alone, Floss allowed her face to fall. Fear and dismay flooded back, and she fought them off, staring out of the fake window. There was the Shard glowing blue in the dark, now accompanied by even taller skyscrapers new since her day. She turned away. The bedroom and bathroom were pristine and equipped with everything she might need. Floss sat at the flash computer screen mounted in silver metal and looked for the On switch. There wasn't one. She'd poked fruitlessly about for a couple of minutes before it occurred to her to say, "Computer."

Instantly the black screen blossomed into cantering horses, which morphed into birds, flew into the sky and fell as snow covering the hills. Winter turned to spring, and the horses reappeared. It was beautiful. Floss watched the sequence three times, before saying, "Google. Records of deaths. Emma Elspeth Dryden."

After ten minutes spent getting used to an unfamiliar interface and hunting about, the page came up that Floss had hoped not to find. Her mother had died on the 3rd August, 2029, aged sixty-three. Tears filled her eyes and ran down her face. She walked to the window and stared into the dark city alive with lights. *I'm going to get back. She'll live longer when she's not grieving for me.*

Floss returned to the computer and looked up her old boss at Zadotech. Bill Caldecot had retired the year before aged seventy, but was still doing some consultancy work. He still lived in the same cottage outside Oxford, where she had once visited when he threw a party for the department. It was strange to see him so old in the photos.

Floss suddenly realized she felt exhausted, wiped out, ready for the temporary oblivion of sleep. Quickly, before going to bed, she looked up her own name. Google offered her various other Florence Drydens, mostly from the nineteenth century; Florence was an old-fashioned name. But though she searched for quite a while, she found nothing about her disappearance. In a way it was a relief; but odd. Very odd.

CHAPTER 25

Mutual charm offensive

In spite of his avowed inexperience, Quinn proved fun to go shopping with. He took Floss to exclusive boutiques in Bond Street and picked out garments for her with a flourish, some of which she liked and some she laughed at and replaced with her own finds. He sat on small buttoned sofas outside fitting rooms, looking both out of place and completely at ease, insisting she emerge to model everything for him, and egging her on to be extravagant.

"Take both," he said, when Floss was undecided between two silk tops. "After all, how often does a government department buy you clothes? Make the most of it. Try this next."

He handed her a dress on a hanger; blue/grey, floor length, cobwebby. Floss took it into the changing room. There was no doubt Quinn had a good eye; the dress might have been made for her. Fitted to the waist, floating as she moved, drifting round her shoulders, it made her look like a ragged angel. She gazed at her reflection, then went to show him.

"That one you must have."

"It's awesome, but the price . . . and when would I wear it?"

"Dinner at the Ritz with me. We'll take it. I think after this we should get you a hat. Either something huge and shady, or tiny and ridiculous worn above one ear."

"I think not." Floss gave him a quelling glance. "I am not minor royalty."

"As you wish. We'll do boots and shoes instead."

They spent all morning shopping, then Quinn took her to a restaurant. Floss wore one of her new outfits; beautifully tailored trousers, wide in the leg and fitted to hip and waist, neat ankle boots, a plain top and a cashmere coat. Quinn arranged for her old clothes and their new purchases to be sent back to her flat. Over their second meal together, Floss tried to analyse Quinn's charm; perhaps it was the way he focused his entire attention on you, listened to what you said, and always had an interesting response. He did not seem to regard this as an investment on which he would expect a speedy dividend.

After lunch he took her to be registered and have a chip implanted in her arm. He bought a dataphone, used it to open Floss a bank account and transferred £500,000 into it.

He handed her the phone. "You are good to go. Welcome to 2050. Now for your new job."

Back at IEMA's headquarters, Jess was waiting in the lobby looking restive, as if she had been there some time. At their approach she rose and smiled with annoying solicitude at Floss, as if she was recovering from an illness, and pretty much ignored Quinn. He left for his office, after telling Floss he had not realized shopping could be such fun, and they must do it again in the near future.

Once they were alone, Jess said, "Florence! You look very well. 2050 seems to suit you. I hope you are nicely settled in in your new flat?"

Floss's suppressed resentment at her abduction bubbled up. *Bloody counsellors, paid to pretend to be your friend, thinking they know best the whole time, treating you like a child . . .* Unable to make herself be pleasant to this woman, she decided not to care. Let her earn her money. "Not really. A, I don't want to be here, and B, if I *am* stuck here, I'd prefer a flat with real windows. Can you get me one?"

"Now that might be a little difficult. We did use the whole of the housing budget allocated –"

Floss looked her straight in the eye and lied. "I suffer from claustrophobia."

"Oh. Well, in that case I'll see what I can do. We might have to move you a little further out . . . Leave it with me. Now, I've found you a job with a pharmaceuticals company. Let me just order a pod, and I'll take you there and introduce you to everyone."

The company occupied a modern building in Leytonstone, with BIOPHARM in big steel letters above the entrance. Floss's spirits lifted; this looked promising. She had enjoyed her work, and looked forward to finding out about all the fascinating discoveries that must have been made in the past thirty-five years. Inside the spacious lobby, Jess spoke to the man behind the desk and he logged their chips. Then they went up in the lift to the first floor, a vast white space with windows all round and a vista of grass and roads. Jess led her past glass-walled offices with elegant desks, all appropriately futuristic, to an area at the far side with ranks of work stations in white and raspberry. Jess stopped at an unoccupied desk.

"This is yours. And you're next to a lovely view!"

Floss, who had been expecting to be taken to a laboratory, became suspicious. "What is my actual job?"

"You'll be Junior Operations Manager, working with the C.O.O. – the Chief Operating Officer – for the senior management team."

There was an ominous pause while Floss deciphered this information. "So you have found me a job working as a P.A. to a P.A.?"

"I wouldn't exactly describe it that way . . ."

Floss scowled. "I am a fully qualified research scientist, and this was the best you could find for me?"

Jess's lips pursed. "It is a pharmaceuticals firm." The Teflon smile reappeared. Unlike most people, Jess was able to smile and talk simultaneously. "I'm afraid you're forgetting your qualifications are thirty-five years out of date, Florence. You wouldn't be able to cope with the equivalent of your 2015 job."

"I'm fast. I'd catch up. I'm prepared to work as many hours as that would take."

Jess was already shaking her head. "I think we have to face facts, here, Florence. No one's going to employ you without an up-to-date degree or recent experience. Why don't you just give this a go for a week or two and see how you get on? You might find it more rewarding than you think."

Floss took a deep breath and made up her mind not to bother. Did it matter, really? She was not intending to stay in 2050, after all. Though she would have loved to find out about the advances in her field, she could always look them up on the internet.

"I'll give it a trial for a few days," she said, grudgingly.

A few days was all it took for Floss to decide she had had enough. That Thursday, her tasks for the day completed early, she waited for five thirty and brooded. Not only was she overqualified and underused, but here there were zero opportunities to get her hands on a TiTrav. She was marking time. Now if she worked at IEMA . . . Suddenly she thought, why not? Why not try to manoeuvre Quinn into giving her a job? Subtly, so he'd think it was his own idea . . .

She called into the C.O.O.'s office, then left the building, ringing Quinn's number as she walked along the road in the early spring light. His pleasant low voice answered immediately.

"Floss. How nice to hear from you. How can I help?"

"I've done something dreadful. I hardly like to tell you."

"And I can hardly bear the suspense. What have you done?"

"I've given in my notice. This job is ridiculous. I've decided to go back to university and take another degree so I can work in my own field."

"But that's an excellent idea. Is there anything I can do to help?"

"Your advice would be appreciated, of course. But it's too late now to apply to start this September – assuming the process hasn't changed?"

"No, you have to apply by mid-January, mid-October for Oxbridge."

"I went to Cambridge – Corpus Christi – before."

"It's just possible I might be able to get your application considered for this year. I have contacts at Cambridge. I'll see what I can do."

"That would be awesome!" Floss attempted flattery. "You are so kind, I feel like you're my only friend here."

"Just the first of many, I'm sure."

"There's one problem – what do I do while I'm waiting? I can't sit staring out of my virtual window all day. I'd be happy to do a boring job knowing it was a temporary measure . . ."

"Hmm . . . I have an idea."

It was as easy as that.

The following day, Floss started work at IEMA in the timecrime department as a dogsbody. She cheerfully accepted being the lowliest member of the team, doing nothing for the first few days except make herself useful and friendly, leaping up whenever anyone wanted coffee, running errands, printing things out, updating records. Making it clear to Quinn that his idea had been a brilliant one. Everyone was pleasant; but a few times she looked up and caught Kayla, the head of the department, eyeing her. Maybe she resented Quinn giving Floss the job without consulting her.

Kayla was not happy about having this girl dumped on her. True, Floss was a willing and efficient worker, good at noticing things that needed doing, and doing them before she was asked. She was very little trouble to supervise. But Kayla's suspicions were aroused. She couldn't help suspecting that Quinn would not have taken Floss on had she not had those looks. Whenever he dropped into the department and paused by Floss's desk, Kayla would watch and listen as much as she could without appearing to. They always seemed to be laughing together at some private joke. Kayla resolved to ignore it and say nothing. This resolution lasted a fortnight.

They were in Quinn's office after working hours to discuss the pay rise Farouk had put in for; after that, Kayla expected they would probably eat out together or go to Quinn's apartment. His decision made – Farouk got his rise, a little less than he'd wanted – Quinn said in passing how Floss's presence seemed to have speeded up routine matters in the department. "The weekly digest never arrived on time while it was Farouk's responsibility. Now it's in my inbox by nine o'clock every Wednesday morning."

Kayla tried to sound nonchalant. "How long is she going to be here?"

"Not very long." Quinn looked up from his screen. "She'll be going to university in September, most likely. Why?"

"I wondered, that's all." Kayla paused, then was unable to resist saying, "I've never quite understood what she was doing here in the first place. Why didn't you leave her in the job that counsellor, what was her name, Jess, found for her?"

He responded to her words, not her underlying emotion. He said calmly, "Floss didn't like it. She's too intelligent, she got bored."

Kayla's voice sharpened. "If she finds filing and fetching cups of coffee at IEMA rewarding, I can't imagine what they had her doing. Scrubbing the floor, perhaps?"

Quinn gave her an assessing glance, his eyes cold. "If you're curious, why not ask her?" he said, getting to his feet and putting on his jacket. He smiled in a perfunctory way and left the building alone. Kayla cursed herself, deeply regretting her failure to play it cool, knowing Quinn disliked any sign of proprietary behaviour on her part.

After a week, discreetly, in the intervals of gofering, Floss started investigating leads. She had already attempted to find Ben Culcavy's address. But he was clearly a dedicated and successful recluse; there weren't even many photos of him on the internet, and they were shot from a distance and blurry. Only the student ones looked as if he was aware a photo was being taken and didn't mind. Out of curiosity, she looked up the Daily Mail article, which made her feel quite sorry for Culcavy. After that her quest had led her into the strange online world of celebrity address websites. She'd typed his name into half a dozen search boxes, and got half a dozen variants on No Results. For the moment, she had given up this line of enquiry.

She was excited to learn that the department had its own TiTravs used for collecting data from the future, plus a small black museum of illegal devices confiscated from time criminals. Farouk told her these used to be on display behind half-inch thick glass, until a couple of attempts to break in and steal them. They now resided in the vaults, locked behind foot-thick steel walls, and she could see that realistically there was no way of getting her hands on one. Tantalizing. Nor was anyone likely to leave a TiTrav on her desk while stopping for a chat. But you never knew . . .

And there were other possibilities. Just occasionally, an illicit TiTrav surfaced. There were, in IEMA's estimation, between six and twelve of them on the loose. The last one to show up had been five years before. Floss raised her eyes from studying the department's records on her computer. Everyone was out of the office except for Farouk, who occupied the desk next to hers. He was scrolling through a property website in his coffee break, hoping to find a bigger flat before his first child was born; a hopeless enterprise that always left him glum and uncommunicative. She'd be doing him a favour distracting him.

"Hey, Farouk, the illegal TiTrav that was found five years ago – were you here then?"

Farouk raised sober brown eyes. "Yes indeed." He shook his head. "It was a very big scandal. And we never actually found it, either."

"Tell me about it."

Farouk told her, in detail. Floss listened carefully, memorizing names and places. He finished by saying, "I liked Jace. He was the last person you'd expect to go off the rails like that. It goes to show you never really know someone. Even Kayla had no idea."

"Why, was Kayla . . . ?"

"His girlfriend, yes. She and Quinn only got together much later."

Quinn and Kayla an item . . . This was news to Floss. Though the possibility had crossed her mind once or twice, there was little in their behaviour in the office to give them away. It explained why she noticed Kayla looking at her from time to time. "What happened to Scott?"

"He left soon after. I think he felt bad about killing Peter McGuire, his heart went out of the job after that. He never got the chance to settle in here."

"And did you ever pin anything on Ryker?"

"No. As far as I know, he's still in his workshop under the arches. We haven't had reason to investigate him since."

Farouk smiled politely and returned to Yourplace.com, his brow furrowing over videos of apartments in undesirable parts of London, all of them undersized and expensive, and most requiring considerable work.

Floss went back to the records of the raid that Farouk had told her about. If anyone asked what she was doing, she could tell them Farouk's story had made her curious. The people involved, apart from those she saw every day in the office, were Scott Winchester, Jace Carnady, Saffron McGuire, and Ryker, who didn't seem to have another name. Helpfully, their 2045 contact details were there.

Floss wondered if there was more to Scott's leaving IEMA than Farouk supposed. She looked him up in the department's records and found his date of birth, his photograph, and his employment dates. He was young, clean shaven with an open face and dark crinkly hair. He had worked at IEMA for only three months. Aha – here was the copy of a request for a reference for Scott from the Metropolitan Police. All at once Floss saw the flaw in her plan. If she looked up Scott and tried to pump him for details of the raid five years ago, he'd naturally want to know why. And she could hardly explain to a policeman that she was hoping to get her hands on an illegal TiTrav in order to get back to her own time.

Okay. So she needed to find someone involved on the other side of the law. Ideally, she wanted to find Jace Carnady, the likeable (according to Farouk) guy who had stolen the TiTrav and presumably still had it, and ask him to take her back to 2015. She Googled his name. To the right of the page were half a dozen photos of him. She moved closer, then clicked on Images. Carnady had dark eyes, a straight nose and a firm mouth in the few photos where he wasn't smiling and showing good teeth; his hair had a Byronic curl, his jaw varied between stubbled and lightly bearded, his shoulders were broad in the high collared jackets of the time. Farouk hadn't mentioned that Jace Carnady was hot.

Below the photos it said:

JASON CARNADY is a British man alleged to have stolen a TiTrav May 2045. He has never been found, and nor has the TiTrav. His last known address was London.

Born 15 October 2016 ~

He hadn't been born yet, in Floss's own time. Staring at his photos, she told herself this was probably not a useful lead. If the authorities had failed to locate him at the time, and were still looking, how much chance did she have now?

What about Saffron, McGuire's daughter? If her father had been a criminal, she might know some of his contacts. She hadn't talked to Kayla, but she might talk to Floss.

CHAPTER 26

A night at the opera

Floss poured Quinn's mint tea from his special teapot into a glass, put it on a tray with a small bowl of mixed nuts and raisins, and carried it down the corridor. Quinn's office occupied the corner of the building, and was the largest and best on that level with windows on both sides. The door was open, and as she got nearer, Floss could see Kayla's back view. She was standing in the doorway facing into the room, hand on the door knob. Instinctively, Floss froze. Kayla spoke, sounding exasperated, as if she had been trying to convince him of something for some time, and had got nowhere.

"You're being naïve."

"*Naïve?*" Quinn's voice, calm and amused. "That doesn't sound like me."

"You can't see she's got her own agenda! D'you think she *likes* fetching you cups of coffee? She's just hoping for an opportunity to get back to her own time."

"I don't see how fetching me cups of coffee would further that aim."

"I'm not saying it would, just that's what she thinks! You're Chief of Intelligence, she knows you get to time travel. She's trying to manipulate you."

"It's thoughtful of you to warn me. I shall take care not to be manipulated." Pause. "By anyone."

Quinn's tone was a dismissal in itself. Hearing this, Floss turned and practically ran back the way she had come, careless of slopping the tea, until she reached the far end of the corridor. She swivelled, and when Kayla emerged, expression stormy, Floss was walking slowly towards her from twenty feet away. Floss gave her a sunny smile, and received a curt nod in return. Kayla was clearly too cross to keep up appearances.

Floss knocked on the door and went in.

Quinn looked up and smiled. "Ah, a cup of your mint tea, just what I need. No one else makes it quite as well."

"I'm afraid I've spilled it a bit." Floss put the tray on his desk and made to leave.

"Sit down a minute, Floss."

She sat opposite him.

"Do you have any plans for your birthday?"

Floss was going to be twenty-six on the following Saturday, 9th April. Or of course sixty-one, if you counted the years from 1989 to 2050. "No . . ."

"In that case you must let me take you out to celebrate. We'll have dinner and go to the opera. You can wear that long dress you look so ravishing in."

Floss was not particularly musical, and didn't like opera. She hoped it wasn't a long one. Wagner, she knew, could go on for four hours, not counting intermissions. But she did like eating out, and it was nice of him to remember her birthday from the details he must have studied about her. This was a kind offer, and much better than staying in on her own in her flat on her birthday.

"Thank you, that's very kind of you, I'd love to."

"Splendid. I'll pick you up on Saturday at five thirty."

Saturday morning Floss's doorbell woke her up. Clambering

out of bed to answer it, she remembered that today was her birthday. She opened the door and took delivery of a large bouquet of white flowers; roses, lilies and gypsophila. Rather bridal, she thought. The note read:

Happy birthday.
Looking forward to tonight,
Q

Floss found a vase, put the flowers in water and arranged them on her desk. They took up most of the space, but there wasn't anywhere else to put them. Their heady scent filled the apartment, a constant reminder of her birthday outing that evening.

Quinn collected her at exactly five thirty. Floss opened the door to him having made a special effort with her appearance; she wore the cobwebby dress, and her hair up. He was looking his smoothest in a waisted black tailcoat and britches, with a white cravat and a red carnation in his buttonhole.

"Hi," she said.

Quinn ran his eyes over her appreciatively. "You look . . . delightful."

"Thank you for the flowers, they're lovely."

"My pleasure."

Floss had never been to The Royal Opera House, though she had often passed it. Their pod dropped them in Bow Street, immediately outside the huge pillared façade. The building had hardly changed at all. Quinn escorted her to a table in the Amphitheatre Restaurant and sat opposite her.

"We can take our time. The table is ours for the evening."

Floss sat up schoolroom straight amid the lavish surroundings, a little uneasy at being out with a man who had a girlfriend; she was not entirely sure of his motives. She hoped he was just being friendly . . . but maybe he was not. A waiter handed her the menu, and Quinn ordered champagne. The food was delicious, and the attentive waiters and civilized bustle of the restaurant around them made their tête-à-tête seem less like a date. Quinn's manner was companionable rather than flirtatious, and Floss began to relax and enjoy herself.

The hors d'oeuvres and a light main course eaten, it was time for the (from Floss's viewpoint) less appealing part of the evening. Quinn put his hand lightly once or twice on her waist to guide her towards their private box in the Grand Tier.

The box was to the left of the auditorium, and decorated in red velvet and gold leaf. Floss sat and leant her elbows on the broad plush surface, looking around. They had a superb, if angled, view of the stage and the orchestra. The other boxes were all occupied by four people. *My God, what is this costing him?* Everyone in the audience, even the stalls, was dressed up, much more so than they would have been in her own day.

She glanced at her programme. They had come to see *Le Nozze di Figaro*. By Mozart, composer of one of Floss's all-time least favourite tunes, *Eine kleine Nachtmusik*. No need to tell Quinn that. Floss was determined to keep an open mind; this would be a really good performance even if she didn't appreciate the actual music. People who knew about music all thought Mozart was the bee's knees.

"I'm deplorably ignorant about opera. Tell me five interesting things about this one."

"Let me think. *Le Nozze di Figaro* is currently number seven of the most-performed operas worldwide."

"What's number one?"

"I think that's Carmen – or just possibly La Traviata."

"Go on."

"Two, Beaumarchais's play on which the opera was based

was banned for licentiousness. Three, Mozart was paid four hundred and fifty florins for the piece –"

"How much was that in those days?"

"The equivalent of two or three years' salary. Four, Brahms described each song in *Figaro* as a miracle. Five . . . hmm . . . okay, hardly interesting at all – I saw my first production of *Figaro* when I was ten."

"Did you enjoy it?"

"Indeed I did. I've been a fan of Mozart ever since."

The house lights dimmed and the audience grew quiet. The orchestra played the overture, then the curtains swung apart and the performance began.

The trouble with opera, Floss thought, is that the cast keep stopping to sing all the time. And the acting isn't up to much; so arch, so over the top. Then there was the story. The tedious misunderstandings, the mistaken identities, the ludicrous complications of plots and subplots, the hiding behind furniture inadequate to the task. It went on and on. And Quinn sat to her right, and because they were at an angle could see her as well as the stage, so she was obliged to maintain an appreciative expression the whole time. She was relieved when the curtain went down for the intermission and Quinn led her to the champagne bar, which resembled a smaller Crystal Palace. They chatted and laughed together, and the bell summoning them to the next act rang too soon.

As they resumed their seats and the house began to hush, Quinn gave Floss a shrewd look. "You're putting up a good front, but this really isn't your sort of thing, is it?" Before Floss could get out her insincere protestations, he said, "No need to be polite. You hate it. Let's go somewhere nice and have a drink." He stood up.

Floss got to her feet too. "But these tickets must have cost a fortune!"

"It's only money. And it's your birthday. Come on."

"But you're enjoying it and we've only seen the first act."

"It's okay." He smiled at her, ushering her out. "I know what happens."

They paced along the deserted corridor, glanced at by the odd member of Opera House staff.

"What does happen?"

"D'you want to go back and find out?" He was laughing at her. He summarized the rest of the plot for her benefit on the way out.

They walked into the deepening twilight of Covent Garden. Floss stopped to peer in the windows of a raffish cocktail bar she remembered going to with Chris in her other life, thirty-five years ago.

"Wow, I'm amazed it's still going strong. I've been here – it was fun. Looks like it's hardly changed."

"Let's revisit your past."

Party music greeted them as they went down the stairs to a low-ceilinged, brick arched space crowded with people. Quinn seemed sublimely unconcerned as heads turned to look at them; their dressy clothes made them stand out in the casual crowd. A small group rose to leave, and they were able to grab seats at a table.

"What will you have to drink?"

"You choose for me."

Quinn pushed his way to the bar. Floss looked around her; though the layout and all the details were different, the wacky atmosphere had changed very little.

A young man said, "Are these seats taken?"

"Just these two."

The man sat down while his companion went to the bar. Floss studied him covertly while he checked his phone; his face was curiously familiar. For a moment she couldn't place him, then she recognized who he was; Scott Winchester, the IEMA operative who had shot McGuire and killed him, and left the department soon after. He still looked exactly like his photo from five years before. Floss's heart rate doubled. She glanced towards the bar; luckily it was packed, and Quinn was not yet being served. She turned back and opened her mouth to speak. At that moment he looked up and caught her staring at him.

He smiled. "Do I look like someone you know? I'd remember if we'd met."

"I work for IEMA doing filing and stuff. I think I've seen your photograph in the records. Scott Winchester?"

His face clouded almost imperceptibly, then he smiled, a little guardedly. "That's me. I worked there once, very briefly. It didn't suit me, so I left." There was an awkward pause, then before Floss had worked out what to say he added, "You probably read about it. It was all over the web at the time. They said I killed a suspect by accident."

"Yes . . ." Floss hesitated before asking his opinion on who stole the TiTrav. IEMA was clearly a painful subject for him; it would be considerate if she dropped it. But this was a heaven-sent opportunity to find out more, and she had to be quick before Quinn came back with the drinks.

Before she could speak he said in a rush, looking down at the table, "Everyone was very understanding. Except the thing is, I didn't kill him. That's why I left." He looked away towards the bar, then made a visible effort to lighten up. His eyes crinkled in a smile and he sat back. "It's been five years. I should be able to let it go, not bore total strangers in bars with protestations of innocence. But it's still eating me."

Floss abandoned subtlety. "Do you think Jace Carnady stole the TiTrav?"

"That's what everyone thought at the time . . ." His gaze went over her shoulder. Quinn had returned holding two elaborate cocktails. Scott did not look as if his evening was improving.

Quinn said, "Scott! How nice to see you. How are you doing these days?"

"Very well, thank you. Really enjoying the work."

"You're still with . . . ?"

"Yes. You'll excuse me, I must go and see what's happened to my friend." He turned to Floss. "Nice to meet you." He walked away.

Floss decided to think about this later. She took the drink. "What is it?"

"That one's Boom Ting, this is Grounds for Divorce. I chose them purely on their names. We can swap if you like."

"What's in it?"

"Guess."

The evening over, alone in her flat, Floss's mind buzzed over what Scott had told her. She had not seen him again – he had not returned to their table. Could he really believe that Quinn had made the mistake that resulted in a man's death, or was he deluding himself? She imagined if you did kill somebody in error, you would really want to believe you hadn't, and if you could convince yourself, it might give you peace of mind. Except Scott hadn't seemed particularly peaceful on the subject. It was still rankling. Maybe to feel okay about it, you needed to convince everybody else as well.

CHAPTER 27

Exploring London

Tuesday, 12th April 2050

It was time to put her plan to visit Saffron and Ryker into action. Floss rang Quinn shortly after nine am and told him she had a migraine. He was all concern, which made her feel a little shame-faced. Not enough to change her intentions, though.

"Is there anything I can get you? Shall I call a doctor?"

"No, it's nothing, I get them from time to time." This was not true – Floss seldom even had a headache. "Just a bit of a bore. I'll be fine if I rest in a dark room till it goes away."

She had memorized the routes to Saffron's home and Ryker's workshop the night before. Floss had to assume she was under some sort of surveillance – probably nothing too extreme – after all, what threat did she pose? What could she do? And she'd taken pains to appear reconciled to her transplanted life; reasonably reconciled, not suspiciously so. But this was a society where citizens were microchipped. She would leave her dataphone in her flat, just in case IEMA was using it to track her. There was bound to be documentation of pod journeys, so she intended to wear her low-heeled new boots and walk. The weather was good for March, bright and blowy. It would be nice to see more of London.

The walk to Haggerston took twenty minutes, with streets morphing from immaculate Victorian terraces with manicured gardens, to 1970s unloved low-rise red brick, to glittering new skyscrapers and depressing old ones. Were architects ever less inspired than in the 1950s, 60s and 70s, Floss wondered. Population, litter and graffiti levels rose and fell as she walked from well-heeled to poor areas. The disparity between the two seemed more extreme than in her day.

When Floss reached Saffron's block, it turned out she no longer lived there. A man answered the intercom and told her she'd moved out. He didn't ask who Floss was, but volunteered Saffron's current address, the White Horse in Hackney. It took half an hour to walk to Mare Street and find the pub. It was closed, but a door to one side had four bell pushes, and the top one had a new handwritten label in red ink: S. MCGUIRE. Floss rang the bell. Nothing happened. She wondered whether to ring again, or try one of the other bells. Saffron might be out. Then she heard the thud of feet on stairs. The door opened and a slight girl stood there hugging a towelling robe round herself. Her feet were bare, her pink/red hair was tousled, her eyes sleepy, and she regarded Floss with mistrust.

"Hi, are you Saffron?" The girl nodded. "I'm Floss. I'm hoping you can help me."

"What with?"

Floss didn't want to come right out with her story until she'd got more of a feel for whether she could trust Saffron. "It's to do with your father."

"My father's dead. Who are you? What do you want? How did you know my address?"

"It's a bit complicated to explain. Can I just talk to you for a minute?"

Saffron paused, eyeing her. Apparently Floss passed her

silent appraisal, because she said, "Okay. You'll have to talk while I get ready. I start work at half ten." She stood back to let Floss in. They climbed three flights of stairs to the top of the house, then ascended a ladder which led through a hatch in the ceiling into a minuscule room under the eaves. To the left of a small round window in the only non-sloping wall was a narrow bed, and a long mirror with cheap jewellery hanging from each corner. To the right a rail of clothes, a filing cabinet, a table and a chair. These things only just fitted into the space, but at least Saffron had a window that was real and opened.

"I took this bar job because the room came with it." Saffron perched on the end of the bed facing the mirror and began to backcomb her hair. Floss sat on the chair, to be out of her way. There was a small silence.

"Well?" Saffron said.

Floss realized it was not going to be possible to make small talk until she'd made a decision about Saffron's reliability. She'd have to take a chance. "This must sound crazy, but I'm from 2015 –"

"You don't look as if you're from the past."

"IEMA bought me new clothes. About three weeks ago they abducted me from my own time. They had a theory I was a catalyst for something bad that was going to happen in the future."

Saffron had darted a quick look at Floss through the mirror at the mention of IEMA. "What sort of bad thing?"

"They wouldn't tell me. And now they won't take me back to my own time, even though it turns out I wasn't the cause of the problem."

Saffron snorted. She had finished with her hair and started on her makeup, dusting pale powder over her face. "That's typical of those bastards. They screw up your life and wander off. So what do you want me to do about it?"

"I'm trying to find someone who has a TiTrav, who might be willing to take me home. There aren't many of them around."

"I haven't got one."

"I know..." Floss hesitated, not sure how to put the next bit. "I don't want to upset you... but I read up about your father being shot five years ago. They said he had a TiTrav. Have you any idea what happened to it?"

Saffron's face was expressionless as she started to paint black lines around her eyes. She didn't say anything.

Floss said, "I'm sorry. I know how awful it must have been for you, losing your father... you probably don't want to talk about it."

"They say you'll get over it. But you don't. I think about him every day."

"I know. My father... he was run over... when I was ten..."

There was a short silence.

"I'll tell you what I know. It's not much." Saffron put her brush down and swivelled to face her. "Dad met me after school the day before they killed him. He looked sort of smaller, sad. He wouldn't tell me what was up, he held my hand and said we'd be all right, whatever it was didn't matter. He told me I was the best thing in his life." She was crying now. Floss moved beside her on the bed and patted her shoulder awkwardly. "He did have a TiTrav, he was going to sell it and buy me my own place and pay for university. Ryker told me. But someone took it off him. I think it was someone from IEMA, then they killed him to cover up." Saffron moved away and blotted her eyes with a tissue, then applied lipstick.

Floss thought of Scott, who'd taken the blame for killing Saffron's father. But if you had a TiTrav, you'd be rich, and he hadn't looked particularly flush, nor had he seemed like a murderer. She said dubiously, "Scott Winchester?"

"Maybe, I don't know."

"What about Jace Carnady?"

Saffron shook her head. "Ryker said it wasn't him, he was poking about because he thought someone in IEMA had gone rogue. Then he disappeared. He was the fall guy, Ryker reckoned. That's all I know. I'm going to get dressed now." Floss took the hint and stood up. "If I were you I'd talk to Ryker. If anyone can get his hands on a TiTrav, it'll be him. You can trust him. And he's nice, he'll help if he can. Have you got his address?"

"Yes, that's where I'm off to next."

"He'll be there unless he's walking Curtis. That's his dog, a huge German Shepherd." She picked up a Guinness beer mat and scrawled *Saffy* and a number in silver pen on the black background. "Here. Let me know if you have any luck. Or if you find out anything."

Floss gave Saffron her own number. "Thanks, Saffron. You won't tell anyone about me?"

"Saffy. Course not."

CHAPTER 28

A walk in the park

Curtis picked up his latest stick and came and sat beside the milling machine, eyes fixed on his owner. Ryker, totally absorbed in watching his new toy go through the moves he had programmed, didn't notice. Vadik had returned Quinn's TiTrav and paid the other half of Ryker's fee, letting him know in his sombre Russian fashion he was well content with the deal. The minute he'd departed Ryker had ordered the machine. It had arrived the day before and he'd spent all day setting it up.

Curtis made a small polite noise in the back of his throat. The deep buzz of the motor drowned it out, so he put a paw on Ryker's thigh.

"Hang on a minute, nearly there..." The cutter made a couple more precise sweeps, swivelled and put itself away. Ryker pressed the Off button, released the machined piece of steel, wiped it on a rag and admired it. "Oh yes. This is real class. The business." He showed his test piece to the dog. "Who says crime doesn't pay?"

Curtis was not to be distracted from matters of greater importance. He gazed at Ryker with trust and anticipation in his topaz eyes.

Ryker put the steel down and stretched. "Okay, I could do

with a break. Let's go."

Wyck Gardens was nearer, but both Curtis and Ryker favoured Ruskin Park, which was bigger, had more trees, fewer children, and a pond. They emerged into the main road, turned right, and had not gone more than a few yards when a young woman caught up with them.

"Excuse me, are you Ryker?"

Ryker screwed up his eyes against the sun and gave her a once-over. Young, nice-looking, brand new clothes, posh accent. Out of place round here. Seemed to be on her own. He said with automatic caution, "Who wants him?"

"I'm Floss. Saffron – Saffy suggested I talk to you. She said you might be able to help me."

"I'm going to the park. You can come too if you like and tell me about it."

On the way, as they walked down the gusty street past massive building sites and run down terraces, Floss told him about herself, and how she had got here. He listened and asked the odd question, but didn't say anything else until they turned into the park.

"D'you want to sit down?"

"Yes please! I walked here and it took an hour and forty minutes. That's after I walked to Saffy's."

She must be starving, unless she stopped on the way. "Fancy a coffee?"

"And a doughnut. Let me buy you one."

Nice manners. Ryker was rather taken with Floss. She hadn't moaned or whined, just told him the facts, and he approved of that. He led her to the booth. Not taking up her offer, he paid for two coffees, plus a Mars bar for her as they didn't have doughnuts. They sat side by side on a sunny park bench in a sheltered corner, and he threw Curtis's stick for the dog to retrieve.

Floss watched him bound off into the distance. "Does he take his stick everywhere with him?"

"He does at the moment. He goes through phases. He's in a stick phase right now, won't leave home without it." There was a thoughtful pause, then Ryker said, "Quinn's been all right with you, then, has he?"

"How d'you mean? I don't know him very well, obviously, but he's gone out of his way to be kind to me. He seems really sympathetic and friendly."

Ryker gave her a sidelong look. "And you want to find someone who's got a TiTrav and persuade him to take you home?"

"Yes – that seems more possible than stealing one. I was hoping you might know someone . . ."

"Thing is, I only know of one illegal TiTrav knocking about. This is just between me and you, right?" She nodded. He watched her, interested to see how she would react to what he said next. "Quinn's got it."

Her eyes widened. "*Quinn* has got a TiTrav? The same Quinn, Ansel Quinn?"

"Yup."

"But . . ." She stared at him, then her brows drew together, and he could tell she didn't believe him. "He works for IEMA. His job is to *stop* time travel."

"Yup."

She shook her head. "I'm sorry to . . . the thing is . . . I've only just met you, and for all I know you could be saying this to make trouble for him. I know you don't like Quinn, he searched your workshop that time . . . he seems okay to me." She hesitated and said, "What makes you think he's got one?"

Ryker finished his coffee and dropped the carton in the bin. "Because he brings it to me when he wants it fixed. I had it in the workshop last month."

He watched Floss frown as she assimilated this information and put it together with what she knew already, as if doing a jigsaw puzzle. She was no fool. He could see the exact moment when doubts began to infiltrate her mind.

"Did he steal it from Saffy's father?"

"Yup."

"And shot him? So it wasn't Scott Winchester doing it by accident at all, though he got the blame, but Quinn?"

He nodded. "Saffy doesn't know that. I haven't told her. She might do something stupid if she knew."

"Bloody hell. Why do you fix it for him?"

"Because I don't have much choice. He'd fit me up if I didn't."

"So what happened to Jace Carnady, if he was innocent?"

"I don't know. But he was on to Quinn. He came to see me." Curtis brought his stick back and Ryker threw it again. "I reckon Quinn offed him, then maybe dumped his body in the past."

Floss summed up what she had learned. "You're saying *Quinn* killed Saffy's father and maybe Jace Carnady and has an illegal time travelling device which he blackmails you to fix. So he's a total double-dealing psychopath. And when he was all sympathetic about me being stuck here, when he said if there was anything he could do he'd do it, it was complete bollocks, because he could take me back any time he chose to."

"Yup. And he could do it without anyone knowing, too, so that means either he doesn't give a toss, or he wants you here for some reason. Whatever the reason is, it'll be all about him."

Floss's lips tightened. She said, "How often do TiTravs need mending?"

Ryker laughed. "Hardly ever." He looked sideways at her. "Unless they've been got at. This particular one will be showing an error message Thursday April 14th, because I programmed it to do that. There won't be anything wrong with it, but it'll bring Quinn round to my place for sure. I'm going to tell him it'll take a day or two to fix."

Floss's face lit up and her voice trembled as she said, "While it's here, could you use it to take me home?"

"No." Ryker felt bad saying this, seeing the hope fade in her eyes. He should have thought before he boasted about putting one over on Quinn. "He's not an idiot. If you vanish while I've got his TiTrav, he's going to guess what happened. He'd take me to pieces."

She said tentatively, "You could go somewhere else out of his reach. Then you could keep the TiTrav."

"Yes, but this is my home. I like what I've got. I don't want to relocate any more than you did. Sorry."

She swallowed and nodded. "I can see that." Ryker's respect for her increased. A lot of women would have burst into tears when he said that, accusing, entreating; embarrassing him. After a moment she said, "How about . . . I realize it's a big favour . . . would you just take me back to see my mother? Then I could tell her I was okay, and if she never saw me again at least she would know I was still alive, just living in the future."

Ryker thought about this. "On the level? You're not planning to run off the minute we got there?"

"I wouldn't do that. I wouldn't want to get you into trouble with Quinn, especially not after you'd helped me."

"Okay then." He grinned at her. "Come to the workshop on the 14th, in the evening, and we'll time travel."

CHAPTER 29

An idea and an inference

On the walk back, Floss brooded over the revelation that Quinn was not at all what he seemed. She had always believed herself a good judge of character, and yet Quinn had taken her in completely. She had thought him, not just able and intelligent, but good natured and kind; yet according to Ryker he was totally self-centred, a liar, a hypocrite and a murderer. Oddly, it was his sense of humour that made his villainy so unlikely and hard to believe. Humour is a sign both of humanity and a sense of proportion. One expects a baddie to be humourless.

She considered – assuming Ryker was telling the truth, and she had to assume he was, else he wouldn't have agreed to take her to see her mother – why Quinn might want to keep her around. It wasn't for her outdated scientific credentials. He was attracted to her, she knew, and before Ryker's assertions she'd found him quite attractive, too. Not knowing exactly how his relationship with Kayla stood, she had suspected he might ask her out; had given him brownie points for being too considerate to do so until she was more settled in her new life. Now she viewed him with acute mistrust, and any increase of intimacy was out of the question.

Floss turned to happier thoughts. She was hugely comforted by the thought of Ryker taking her to see her mother, so Floss would not have to worry about her if she never managed to return. She decided to take some photos of 2050 to show her, and began by snapping the quiet streets with no parked cars, the futuristic pods, and the tall buildings glittering in the background against the sky.

She was nearly home when an idea came to her so brilliant that her feet stopped moving of their own accord and she stood transfixed in the middle of the pavement. Ryker was an engineer, and was going to have access to Quinn's TiTrav on the 14th April. What was to stop him putting some kind of receiver inside it, the sort of thing you get in a key finder? Then all she would have to do was find a way to be on her own in Quinn's apartment – she assumed that's where he kept it – and use the transmitter to locate and steal the TiTrav. Ryker would be in the clear, especially if she left a note where she found it letting Quinn know she was the thief. Something along the lines of "So long, and thanks for all the fish, Floss". There'd be bugger all Quinn could do about it, either, in his private capacity.

Of course, it was possible IEMA might come looking for her in 2015. She wasn't sure what the rules were. But surely, if she lay low for a few weeks, and there were no undesirable repercussions in their time, it would become clear to them that a second abduction was unnecessary? And it would be in Quinn's interests to do what he could to stop them; he wouldn't want her telling them about how she'd escaped using his illegal TiTrav.

Also, she'd have the TiTrav all to herself for a bit, though obviously she'd have to let Ryker keep it for his help. She wasn't particularly interested in time travel, but the thought of one thing she could use it for made her heart flutter with longing in a way that was almost unbearable.

Back in her tiny flat, her mind buzzing, she ordered a late lunch. Sitting on the sofa with her feet up, a cup of tea, a sandwich and an apple on the coffee table, she considered her plan. Its only downside was that she would need to get closer to Quinn and gain his confidence. Going to bed with him would be the obvious way to get time on her own in his apartment, but the thought revolted her; she had no intention of sleeping with a devious murderer. Even the light flirtation that was the most she could see herself managing would strain her thespian abilities to the max. Perhaps she could break in to his apartment . . . if she got herself invited there, she could check out the door lock, and see if he had an alarm.

After finishing her meal she took some photos for her mother of the flat, then looked up Jace Carnady on the internet, staring at one image after another, and finding new ones she hadn't seen before. Now Ryker had told her what he thought had happened to him, looking at his handsome smiling face pained her, gave her an almost personal sense of loss. Her feeling of outrage towards Quinn increased. To take her mind off him she read for a while, then began to find the flat oppressive, and looked up the cost of apartments with windows. Their prices gave her a new sympathy for Farouk. Unable to go out in case Quinn rang to see how she was, she drifted off to sleep on the sofa.

The room was dark when the doorbell woke her, city lights gleaming in her virtual view. She walked to the entry phone, and got a nasty jolt when she saw Quinn's face on the screen. Fighting her feeling of revulsion, striving to sound natural, she said, "Hi . . ." and yawned, half-deliberately.

Quinn's mellow voice said, "I hope I didn't wake you."

"It doesn't matter. Lucky you did wake me or I wouldn't sleep tonight." After a moment, Floss realized it would look odd if she didn't ask him in. Reluctantly, she pressed the door release. "Come up."

She turned on all the lights and ran her fingers through her hair, apprehensive about seeing him now she suspected what he was like, not feeling ready for this. She worried that he might read her knowledge in her eyes. The door buzzer sounded, and she went to let him in.

"How are you feeling?"

"I'm fine now. Just a bit tired."

"I won't keep you long. I wanted to make sure you were okay, and I practically pass your building on my way home." He smiled.

It was all right. He hadn't read her mind, though she was finding it difficult to look him in the eyes. She felt obliged to ask him to sit down, and offer him coffee.

"Wine would be better. It's been one of those days."

"Australian Chardonnay or Australian Chardonnay?"

"Let me see, I think . . . Australian Chardonnay would be nice." He sat on the sofa and picked up her Kindle while she fetched the bottle and glasses. "Shakespeare. *Measure for Measure*. An interesting choice."

"Yes. It's a play you can read in many ways. Even the 'good' characters behave appallingly. *Especially* the good characters, come to think of it. What was wrong with your day?" She sat at the far end of the sofa, and passed him a glass, looking at it rather than him. Talking was okay, she was able to sound quite natural, but meeting his eyes was another matter.

"I don't expect you to have any sympathy with my problems, given that they're the repercussions of lifting you from your own time. I've been getting flak about it. The violation of your human rights, the enormous expense of relocating you, the possible unwanted ramifications, but mainly," and here he smiled wryly, "the fact that I got it completely wrong."

Floss nervously smoothed the cushion next to her. "I know you'd put it right if you could," she lied with as much conviction as she could muster, curious to hear his response.

"I hope you know that if there's anything at all I can do to make you happy in your new life, you have only to ask." His voice went lower as he held out his glass. "To . . . the future."

Floss, who had feared he was about to say, "To . . . us," raised her glass to clink his, fingers trembling. It would seem strange if she kept looking down, so she compelled herself to meet his gaze. Her cheeks felt hot. Quinn swallowed a mouthful of wine, looking deeply and intimately into her eyes. His were warm, shrewd, and coming to some conclusion, a conclusion that made him smile. Floss read his mind.

Oh God, he thinks I'm embarrassed because I've fallen in love with him.

She felt her blush deepening.

CHAPTER 30

Mini-break in 2015

"He got a bit ratty," said Ryker. *Ratty* was understating it.

Floss grinned. "Oh dear. Was it bad?"

Ryker was not going to admit to finding Quinn intimidating at times. He could handle him. "Nah. He had a bit of a rant, that's all, threw his teddy out of the pram. Who else is going to keep it working for him? He can't afford to do a flounce, he'd lose too much face when he came back, so he just had a go at me."

"And he doesn't suspect?"

"I don't think so. But I'll leave it a bit longer next time, just in case." Eight months seemed reasonable. Not too long, but not so quick that Quinn started to suspect he was taking the mickey.

Floss was excited, Ryker could tell. Her cheeks were pink, her eyes bright, and she was clutching a folder full of stuff to give her mother, evidence so her mum wouldn't start thinking after she'd gone that her visit had all been a strange dream. She'd shown him what was inside. Printed-out photos of herself, her flat, and bits of London her mum would recognize, showing the changes of thirty-five years. The temporary phone Quinn had given her was in there, a solar powered toy pod, and a holo cube with images of London – tourist tat, but they probably didn't have them back in 2015. A silk scarf, with its receipt, in a blue and gold Harrods bag. A Royal Opera House programme from an opera Quinn had taken her to on her birthday the week before, and a silver bookmark which Floss had chosen for the 2050 hallmark. She hadn't shown him the letter she'd written to her mum explaining everything, but he'd caught a glimpse before she moved it below the rest, and it covered two pages and had lots of kisses at the end.

"Here, take this." He held out a twenty-pound note. "No one could fake that. Well, they could, but it'd be hard."

"Oh thanks, that's great. I wanted to put some money in, but didn't know where you get it from. No one seems to use it, even for small things."

"Yup, you've got to be down and out or off the grid to have a use for cash. Ready?" She nodded. He thought of something. "Some people get motion sickness."

"Yes, I did when Quinn brought me here. I bought patches. I don't want to alarm Mum by turning up and being sick as a dog on her doorstep."

"Okay. Thursday, 23rd July, 2015, 8 pm, 15 Highbury Street, N5 1UP, exterior?"

"Yes. What happens if we materialize and someone's standing right there and we land in the middle of them?"

"We won't. It's got compensatory fuzzy logic. It won't land us in the middle of a wall or ten feet up in the air, either. Hold my hand."

Floss gripped his left hand, eyes wide. Ryker grinned at her and pressed the two buttons simultaneously. Blackness, silence, a whirling sensation; then light again, the golden light of a summer evening shining on Victorian stucco to their left, and a park with big trees on their right. Floss let go of him and her face broke into a huge smile.

"Awesome!"

Ryker smiled and looked around to conceal it. The old-fashioned words she came out with amused him. "Nice here. Should have brought Curtis. Which one's your mum's?"

"This one, right here."

He followed her under a spindly iron arch with a hoop (designed he guessed to hold some sort of light – probably not for a Victorian version of basketball) and up three steps to an imposing door with a fanlight. Floss pressed a bell. "It's me." The door latch released and they went upstairs.

Floss's mother looked quite like Floss, only older. She was slim and elegant, with nicely-done hair and makeup. Floss hugged her for a long time.

"What was that for?" she said when Floss released her, smiling at Ryker and giving his clothes an almost imperceptible once-over. "Lovely to see you. I like your new outfit. Have you eaten?"

"Yes. This is Ryker. My mum."

"I'm Emma," said her mother. "Do come in."

Once they were all sitting down, drinks in hand, in a classy living room with high ceilings and two big windows looking over the park, Floss explained to her mother what they were doing there. Ryker had to hand it to Emma; she was cool. She listened carefully, asked sensible questions and took very little convincing. She looked through the folder and examined the TiTrav on his wrist with interest.

"Ryker brought me to see you just in case I can't find a way to get back from 2050. I'll do my best, but if I don't, I'm going to go to university again, requalify, and start all over. I'll be fine, so you mustn't worry if I don't manage to get back."

Emma nodded. She seemed to be taking this very calmly. Perhaps her and Floss weren't that close... Suddenly to

Ryker's alarm her face began to quiver, then it crumpled and her eyes flooded with tears. She turned away shaking and sobbing. Floss put an arm round her.

"It's all right," Floss said.

"I'm sorry . . ." she gasped through her sobs, "It's just the thought that I'll know if you don't come home in the next week or so, I'll never see you again . . ."

Ryker got up, mumbled something and left the room. He found the bathroom along the corridor and had a pee, washed his hands and face with great thoroughness and hung around for ten minutes gazing out of the window to give them a bit of space. When he returned, they were falling about laughing as Emma filmed Floss with her camera. Floss was pulling faces and her mum was trying to get her to stop messing about. The camera swung in his direction. Ryker's native caution made him unhappy about being recorded on film in a time that wasn't his, digital evidence of timecrime that might still be around decades later. Even just Floss being filmed incriminated him. But he couldn't ask Emma to delete it.

When they got back to his place, Floss went a bit quiet. Fretting about her mum, he reckoned. Then she told him the idea she'd had.

Ryker thought it over. No reason why it shouldn't work, in theory. He could fit a receiver into the TiTrav, no problem. Of course, he'd lose a source of income – but then on the plus side, he wouldn't have to deal with Quinn again. Floss would end up the new owner of the TiTrav. She had as much right to it as Quinn or Pete. He wondered if she'd use it. Difficult to resist . . .

"How are you going to get time alone in Quinn's flat?"

"I don't know. How difficult d'you think it would be to break in?"

"For starters there'll be CCTV in the lobby, recording everyone in and out."

"That wouldn't matter, though. I'd be gone before they looked at it. Anyway, he can hardly report the theft, can he? I thought maybe I could jemmy the door. It's a penthouse, people don't come up there unless they're visiting Quinn, so no one would pass by and see the damage."

Ryker laughed. "Do that a lot, do you, jemmy doors? And it'll be a smart lock. Ritzy apartments always have them, they come with the robotics. You break in, it'll send a message straight away to Quinn's phone and the nearest cop shop. So will the burglar alarm. And Quinn'll be able to watch a video of you in his flat from his phone."

"Ah." She paused, eyeing him sideways, and he could see what was coming next. "You're really good at robotics, aren't you? I don't suppose . . ."

He gave her a look. "I could get in there okay. That's not the point though, is it? You'll be safe in the past afterwards. I'll still be here when Quinn finds out he's been robbed."

"Couldn't you hack into the building's CCTV and delete the film? Actually, it would be really good if you came with me because I want to get into Quinn's computer, and you could do that, couldn't you? You could wear a disguise, if you're worried about being recognized. We both could. We could pretend we're going to a fancy dress party. I could be Princess Leia and you could be Darth Vader, so you'd have a mask on and no one would recognize you."

Ryker gazed at her, speechless. He didn't know where to start with this – she couldn't be serious. She was very bright, he'd seen that for himself before he knew what she did for a living, but this reminded him she was only young, not much older than Saffy. Her suggestion sounded more like it belonged in a heist movie than reality. Ryker liked a quiet life, and that didn't mean a quiet life in jail. He liked things the way they were.

Finally he said, "So your plan to not be noticed is us dressing up as Princess Leia and Darth Vader?"

"It doesn't matter if they *notice* us, as long as they don't *recognize* us – you. But if you wiped the recording it wouldn't matter. Quinn can't use IEMA tracking for personal stuff, can he?"

"Don't think so, not without leaving a trace." Floss looked eager at this, and Ryker felt things had gone far enough. It was high time to disillusion her. He said firmly, "Look, it's not that I can't do this; I don't want to. I could hack into the flat's systems and from there to the building's. I could reset the surveillance so there'd just be a repeated section from the day before that if you're lucky they might not notice. If we were careful, Quinn wouldn't know he'd been robbed till he looked for his TiTrav and it's not there. But if anything went wrong, anyone saw me and Quinn did get to hear about it, I'm screwed, and it's not as if I'm getting anything out of this, either. As far as I'm concerned, it's too big a risk for nothing. Why d'you want to get into Quinn's computer anyway?"

"To read his journal. To find out what the disaster is that's going to happen to humanity."

"Why?"

"I'm curious. After all, they thought I caused it. I want to know why they thought that. Maybe I can do something to stop it."

"You don't even know he keeps a journal."

"Yes I do. He told me when we went to the opera. *The unexamined life is not worth living*, he said. Socrates."

Ryker shook his head, unconvinced.

Floss said, "We could use the TiTrav to come back here after to drop you off. Then I'll use it go home. If you like, I could bring it back to you in the future, in a few months' time when any fuss has died down. Then you could take me home and hang on to it. I don't need a time machine –" he sensed her making some private reservation here. Was she planning to win the lottery first? "– so I could do that the same day, and you'd know I'd be there on a date and time we agreed."

This would mean he'd get the TiTrav in due course. He had to admit, that was quite a big incentive. Quinn would think she'd stolen it so wouldn't come after him, and he could make enough money to sort Saffy out the way Pete had been going to, save her from scratching a living in that dead end job. He trusted Floss; she struck him as honest. If she said she'd bring the TiTrav back to him, she would. The balance wavered, and tipped in her favour.

But it was still a mad scheme.

CHAPTER 31

The mad scheme

Thursday, 5th May 2050

Floss hadn't really thought Ryker would come with her. The moment she realized he was agreeing her heart began to pound with excitement and trepidation, because with his expertise her plan was much more likely to succeed and she'd be going home. It was nice of him; of course, he stood to gain a TiTrav, but all the risk was his. The worst she could be accused of was breaking and entering, and that only if they caught her. With luck, she wouldn't be hanging around long enough to be prosecuted for timecrime.

They walked together up the City Road shortly after nine am. Floss had a backpack containing her 2015 clothes and the cobwebby evening dress she could not bring herself to abandon. Ryker had turned down her idea of wearing a Darth Vader helmet; instead he'd put on a sort of hoodie under his jacket, pulled up the hood and kept his head down. Luckily it was a grey cloudy day threatening rain. He stayed a few paces behind her as if they just happened to be walking in the same direction. Floss's breathing was rapid, and her stomach lurched every time she thought of what they were about to do. She felt she could not bear the disappointment if the TiTrav was not there and she had to stay in 2050 after all.

Near the entrance to Quinn's building they slowed to a dawdle, watching as planned, until they saw a woman heading for the main entrance. Ryker closed the gap between them.

"Keep behind me," Floss muttered. Few people are prepared to shut a door in another person's face, unless that person looks disreputable. Floss knew she looked respectable; she wasn't sure that Ryker did. She accelerated towards the door, gave a friendly smile to the woman and followed her inside. Ryker sidled in at her heels.

They didn't see anyone on the way up to the penthouse. In the elevator, they shared a tense silence. Once outside Quinn's door, Ryker skulked around the corner while Floss rang the bell. When no one answered, she kept watch while Ryker got working on a small tablet, looking jumpy. Her palms sweated. Minutes trickled by. She'd rung Farouk and told him she'd overslept and would come in as soon as she could; she glanced at her watch. She hadn't realized this would take so long. Still, Quinn would be at work. Immediately she had a vivid image of him sitting inside his flat, looking up as they walked in. But if he was there, he'd have answered the door . . . unless he had been into the future and knew what was going to happen, and was waiting to arrest them. Floss felt hot all over. Why hadn't they thought of this? She walked towards Ryker to share her fear, and the lock made a small whirring noise, and rotated.

"Suppose he knows we're coming?" she said in a low voice. "He's got a time machine."

Ryker grinned. "Suppose he doesn't? Let's find out."

"Have you turned off the alarm?"

He nodded, opened the door and they went inside. Floss tiptoed to the living room, heart pounding. Empty. Behind her she heard Ryker close the door softly and the lock click and whir. He glanced at her.

"No one can get in. We'll check out the gaff, then you'll relax a bit," he said. "If you touch anything, put it back the exact same place."

Floss hadn't seen Quinn's home before. He'd invited her to come up there for coffee and liqueurs on her birthday outing, but she'd made an excuse. He had a girlfriend, and she had not been totally certain that coffee and liqueurs would be the only thing on offer; she had chosen to avoid the possibility of embarrassment.

The apartment was quite something. Just the size of it impressed, after her studio flat. In the living room were vast expanses of polished marble floor, full-height windows showing a grey sky with clouds whisking by above a city panorama, long sofas and velvety rugs in rich colours. Beyond an archway was a large and pristine kitchen. There were three bedrooms, three bathrooms, a dressing room and a study, plus a terrace on two sides of the building. When they had checked every room, they went back to where they had started.

"Moment of truth," Ryker said, fishing the transmitter out of his pocket. He pressed the button, and immediately the faintest of beeping noises responded, just audible in the quiet. They exchanged nervous yet triumphant grins and followed the sound.

This must be Quinn's bedroom, Floss thought. Twice as big as her entire flat, lined in dark hardwood panels that gleamed expensively. The king-size bed had a wolf fur coverlet at its foot that might even have been real. The beep was louder now, coming from behind a panelled door. She stepped through. Beyond the door was a walk-in closet you could comfortably live in, immaculately kitted out with shelves, drawers and hanging rails. Quinn had a lot of clothes, and rows of footwear. At one end was a window, and opposite that an expanse of mirror. Running down the middle of the room was a buttoned leather ottoman, presumably for Quinn to sit on while pulling on his boots.

The beep was coming from the ottoman. Floss crouched and felt underneath until her fingers encountered a slit in the canvas. She slid her hand inside and touched cool metal; the TiTrav, nestled on top of a wooden strut. She handed it to Ryker, replacing it with an envelope addressed to Quinn containing a brief note she'd written earlier.

They went back into the living room. Ryker sat at the computer and fitted some small gadget into a port. After less than a minute's tinkering with scrolling code, the screen displayed a blue and green underwater scene, with a succession of sea creatures, each eating the one before. There was only time for the octopus, having eaten a starfish, to be eaten in turn by a shark, before Ryker located Quinn's journal and circumvented the demand for a password.

"There you go. You've got a few minutes to poke around while I get this unlocked and sort out the CCTV."

Ryker settled himself on the sofa while Floss read Quinn's journal. She was briefly sidetracked when she noticed her own name on the latest page and couldn't resist reading:

... Floss now displays a certain uncharacteristic sweet timidity when in my company, and the exquisite curve of her neck as she turned to avoid my eye made me want to rip her clothes off and take her then and there on the floor of her tiny flat. But I can be patient when the prize is worth the wait ...

Floss recoiled. *Sweet timidity?* And he referred to her as a *prize?* Yuk, gross. She really didn't want to read this. Besides, Quinn's delusions about his chances of seducing her were not what she was looking for. She typed 'disaster' into the search box. Nothing came up. 'Humanity' yielded the same result. What else had he said? "We know there is a problem heading our way. A big problem." She tried 'problem'. El zippo.

Floss glanced at Ryker, who was absorbed in his task. The TiTrav was now on his wrist, and he was tapping away at his tablet. She hadn't got long. While thinking what to try, she scrolled through the pages. Quite a few women's names jumped out at her . . . Kayla was far from the only woman in Quinn's life. Did she know he was two – no, multiple-timing her? She'd probably been better off with Jace Carnady. The photos Floss had seen of Jace on the internet came into her mind. On impulse, she typed 'Jace' into the box. Lots of results; she chose the entry for 20th May 2045. May 2045 was when the TiTrav had vanished and Jace got the blame. She started reading. Funny how ornate Quinn's writing style was; he didn't speak like that at all.

20/5/45

Heraclitus observed that big results require big ambitions. And sometimes big decisions, too. Not the easiest of days, and I was obliged to modify what I flatter myself was an extremely elegant plan. This irked me; Scott was the ideal scapegoat, given he shot McGuire. I wish Jace had not guessed. But at least I encountered him before he'd spoken to Scott, else I'd have had to get rid of both of them, and I'm not sure IEMA investigators would have swallowed the idea that they'd worked in collusion.

It pains me to lose Jace. I liked him a lot, and he'll be a loss to the Department. On reflection, it's a pity I let him get under my skin. I hadn't had time to decide whether to untie him or administer a coup de grâce before I left, and being angry, I did neither. I'd have shot Scott. It wouldn't have been much of a life for Jace, alone in London, had I released him. The last human died around 2170.

As she read this, Floss became very still. In her brain, synapses and neurons processed new information. She read on.

It's interesting to speculate in what sense Jace is dying in the London of the future. The ability to time travel changes things. I feel as if he is lying there dying now, since I left him less than an hour ago; though you could argue he will not begin this process for more than a century. But in that case, where is he now? A question for a philosopher.

"Ryker!" He got up, alarmed at her expression, and came over. "Read this!"

He bent to the screen. "The evil scheming bastard . . ."

"We have to rescue him! He left him tied up, dying slowly of thirst and starvation. We can go into the future and save him." Floss leaped to her feet, in a fever to be off.

"Hang on a minute. I haven't sorted out the CCTV yet. Does he say where he left him?"

"London." Leaning in to the computer screen, Floss scrolled down frantically, as if Jace would die if she didn't hurry. "I can't see anything more . . ."

"Perhaps it's in the history." Ryker tapped and swiped at the TiTrav's display. "Nope. He's wiped it. There's nothing in here. Does he say the date he left him, I mean the future date?"

"I don't think so . . ."

Ryker turned his attention from the TiTrav to stare at Floss. "London's a big place. We can't rescue him if we don't know where or when he is. If he's tied up, we've only got a window of a few days to turn up before he's had it . . . how lucky would we have to be to hit that?"

"It'll be after 2170. Probably Quinn allowed a bit of leeway to be certain of not meeting anyone. We don't have to get it right first time. There might be remains and we could work out from the state of them when to go back . . . you finish that, I'll go on looking."

She put 'contraceptive virus' into Find. As she had guessed, this was the cause of humanity's demise, and the reason IEMA had thought her responsible. Confirming her theory took only seconds, and she went back to looking for clues to where Jace had been left. She skimmed the journal for place names, then checked everywhere Jace's name cropped up after May 2045. He got a mention when Quinn went to the Colosseum; then another when Quinn moved in on Kayla and started doing the sympathy routine with which Floss was familiar. It seemed to have worked fine, if slowly, on Kayla. Then a passage where Quinn recounted a recurring bad dream he had of Jace, filthy, in tatters and vengeful, appearing from behind overgrown tombstones and moving menacingly towards Quinn who then woke up. Nothing else.

Tombstones . . . Something clicked in Floss's brain. She remembered Quinn turning to stare out of the pod window on the way to the restaurant that first evening.

"Bunhill Fields. He left him in Bunhill Fields."

CHAPTER 32

Missing person

Ryker set the TiTrav for 2175, June 1st. "Might as well have nice weather for it."

They were back in his workshop. After checking no traces remained of their visit to Quinn's apartment, they had left discreetly via the TiTrav. Ryker got out a long wrecking bar, and tucked it in his belt. Floss wondered if she should have a weapon too. Ryker hadn't suggested it.

"Bunhill Fields is quite big – how will it choose which part to take us to?"

"It'll go for the clearest space."

She held his belt with one hand and his arm with the other. He pressed the buttons.

They materialized into a grassy clearing, scattering rabbits. Floss looked around her, and the more she looked, the more astonished she was by the beauty of the place. Left to its own devices, nature had turned this corner of London into an earthly paradise. Dappled sun shone through the leaves of trees that soared, unspoiled by chain saw, towards a blue sky. Different textures and shades of rampant green covered everything, ornamented with the white of bindweed trumpets and the brilliant massed purple of buddleia flowers. The sweet-scented air was loud with birdsong. There was no litter. Litter, like humanity, had been and gone. A movement caught Floss's eye; a mallard led her six yellow ducklings between ox-eye daisies towards the iron gate.

Ryker was not admiring the view. "We can't do this," he said, gazing around. "A dead body would get covered up in no time, even if it didn't get eaten first. It might take hours to find."

"I don't know, if this is the only clear spot, wouldn't the TiTrav have brought Quinn here too? He'd most likely have left Jace where they arrived, if he was tied up. And even if animals did disperse the remains, there are two hundred and six bones in the human body. Bound to be a few still here. I think we only need to check the edges."

"Right." Ryker did not sound convinced. Using his wrecking bar, he began to cautiously part the thicker undergrowth that bordered the clearing. Floss got herself a stick and did the same the other side.

"I've found a bone."

Floss went to see. "That's a rabbit femur," she said, remembering old biology lessons. "Let's try a year later."

June 1st 2176 was grey and spitting with rain. Twelve months' growth was marked by taller saplings and an advance of the encroaching ivy. The stick she'd dropped the year before was still there, softened by weather and in pieces.

After a quick and unproductive search, Ryker said, "I reckon people think in round numbers. Why don't we try 2180? Or 2185?"

"Good point. Let's go for 2180."

June 1st 2180; a breezy, sunny day with scudding clouds. Again, they found no trace of a body. Floss's first urgency to find Jace had diminished a little; she was losing her feeling that he was dying *now*. She felt curious to see more of London in the future, and wondered if the skyscrapers were still standing.

"I'm just going to have a quick look outside," she said.

"Okay. I'll carry on poking around here."

Floss picked her way to the gate and climbed up. *Wow, amazing.* To see nature reclaiming her own was a mixture of entrancing and strangely upsetting. She dropped to the ground, and walked towards a pond that covered half the ruined road leading to the heart of the City. At this distance, the skyscrapers looked much as they had in 2050.

The pond was more interesting. Grass and ferns surrounded its margins, with narrow tracks leading through the vegetation. This must be the local animals' watering hole. A frog plopped from a brick into the water at her approach. Floss walked to the edge and stared below the surface. Newts darted about; one gulped down a tadpole head first as she watched. Her gaze travelled across the road to where the far pavement had once been. A few York stone slabs could still be made out under the carpet of ivy. Sycamore saplings competed with tall grasses and bamboo escaped from a City garden . . .

Something made her look twice, not sure of what she was seeing. The light changed as a cloud swept across the sun. She stared. The something blinked; a pale green eye, watching her among the undergrowth. Peering, trying to identify the animal, she made out black and white V-shaped stripes some way below the eye, then long tawny forelimbs . . . she looked back at the face. The tiger licked its nose with a big pink tongue, still watching her.

Little by little Floss backed towards the gate, maintaining eye contact, her heart banging about in her chest. If you ran they gave chase, she'd read somewhere, or was that polar bears? The ground was uneven, and tripping would be fatal, literally fatal. Very slowly, hardly moving, the tiger got smoothly to its feet, head lowered, staring at Floss. Still in slow motion, it emerged from cover, looking a lot larger than tigers do on television or at the zoo. From this angle, she could only see the massive head, the hump of its shoulders and the big front paws crossing each other to land softly, almost hesitantly, on the ground as it felt its way, eyes never leaving her. The tiger was imperceptibly accelerating, shortening the distance between them. Pure terror nearly robbed Floss of the ability to move, but she forced herself to back away a little faster. Halfway across the road the tiger dropped to a this-means-business crouch, focused and intent. Floss froze. Suddenly there was a great clanging and shouting behind her; Ryker was running his wrecking bar along the railings like a maniac and yelling his head off. With dignity the tiger rose, turned, and sloped back into the undergrowth.

Floss hurried to the gate and grabbed Ryker's outstretched hand. She clambered over, sweating and palpitating. "D'you think they can get in here?"

"Let's take a look."

Together they walked round the perimeter of the Fields. Though the edges were overgrown they could make out that all the walls and railings were still intact. The gate at the far end from the one Floss had climbed was padlocked.

"Maybe that's why there are so many rabbits."

"I dunno, foxes and cats can get in between the bars."

"Shall we try another five years' time?"

"Okay." He thought of something and turned towards her. "How long are you thinking of spending on this?"

"As long as it takes."

"It could take weeks. Longer. Look, I'm sorry for the geezer, but I got stuff to do."

"You don't have to come with me. I'll be all right on my own."

Ryker's eyebrows went up. "Oh yeah? I just saved you from being a tiger's dinner. I can't save you if I'm not here. If we don't find anything in 2185 let's go home and talk about what to do next over a cup of tea."

Thursday, 5th May 2050

Quinn wasn't told that Floss had failed to come in to work until he was about to go home, an hour later than usual. He'd had a lunch appointment with the Secretary of State, and meetings all afternoon and into the evening; he was just clearing his desk before leaving when Kayla knocked and walked in to his office.

"Ansel, I thought you'd want to know. Floss hasn't come in today. She called Farouk to say she'd overslept and would be in late, but she hasn't arrived and she's not answering her phone."

Quinn frowned. "You should have told me earlier. Why didn't you ring me?"

"I did. I rang this afternoon. If you checked your phone more often . . ."

Quinn ignored this. "Maybe she's ill. Have you sent someone round to her flat?"

"No. I couldn't see the point." Kayla added, barely concealing her satisfaction, "Perhaps she's run off. She didn't want to be here, after all."

"Where could she go? She doesn't know anyone here. You should have done something this morning."

"D'you want me to send someone to her flat now? Farouk's still here."

"No." Quinn got to his feet. "I'll go myself."

On the way Quinn rang Floss, and got her voice mail. He wondered what had happened. Even Kayla admitted that Floss was a conscientious employee; if she was ill, she would have rung the department. Perhaps she'd had some accident. It even crossed his mind she might have attempted suicide; though she seemed level-headed enough, he did not know her well and she might be more fragile than she appeared. If, as he was convinced, she was in love with him, she might have heard that Kayla was his girlfriend and despaired, alone in a strange world. He remembered her telling him he was her only friend.

He reached Floss's block of flats and pressed bell number 633, paused, then rang it again, allowing plenty of time for her to answer. When she didn't, he went inside and explained the situation to the concierge, prepared to write a warrant if the man was awkward. In the event he was helpful; he got out his master key and went up in the lift with Quinn, opened the door and let him walk in first.

The place was just as Quinn remembered it; as neat and tidy as if she had never been there. Then he noticed her phone lying beside the computer. He checked the bathroom; empty; then looked inside the wardrobe. The clothes they had bought together were hanging there. No note. The concierge, though he recalled Floss, could not remember when he last saw her. Quinn got rid of the man and opened her computer. Nothing at all; it had been restored to factory settings. His frown deepened.

Quinn left the building. Whether something had happened to her or she had run off, he would have to alert the police. He did this on the short walk between Floss's block and his own, sending them a photo of her and confidential details of her move from 2015.

Back in his own flat a couple of hours later than usual, he poured himself a Glenfiddich single malt and ordered a meal. He remembered it was a Thursday, his day for checking out the future. Perhaps his journal could throw some light on Floss's disappearance. Before writing up the day's events as he would normally do, he went into his dressing room, knelt by the ottoman and reached for the TiTrav in its hiding place. It was not there. He felt around, thinking it had slipped off the ledge. His fingers encountered stiff paper. He pulled out an envelope with his name handwritten on the front, and tore it open.

Hi Ansel,

You always said if there was anything you could do to help me, you would – so I imagine you must be pleased to find there was a way after all. Fancy your turning out to have a TiTrav, the very thing I need!

Thank you so much,

Floss

X

Quinn sat down heavily on the ottoman, staring at the disingenuous note. He'd misread Floss; had thought her resigned to her new life; had missed her determination to return to her own time. Had he even guessed right, thinking her in love with him? This no longer seemed likely to be the case. She'd played him. He'd known she was intelligent; had not realized she was intelligent enough to run rings around him. He didn't understand how she had got into his flat and discovered his TiTrav. No one knew about it except Ryker, and he didn't know where it was hidden. And Floss didn't know Ryker. Even if they'd somehow met, he had no reason to help her – he was a self-serving cowardly little rat. And if Ryker *had* been involved, what could Quinn do? Blustering at him would be humiliating and achieve nothing; shooting him would be foolish. He would need Ryker once he had got the TiTrav back or obtained another one, which he was determined to do.

Floss now had proof that he, the Chief of IEMA Intelligence, was involved in timecrime. On the plus side, she was unlikely to use this knowledge. Having got what she wanted, she had no reason to return to 2050 to make trouble for him. All the same, he went to the living room and sat at his desk. With the TiTrav gone, the only incriminating evidence that remained was his journal.

"Computer."

Quinn had an emergency deletion system already in place. He now went through the process, which overwrote the files multiple times, scrambled the file name, and truncated the file size to nothing before finally and irrecoverably unlinking it from the system.

He fetched a lighter, went on to the terrace and set fire to the edge of Floss's note. A crescent of flame, bright in the twilight, spread across the paper, consuming her writing. Grey flakes scattered in the wind, until only the corner he held remained, burning his fingers. He let go and watched it swirl away from him into the heart of the city.

CHAPTER 33

Gone fishing

June 1st 2185 was hot and humid, but the temperature wasn't the first thing that struck them. Bunhill Fields had changed. There were trodden pathways through the trees, and stacked timber and galvanized water tanks surrounded the warden's house. A sizeable pyramid of empty wine bottles glinted greenly in the sun. Behind the house an attempt at a vegetable garden doubled as a rabbits' café, with a naked shop window dummy standing in the middle. Probably intended as a scarecrow, she was covered in bird droppings and leaned at a drunken angle with a pigeon on her bald head. Floss and Ryker stood and contemplated this incongruous sight.

"Be fair, it's sort of working," said Ryker. "I can't see any crows."

They walked towards the little house and Floss knocked on the door while Ryker peered through the window into the dark interior. When no one answered, he joined her, pushed the door open and went in. Floss followed him. They were assailed by a badgery smell of unchanged bedding made worse by the heat, and a fly buzzed and banged against the window panes. But the room was tidy and organized; someone had been living here for some time. There were stacks of books, and tools in a row. A church candle burned inside a tall glass jar, strings of onions hung from the ceiling and there was a bowl of small apples on the table.

"D'you think it's Jace?" Floss said. "Or maybe Quinn dumped someone else here, without leaving him tied up."

"Only one way to find out," Ryker said, helping himself to an apple. "Let's wait for a bit, then if he doesn't turn up, try again this evening." He took a bite, then looked closer. "Ugh, this one's got a maggot."

They went outside again. Ryker took off his jacket. So did Floss. They sat on a nearby tombstone under a shady tree to wait.

For a long time after his arrival in 2180, Jace had felt uneasy going more than a few minutes' walk away from the Fields, afraid he might miss a chance of escape. Gradually, as the years went by, though he still wore the locator on a chain round his neck day and night he'd given up hope; he no longer expected Quinn or an IEMA research team to appear. At night he dreamed of escape; but in his dreams something always went wrong at the last moment, and he remained stuck here.

For the last year or two, he had taken to foraging further afield.

On this sweltering June day he had gone fishing in the Regents Canal. While waiting for the float to bob he was doing his best to wash himself and his underwear, an unsatisfactory process without soap, but pleasantly cooling. After ten minutes he levered himself out of the canal and draped his ragged boxers over a shrub to dry. He checked his fishing line and chucked a few more worms in the water.

He had taught himself to fish by trial and error, having no experience of it in his former life. At first he had thought fishing in the abundance of nearby ponds might be easier than trapping rabbits. It was certainly easier than attempting to grow food, as he had later discovered – the sheer variety of pests and blight you could attract with one small vegetable patch had to be seen to be believed. There were plenty of fish swimming about wherever water had gathered, lots of different types he could not identify, all presumably edible. Lacking rod or line, he had attempted to catch them with his hands. The fish were too quick and slippery for him, even in shallow water; he wasted many hours in futile pursuit. Discouraged, cold, his clothes never dry and with each passing day shorter and colder, he had focused his efforts on the rabbits.

He would never forget that first winter; the bitter cold, the gnawing hunger, the constant struggle against overwhelming odds, the loneliness, depression and sense of loss. Bottles of wine and spirits had survived better than almost everything else, and huddled in an indestructible orange nylon quilt each night, shaking with cold, Jace drank to drown out the silence. But after a while he knew he had to stop. His determination not to be beaten mattered to him more than temporary alcoholic escape. He imagined Quinn finding him a bleary-eyed drunken wreck, and putting him down with contempt. Hate was a big motivator to survive.

The next spring he'd got lucky scavenging in derelict apartments, and found a reel of nylon thread. He'd thought he was on the home stretch, and that all he needed now was hooks, which he made out of wire coat hangers bent and filed to shape. But after many hours of fruitless hanging about various pond margins, he had done some research in a tattered encyclopaedia and realized he needed a float – a cork from a wine bottle would do – plus something to weight the line. It had taken him some time to finesse the equipment to a point where he caught his first fish; but time was something he had plenty of.

These days he was quite good at fishing and if the weather

was fine, enjoyed it. The biggest fish lived in the canal.

Seeing the float dip, he tugged the line smoothly towards him, feeling something resisting; then he saw his catch beneath the water and flipped it on to the bank. The fish struggled against the air, twisting silver and white with orange fins. He killed it quickly with a blow to the head from the heavy stick he kept for that purpose. The fish wasn't all that big, about eight inches long, and he needed more. He set the line again, and sprawled idle and naked on the warm stone, reading in a desultory fashion, one eye on the float, until the heat got too much and he moved into dappled shade. He had hacked his beard as short as he could for summer, but it still made him hot. Bees hummed on the flowers, loud in the silence, and he glanced up to see the brilliant blue flash of a kingfisher darting from the greenery. The air smelled of honeysuckle. For a moment he felt almost happy. Summer was his best time, winter a recurring ordeal he avoided thinking about. The heat made him drowsy and his eyes closed. He drifted off . . .

He was lying in bed at home, breathing in the scent of Kayla's hair, her warm body curled next to him . . . the alarm sounded, an insistent beep rousing him from sleep. Time to get up. Jace's eyes opened to sunshine, blue sky and green leaves. The hard ground dug into his hip. For a moment he was disorientated, then he realized what had woken him. The locator round his neck had gone off. He sat up with a jolt and checked the distance and direction. Bunhill Fields. *Shit*. He jumped to his feet. Someone was about to time in, and he was the best part of a mile away, and whoever it was might go before he reached them.

Cursing, he grabbed his britches and zipped them hastily, pulled on his boots, abandoned everything else and set off at a run for Bunhill Fields, hope and fear raging inside him. Though he'd cleared a pathway to the canal, its surface was uneven, tangled with roots and debris. Jace hurtled down the rough track, preferring to chance a broken ankle or an encounter with a lion, rather than risk missing whoever had timed in. He did not slacken speed, sweat stinging his eyes and running down his chest, until he reached City Road. Near the big gates he slowed to get his breath and see who – if anyone – was there, before they saw him. Quinn would have a gun, and use it. If Quinn was there, Jace needed to take him by surprise. If Quinn was there, Jace was going to kill him.

Floss, dressed for April in her smart wool blend trousers, was too hot. She tied up her hair to get it off her neck, and took off her boots and socks. Ryker wandered over to one of the tanks, and splashed his face with water. A black tomcat emerged from the undergrowth and stared at Floss as if he'd never seen a human female before. He probably hadn't. She held out her hand. "Who's a beautiful pusscat, then?" After considering this compliment carefully, the cat walked warily towards her. "Come on, I won't hurt you . . ."

Floss glanced up to see a man approaching. She jumped to her feet and the cat shot off.

The man was instantly recognizable from the photos as Jace; which was not to say he had not changed. He wore only britches and boots, both dirty and the worse for wear; he was sunburnt and sweaty, lean and broad-shouldered, with well-defined muscles. He had a rough short beard and long shaggy hair. As he got nearer she saw his face was different from the photos. Older, of course, and leaner, but also harder somehow; the ready smile was missing. He looked wary and self-contained and his expression gave nothing away as he glanced at Ryker, then around the Fields and back to Floss.

One thing had not changed. He was still hot.

Floss felt herself blush like some silly teenage fan meeting her idol in the flesh. Not that she was infatuated with him . . . it was just that she had thought him dead, and now here he was. A confusing situation. Anyone would be a bit emotional. She said, "Jace Carnady?"

"Yeah. Are you two on your own?" His voice was low, with a rough, husky edge to it, as if he hadn't used it for a while.

"Yes. I'm Floss. Floss Dryden. We came to rescue you."

"How did you know I was here?"

"I read Quinn's diary. Ryker broke into his flat. Quinn said he brought you to London in the future and left you tied up, but didn't say when. We thought we'd have to catch you before you died, and that might only be hours or days. Needle in a haystack stuff. But you must have escaped . . ." He just stood, listening to her. Her voice trailed off. *Shut up Floss, you're babbling. He knows he escaped.*

"I've been here five years," he said bleakly.

"I'm sorry." *Shouldn't he be thanking us? He doesn't seem very grateful.* She shot a quick look at Ryker. "We tried five years ago, but you weren't here. June 1st."

"Quinn dumped me late summer that year."

"Ah. We could go back five years and pick you up then if you like."

Jace stepped towards her and said, "No! Don't go." He took a breath and said more slowly, "It's okay. You're here now."

"You're sure? Because it would be no trouble, we could just –"

"I'm sure." He turned to Ryker. "Thanks for coming to get me."

"Don't thank me, thank Floss. It was her idea. I said, what d'you want to do that for? He's a time cop. Leave him where he is."

Jace smiled at her with reserve, and the contrast with his happy smiles in the photos made her want to cry. "Thank you."

He said to Ryker, "Is that Quinn's TiTrav?"

"Nah. Used to be. It's ours now. Where can we take you?"

Jace thought. "Take me back to just after Quinn dumped me. I'm going to expose him to IEMA."

Floss said, "I don't think you can do that. We came from 2050. If you go back to 2045 and get Quinn flung into jail, he won't get me abducted from 2015 – that's my home time – so I won't be able to come and get you, and it'll set up some illogical time loop or something. Like the grandfather paradox."

Jace growled, "You're right. So what it comes down to is I've lost five years in my own time and I can't get them back."

"Yup," said Ryker. "Think of it like you've done five years in clink. Only with no visitors."

Floss said, "Basically, we can only take you back to some time in the last three weeks. The last three weeks in the time we just came from, that is. Between the 21st March and 14th April 2050."

Jace digested this. "What happened about the stolen TiTrav? I got the blame, right?"

"Yes. You're on the Most Wanted list for timecrime. A reward and everything."

"What about Quinn? Is he still running Timecrime?"

"No, he's Chief of Intelligence."

Jace's frown deepened. He turned to Ryker. "To take Quinn down I'll need fake ID, a chip and a phone."

Ryker said, "I got contacts who could help you, if you've got the dosh."

Jace's face was blank. How could he have any money? Floss thought of the almost untouched £500,000 IEMA had given her, sitting in her bank account in 2050; but knew it would be madness to attempt to retrieve it. She said to Ryker, "We could use the TiTrav to win the lottery."

Ryker looked at her the way he had when she suggested he dress up as Darth Vader. "*We?* You're on the run, and as soon as IEMA notices I won the lottery – and you may not know, but they do automatic checks on all big lottery winners – I'd be screwed. It'd be, Go directly to Jail, do not pass Go, do not collect two hundred pounds."

"I could do it in my own time. You're going to lend me the TiTrav anyway. I could buy gold bars or something with the money, and bring them back to 2050. Jace could stay with you while he sorts himself out."

Ryker shook his head. "Bad idea. I've taken a chance as it is, nicking Quinn's TiTrav. Wouldn't put it past him to come sniffing round my gaff when he realizes you've done a runner. He finds Jace, we're both in trouble."

Jace had stood and watched them during this exchange, his eyes flicking from one to the other. "It's okay." He looked calm and hard, as if well used to dealing with disappointment. "I can do this alone. Just take me back to my own time. I'll cut out my chip. I'll be all right."

Floss really didn't see how he would be, an outlaw with no resources. Surely not having a chip was suspicious in itself in a society where everyone had one? If he got caught it would be his word against Quinn's, and they'd believe Quinn, who was well-connected and part of the establishment. And Quinn was no longer guilty of owning an illegal TiTrav. There was no evidence. Jace would most likely end up in prison for his pains.

Hesitantly, Floss said, "You could come with me to 2015, and stay at my flat for a bit, while we make you some money. If you like. It's only small, you'll have to sleep on the floor."

"Thanks."

She glanced at the others. "Are we off then?"

"Hang on." Jace went into the house and came out putting something small into his pocket. "Let's go."

CHAPTER 34

Back to the past

Thursday, 23rd July 2015

After dropping Ryker in his workshop, Floss and Jace set off for 2015. The TiTrav refused to take them into Floss's flat. They had to arrive outside, in a quiet street round the back. When Jace followed Floss through the duck-egg blue front door and looked around him, he could see why. It was tiny; nowhere was there the 6 by 6 by 8 foot space a TiTrav needed to time in. This was good, meaning as long as they were there, there was no way they could be unexpectedly joined by an unwelcome time travelling guest.

Evening sun streamed through a dormer window into an L-shaped studio flat, with a double bed in the short part of the L. The ceilings sloped. The kitchen was in the corner beside the entrance to the flat. Another door was open, showing a bathroom with a skylight. The flat was decorated in black, blue and white, and though compact had an idiosyncratic appeal. Floss was looking around and beaming, clearly thrilled to be back home. She switched on an old-fashioned laptop and checked the date, got a greyish long dress out of her bag and hung it in the fitted wardrobe next to the bed, then turned to him. He could see his presence alone with her made her shy and she was trying not to show it.

"We ought to get you some clothes. Fancy a trip to Primark? They're open till nine."

"That's a clothes shop?" Jace frowned. "I haven't got any money."

"It's okay, I'll treat you."

Jace wasn't having that. He got the small rusty tobacco tin out of his pocket and carefully removed the lid. Light sparkled and flashed; the tin was half full of loose diamonds, interspersed with a few rings.

Floss's eye widened. "Wow."

"I got them in Hatton Garden." After he'd learned how to stay alive, and before he'd despaired of rescue. "Choose something."

"You really don't have to . . . any one of those must be worth thousands. Primark's cheap."

He picked out a diamond solitaire ring, and held it out towards her. "Take it."

After a moment, Floss took the ring and found a finger it fitted on her right hand. The diamond flashed in the sunlight. "Cool. Thank you." She went to the window and peered down at the street, her expression anxious. "I think we should use the TiTrav. I'm a bit worried IEMA might be waiting outside to get me back."

"I'd like a bath first."

She nodded, went into the bathroom and turned on the bath taps, then got a towel out of a drawer and handed it to him before closing the door and leaving him to it. He stripped and lowered himself into the hot water, smiling with pure pleasure. Only the most upmarket apartments had soaking baths this length in his own time; space was at a premium, and showers took up less. Through the wall he could hear Floss on the phone, sounding happy.

He reached for the soap to scrub away the dirt of years. This done, the water was beige and scummy, so he pulled the plug, ran a second bath and washed again. Once out he cleaned the ring of grime from round the bath, then found a disposable razor in a mirrored cabinet and shaved. His face was leaner, older, and grimmer than the last time he'd looked in a mirror five years before. Maybe he should have let the girl go away and pick him up soon after he'd been dumped in future London, before his hopes and ideals had flaked and rusted away. His nerve had failed; he hadn't been able to face the chance of something preventing her coming back; the possibility of his life going on with the knowledge he'd had an opportunity of escape, and turned it down. This was better.

He put on his grimy britches with distaste. They were filthy, but he had not realized while wearing them year after year, day and night, quite how much they stank. Gutting fish and butchering rabbits was a messy business. Back in 2180, he had been unable to find any garments not already in an advanced state of disintegration. Even clothes he had found stacked in boxes, individually plastic-wrapped, fell apart at the creases as he ripped open their ancient packaging. The aging remnants of humanity had no doubt relied on foraging as the population dwindled; he doubted anything had been manufactured for fifty years or more. Since then, time, damp, light, heat, cold, rodents, moth and mould had done their worst.

After a last critical glance in the mirror, he went to find the girl.

She looked up from her laptop. "Wow. You look . . . several shades lighter." She handed him an oversized black sweater, still staring. "This is the only thing I've got that might fit you. A bare chest would attract attention."

He pulled it over his head. On him it was a snug fit. "I need you to cut my hair."

"I'll give it a go."

She sat him at a narrow desk in front of a mirror. He regarded his reflection disapprovingly; the sweater made him look like a male ballet dancer at rehearsal. She had crossed to the kitchen and came back with scissors.

"How short do you want it?"

"Just shorter."

Floss didn't say anything for a while, combing and snipping carefully, studying the result in the mirror as she worked. She wasn't doing a bad job.

"You're not a hairdresser, are you?"

She laughed. "No. I used to cut my boyfriend's hair at uni."

Now she was back in her own time and had rung her mother (who had told her she and Ryker had just left her flat) and Chris to say she couldn't meet her that evening, Floss felt like dancing about; hugely relieved, triumphant and in celebratory mood. She'd done it, got back to her own time, a mammoth achievement; she just had to sort Jace out, and be a bit wary of IEMA for a while – her mother had reminded her of this at least three times on the phone – then she could get on with her proper life.

Before they went shopping, they took turns to cut out each other's chip. Hers came out easily, if painfully; she had to dig for Jace's. His stoicism was impressive. After that, Floss set the TiTrav to materialize one minute in the future, in a backwater the other side of Oxford Street, hoping it would be secluded. Jace had explained that, though TiTravs needed a certain space to time in, there were no restrictions on timing out. You could leave from under a bed or inside a phone box.

Floss glanced discreetly at Jace just before they left. His trousers were filthy, threadbare and torn, and smelled rank as an uncollected rubbish bag sitting in the sun. Her black sweater with the deep V-neck looked a little odd on him. But he'd probably pass in a crowd; London was full of oddly-dressed people. She felt very aware of the ring on her finger; she seldom wore jewellery. Strange to think the craftsman who made it had been dead for half a century . . . or looking at it another way, had not yet been born.

She held her breath and pressed the two buttons.

One side of Granville Place was a porticoed terrace with balconies, bay trees and wrought iron. Facing these pleasant houses, forming their depressing view, was a massive blank grey wall with a scurf of litter bins and bags at its base. A woman smoking outside a building stared and followed them with her eyes as they left. Floss led the way into Portman Street, Jace walking beside her. After her three weeks in the future, everything looked both comfortably familiar and different, as it sometimes does when you come back from holiday. She wondered what Jace made of it. His expression was stern and inscrutable.

She waited at the lights to cross Oxford Street. Primark was directly opposite. But Jace didn't stop; he stepped straight out into the road in the path of a black cab. The taxi's brakes squealed and it lurched sideways, stopping inches from him. The outraged cabbie leaned out of the window and yelled, "You want to get your eyes tested, mate!"

Floss grabbed Jace's arm, feeling sick, and pulled him back to the safety of the pavement. "Are you crazy? You nearly got knocked down! Why d'you do that?"

"I forgot your traffic. I'm used to cars that stop for you."

"Five people get killed on the roads and five hundred injured, every single day in the UK. You don't want to be one of them." Floss was tempted to take a firm hold of his hand as if he was a child, but didn't quite like to. He was a grown man, and she found his reserve a little intimidating. "Keep with me. Do what I do."

The lights changed and they crossed the road and went into Primark.

When they got to the men's department, Jace, faced with unfamiliar fashions, didn't seem to know where to start; he stood transfixed by a particularly virulent Hawaiian shirt with a repeating pattern of hula girls and palm trees.

"Men wear these?"

"Not men with taste. Let's both choose stuff."

She asked him his size and whisked round the racks. It amused Floss to think that she was now enacting the role Quinn had with her. But then IEMA had been footing the bill. Luckily it was not possible to overspend in Primark, which was why she'd brought him there – though she earned a decent salary, most of it went on her mortgage. Of course, she could always sell the ring; but it had grown on her, so elegant on her finger, sparkling with all the colours of the rainbow, and she didn't want to part with it. Her selection was dark blue straight cut jeans, a plain belt, a black T shirt, a grey hoodie, and white trainers. She totted it up; forty-six pounds. She could afford that. Jace chose boxers and socks, then rounded up his own assortment of garments.

When they'd both finished, Floss looked the armful of clothes he had chosen. "Okay . . . hmm . . . you have to be joking! You don't want to look like a gigolo . . . That's quite nice . . ."

Jace eyed her, and went through her selection critically. "They're kind of plain . . ."

"Welcome to men's fashions, 2015. These are only cheap, but you can get better quality stuff when you've got some money. The main thing's to make you respectable."

"These won't look right in 2050."

"Let's not worry about that now. One step at a time."

Jace went into the fitting rooms. Clothes chosen and paid for, they emerged into a sunset that gilded the buildings and cast long shadows. Floss escorted him carefully across the traffic of Oxford Street and into Selfridges, and waited outside the gents' lavatories while he changed into his new clothes. She realized she was starving. She'd lost track of her real time; wasn't sure if it was lunch or dinner she wanted.

Jace emerged frowning; slightly suspicious, and hotter than ever. He muttered, "Are you sure these are all right? Do I look... normal?"

Floss grinned and his frown deepened. She hastened to reassure him. "Better than normal. You look... very nice. Let's go home and eat."

Back in Floss's flat, Jace used her laptop while she made her fall-back speedy stir fry, doubling up the ingredients. She unfolded the rickety white table and put a chair either side and a candle in the middle as she always did when she had a guest to dinner, then opened a bottle of wine and poured them each a glass.

"To one's own time." They clinked glasses.

Over the meal she tried to get Jace talking. Conversationally, he was quite unlike Quinn; he tended to lapse into silences or make brief responses that gave nothing away. Maybe it was years of brooding alone in future London. Maybe he was still brooding, having got into the habit. Maybe he was focused on the food; his only voluntary remark was, "This is great," waving his fork, mouth full. She told him about her time in 2050, and about her job in 2015. He listened.

In the end Floss gave up what was pretty much a monologue and did a little thinking of her own while she ate; now she had the TiTrav, there was no reason not to put her secret plan into action that same evening. The thought made her excited and nervous. She put the place and date she knew by heart into the TiTrav, and an approximate time, erring on the early side. She stuck a new motion sickness patch on the inside of her elbow. Jace's dark eyes were on her, watching, but he didn't say anything.

They had nearly finished eating when she broke the silence to talk about something that had been niggling her; how he was going to manage when he got back to his own time with no money, the wrong clothes and the authorities looking for him. "Have you got someone you trust in 2050 who'll put you up and help you?"

"Yes. There's a woman I know. Kayla Hartley-Hunter."

"I know her, she was my boss while I worked at IEMA for a few weeks."

He misread Floss's expression and explained. "She'll believe my story and keep quiet about it. Even though she's a time cop."

Floss looked at him. There wasn't a good way to break the news, but she did her best. "Actually, that plan might be flawed. You have to remember, you were away for five years . . ." He flinched and she ground to a halt.

"What? Tell me."

"And everyone thought you'd done a bunk with the TiTrav. You can't really blame her . . ."

"Blame Kayla?" His face set. "Why would I? You're telling me she's married or got a new boyfriend? I sort of expected that."

Floss didn't believe him. She guessed that at least a part of Jace had hung on to the idea of Kayla waiting, hoping against all reason for his return. He'd needed the thought of her constancy to keep him going through the long solitary years.

He said, as if reassuring himself, "I'd have to be really

unreasonable to think she'd wait indefinitely . . . but she'll still help me."

"She might not . . ." *Just tell him.* "She's going out with Quinn."

"*Quinn?*"

Floss nodded. Jace got up, walked to the window and stared out. After a few tense seconds he came back, sat down and refilled his glass. "Five years ago he was married with three kids."

"He got divorced a while back, I think."

Another pause. "What was he like with you?"

"Charming and helpful. Lying his head off. And going by his journal, waiting for the right moment to pounce."

"Two-timing shit. She doesn't know what he's like. I'm going to get the bastard."

Floss heard the unspoken, *and get Kayla back*. In her opinion, this was unlikely; Kayla had crossed Jace off and moved on. Floss knew better than to share this view. Instead she said, "Look, I've been thinking, are you sure you're doing the right thing? You could be running your head into a noose. Suppose no one believes you? You've got no evidence against Quinn. He doesn't have his illegal TiTrav any more, and as soon as he knows I took it he'll get rid of any other evidence. It's a pity I didn't make a copy of his journal – I didn't think to at the time."

"There's Ryker."

"Ryker won't testify. What else have you got? Just Scott maintaining he didn't kill McGuire, and he would say that, wouldn't he? On the other hand, there's plenty of evidence against *you*. As soon as you admit you've time travelled you're in for a mandatory fifteen years."

"You could give evidence of finding the TiTrav in Quinn's apartment."

"Yes, and be done for timecrime too the minute I tell them I time travelled. I've just got away from 2050, I'd be crazy to go back."

"I meant make a video."

"Would that be admissible? Anyway, it wouldn't be fair to implicate Ryker after he helped me, and I don't see how I can leave him out of it if I'm giving evidence. I can see you want revenge on Quinn, but –"

"It's not just that. He's a corrupt cop. I should do something about it. It's my job."

"It was your job five years ago."

"Yes, and it's his fault I'm not still doing it."

For an intelligent man he was being obtuse. She said in exasperation, "You don't seem to see that he's holding all the cards. He's a pillar of the establishment, with friends in high places. He knows Prince – I mean King – William, for goodness' sake! How will you feel if they don't believe you, and he's off the hook and you're in jail?" He said nothing, just looked mulish. Floss gave up on this. She pushed back her chair. "I'm going to wash up."

Jace gave her a hand, and it didn't take long. Floss blew out the candle and folded away the white table and chairs.

"I've got something I have to do. Make yourself some coffee."

He gave her a sharp look. "You're time travelling somewhere, aren't you?"

"I won't be long."

"Tell me where you're going." He saw her eyebrows lift and said, "Okay, you think it's none of my business, but where does that leave me if you don't come back?"

"I'll be back."

"You don't know that. Are you going to the past?" She didn't answer. "If you're going to the past you need a damn good reason. It's risky, not just for you but for everyone. It's not banned for nothing."

"You won't talk me out of it."

He waited. She told him, since he would not talk her out of it, though her reason for going was something she never willingly mentioned or thought about. That didn't mean she didn't think about it a lot.

"Fifteen years ago my father was run over and killed. He'd given me a puppy for my birthday the week before, and we were taking him for a walk. I stopped to do up my shoelace, and let go of the lead. The dog ran into the road and my father ran to get him. A car appeared out of nowhere going too fast and knocked him over. He was killed instantly." Floss tried to stop her voice trembling as the terrible memory played again in her mind, and she was once more her ten-year-old self standing on the pavement watching her father die. "He was only forty-one, a brilliant scientist, and it was my fault. I'm going to save him."

Jace stared at her. "You can't do that! Insanely bad idea."

Floss bristled. "I think your going back to clear your name is pretty dumb. You're still going to do it. I've already been to the past once, with Ryker, and nothing happened then. And what about you, you're back in the past right now!"

"That's different."

"Yeah, right. Of course it would be totally different when you're the one doing it."

"I'm not intending to interact with anything or anyone. You are."

This was just wasting time. "Don't bother trying to change my mind, I'm going."

She got up and moved her fingers towards the TiTrav on her wrist. Jace leaped across the room and grabbed her arm.

CHAPTER 35

Time is, time was, time is past

Sunday, 16th April 1999

When the blackness cleared Jace saw a sunny spring afternoon and a peaceful suburban street, with hedges growing behind low brick walls and a scarlet phone box on the corner. Street trees cast long shadows and a blackbird sang.

Floss was staring at him furiously as if she might hit him. "Why did you do that? Let go of me!" She shook his hand off and glowered at him like an angry teenager. "I don't want you here!"

"I can't let you do this. It's a stupid, crazy thing."

"Why? What difference will it make to anyone except my dad, my mum and me? I wish I'd left you in future London!"

"Too late to take me back now. Let's talk about this."

He sat on a brick wall warm from the sun, and after a few seconds' hesitation she sat sulkily beside him, not too close, keeping an eye on the road and ready to jump up again at any moment. Jace took a deep breath, paused to collect his thoughts, and tried to reason with her. He kept his voice unemotional, hoping she'd calm down.

"As part of my training, I went to lectures by the best physicists in the field. Lectures about time. A lot of it went over my head, but one thing I do remember; time is like a river. If you go upstream and dam it to change its course, then its former course will dry up and cease to exist. There aren't multiple alternative timelines. We only get one, and you'd better be careful how you mess with it. If you save your father's life, there'll be fifteen years of changes his presence will make to the world, all of which will alter our present. Any one of those changes could alter it disastrously."

She said, "Why should it alter the world disastrously? My father was a good man."

"Can't you see you're letting emotion stop you thinking clearly? For an intelligent woman you're being pig-headed." Her eyebrows went up and her mouth opened, but he carried on. "You remember when you came for me in future London, you said you could only take me back within a three week window, in order not to set up a time paradox? Your father's been dead for fifteen years. That's *fifteen years'* worth of potential paradoxes. You have no idea of what will happen if you save his life. You may find you don't have a life to go back to. There may not be a *world* to go back to."

"I'm prepared to take that risk."

"It's not just your risk, it's ten billion other people's."

"A tiny risk. Point nought nought nought something, I'd say."

"Even if you're right, that's a tiny risk of total disaster."

"I don't *care!*" Floss's voice had risen. "What does it matter? Humanity is on borrowed time anyway. Everyone's dead by 2170."

Her eyes filled with tears and she looked about fifteen. Jace suddenly remembered Saffron crying for her father. Without thinking, he reached out and took her hand, speaking more gently. "I know how you feel –" She yanked her hand away and he corrected himself. "I can *imagine* how you feel. But Floss, you're a scientist. You've got to think about this rationally. You can't put your personal needs above the rest of humanity's. I'm not going to tell you that's the worst sort of timecrime, because you don't care – and anyway, we're both technically guilty of timecrime already. But it's unethical. It's wrong."

A short silence was broken by the blackbird's brilliant liquid notes. A pigeon walked past. High above them a tiny silver plane left a thin vapour trail. The fight seemed to have gone out of Floss, and in the still suburban street Jace sensed the atmosphere of a truce. She said in a small voice, "I'm not even sure this is the right place. I remember the phone box, but the road looks different, it's smaller . . . maybe I remembered the name wrong."

Jace hoped she had. Easier all round. "Memory plays tricks. People think of it as a filing cabinet, but it's more like a garden. Things left there change and grow."

They sat for over an hour side by side in the spring sunshine while nothing happened; sometimes silent but mostly talking. Gradually they both relaxed. Floss told Jace about her father, who was the reason she'd become a research scientist in the first place. Like him, she had worked on the contraceptive virus, getting her first job with the same company, Zadotech – which, of course, was why IEMA had abducted her from her own time. She told him about the early work her father's team had done on the Mapuera strain, which they isolated from a bat in South America because it was able to infect other species. The programme was terminated shortly before his death – one Wednesday without warning all work had been stopped on it, and Richard Dryden transferred to different research. The vaccine had turned out to be just too contagious; it spread through the animals like wildfire. Zadotech concluded it was not commercially viable – based on epidemiological modelling, just a few vaccinated rabbits would be enough to treat Australia.

"By the time I joined Zadotech, they'd restarted the programme, hoping to produce a virus that could be tailored to fit any pest species. That's much easier now – and cheaper. We've got way better computer modelling, crystallography and cryo-electron microscopy. I was really pleased. Dad never thought it should be shut down, he could see the possibilities. But it was a business decision, he didn't get a say."

A Red Admiral butterfly zigzagged past. No people had been by. Jace was wondering whether she'd agree if he suggested they went home now, when her whole body stiffened. He turned. They were in the right street after all.

A man and a young girl walking towards them, their progress slowed by a labradoodle puppy who lolloped around, wanting to sniff at everything, winding his lead round the girl's legs. Her attention was focused entirely on the dog, trying to encourage him to walk to heel. The man was smiling as he looked at his daughter with obvious pride and love. A tear ran down Floss's cheeks, and she brushed it away impatiently. Her father and younger self were getting nearer.

Floss took a deep breath, and half rose. Her movement attracted her father's attention, and he glanced their way with a smile as they drew level. Young Floss was too taken up with the puppy to notice them.

Now they were past, now they were walking away, now they were out of sight. Floss continued to sit, staring down at her shoes.

Let's get her out of here. Fast. Jace stood. "Time to go."

A faint thrum in the distance grew louder. The peace and quiet was shattered by the roar of an approaching engine, as a big black four-by-four sped towards them from the same direction young Floss and her father had come from. It shot past and screeched out of sight round the curve of the road.

Floss leaped up and raced after it, feet pounding the pavement. Jace ran after her.

In the distance screened from their view, a screech of tyres, a car's horn blaring, a thump, a high-pitched scream that went on and on. Floss stopped and burst into tears, sobbing uncontrollably, lost in misery. Jace stood, feeling utterly inadequate, wondering whether she'd be comforted or hate it if he put his arms around her.

After a while her sobs quietened and he said, "He looked nice, your dad. I'm sorry. Let's go back."

"I had the chance to save him, and I chose not to. I feel even worse than before."

"You did the right thing."

"Maybe. Doesn't help."

He started to extend a tentative arm towards her, but Floss moved away. Something had caught her eye, and she went and picked it up; a fat little notebook in a blue cover, lying by the kerb. She opened it and turned the pages. He craned over her shoulder. It was hand-written in biro, with dated entries like a diary, and diagrams and formulae here and there.

"It must have fallen out of his pocket." Her brows drew together and she looked Jace in the eye defiantly. "I'm keeping it."

Jace hadn't the heart to argue. She just wanted something of her dad's. What difference could a few random jottings about an abandoned project make? "Okay," he said. "Let's go."

CHAPTER 36

The answer?

Thursday, 23rd July 2015

Back in Floss's flat, Jace made coffee while Floss curled up in the one armchair, poring over the notebook. She took the mug he handed her absently without saying thank you, intent on reading. He let her be. Quinn could wait till tomorrow. He picked an elderly paperback from her shelves, an early John le Carré, and sat on the floor with it. As he opened the book the front cover came away in his hand. The paper felt rough, and was darker cream around the edges. He had got used to these old-fashioned paper books in future London – they were surprisingly durable. Now he gazed at the print without taking it in. He had to admit that, clearer-headed in his case than her own, she'd been right about the problems involved with bringing Quinn to book. Perhaps he should let it go, though to do that went against his every instinct. Plus he hated the thought of Kayla with Quinn. He could go and talk to her, tell her what had happened . . . the trouble was, he'd be forcing her to make her choice between them, and she might choose to trust Quinn. He couldn't believe she'd shop him though . . .

"Jace!" Floss's face was flushed, her eyes bright. "I think . . .

there's something here that might be the answer."

"The answer to what? Life, the universe, and everything?"

"Humanity dying out."

"What is that anyway? A journal?"

"No. It's my father's ideas book. Sort of an unofficial lab notebook. The real ones have to stay in the lab because they're important as a record for patents, they're legal documents with page numbers and a permanent binding. A record of procedures, observations and thought processes, that sort of thing. Dad liked to have something with him to jot things down in case he forgot. He said his best ideas came to him when he wasn't thinking about them. I remember he thought he'd lost it once – the relief when it turned up . . ."

"So how does it help?"

"I'm not certain it will. I'm just guessing. You know I'm working along similar lines of research to my father, even though we're further advanced, obviously. IEMA believed the work I was going to do resulted in disaster, so they removed me before I could do it. But the last entries in this notebook, just the last day or two, show my father was still thinking about the virus. He hadn't written up his ideas in his lab notebook because the programme was closed. They'd drawn a line under it. Then he was killed. No one picked this notebook up. It must have lain in the gutter until it was swept away."

"What does it say?"

"I'll have to tell you the background or you won't understand. At Zadotech they – we – want a virus that's highly contagious and causes infertility in pest mammals, but can't be passed to other animal species. The mumps virus is the right sort of virus, plus it mutates easily, but they couldn't use mumps because its host is human. Instead, they found a related bat virus, and modified that. The Mapuera virus, like mumps, is a single-stranded RNA virus. Obviously there's a bit of a conflict when you need a virus to mutate, but then once you've got it right you want it to resist mutating. It's got to be stable. That's what I'm working on now."

Jace nodded.

Floss went on, "Now suppose we think we've cracked it, but it mutates and infects humans? Which we know now is what actually happened. Will happen. What you'd need then is to develop, fast, a new disabled human vaccine that is highly transmissible, so it'll protect everyone, because some people won't agree to be vaccinated. The worry is that the new vaccine will revert. To avoid this, you have to understand the sequence of mutations that originally gave rise to the contraceptive virus, also the variant that cropped up with the propensity to infect human cells."

"I see," Jace said. "More or less."

"I'm knee deep in genome sequencing data. I've sometimes wondered about sequence data from the first-generation programme, because it would be really useful. They said none exists, that virus samples were destroyed on programme termination, as was normal practice at the time. My dad would have been told to do this. But he didn't. He kept some in an off-site facility, all labelled and coded. He's listed them here. Ten to one they'll still be there. I think they're the answer."

Jace looked at her sitting there, all young and bright-eyed and ready to save the world. She made him feel time-worn, the more so because he could remember when he had felt like that himself. "So what are you going to do about it?"

"Steal the samples and take them to my boss, Bill Caldecot. In 2050. He's retired, but he'll know what to do with them, who to give them to."

"I'll come with you." She narrowed her eyes at him, so he added, "I can help if you get into trouble – say someone gets curious, or wants to check your chip."

"I'm going to appear on his doorstep, no reason I should meet anyone else. Why do I get the feeling you have an ulterior motive?"

She was sharp, no doubt about it. The eagerness in her blue eyes had been replaced by a steely intelligence. He said casually, "I thought I might drop in on Kayla while we're there. Sound her out. See if she'll help me."

He could see her thinking about this. In the end she said, "Okay, but I'm coming with you. I'm not leaving you alone with her. And you have to agree to do what I say. Especially if I say leave. Else I'm not taking you. And I've got the TiTrav."

This last argument was unanswerable. "Agreed. When are we going to steal the samples?"

Floss smiled. "I don't have to actually steal them. I can do this in plain sight, like Dad did, just requisition them from the facility via the usual channels. No one's going to check what they are. I might order some other virus samples at the same time as cover. I'll use the high containment lab at Zadotech to unpack them – I only need a spot of each on filter paper, with a note of the code. Then I can send them back."

"How long will it take?"

"Tomorrow's Friday, so I'll be going in to work. I'll get them couriered over. We can take them to Bill in the evening."

Friday evening, and Floss's flat under the roof was sweltering. That afternoon Jace had been to New River Walk and lain on the grass by the water, watching the ducks and thinking about Kayla. He felt guilty; if only he had told her his suspicions of Quinn . . . she wouldn't have been able to do anything about bringing him to justice, most likely, but she would at least have been wary of him. On the other hand, maybe she'd have been dumped in future London too . . . which would have made his stay considerably more pleasant . . .

He fell asleep, and for a nasty moment on waking thought he was in future London, until the sound of an ice cream van's jingle welcomed him back to civilization. He strolled through Islington, marvelling at the endless lines of vehicles parked at the kerb, making the streets so narrow that in places a car couldn't pass a bicycle. London was one big car park. The main roads were not much better; the cars moved sluggishly, with massive tailbacks at road works. No wonder the drivers all seemed bad-tempered.

He returned to the unbearably hot flat, opened the windows wide and had a tepid bath, tried to get into a book, and was really pleased when he heard a key in the lock. Floss was flushed and windblown from the bike ride. He noticed she was still wearing the ring.

"Did you get them?"

Floss nodded. "Ready? Let's go."

CHAPTER 37

Reunion

Friday, 6th May 2050

Kayla hung her jacket in the wardrobe and slipped off her high heels, glad to be home. The day was windy, and one of the pair of olive trees on her balcony had blown over; she went outside, picked it up and noticed how dry the compost was. The automatic watering device must have failed days ago. Annoyed – it had been that sort of week, one petty frustration after another, culminating in Floss Dryden's disappearance – she fetched a jug from the kitchen. Plants watered, she had a quick shower, redid her make up, applied perfume and put on a svelte black dress in case Quinn should want to take her to dinner. She sat on the sofa, thinking she'd give him an hour before eating alone.

When Quinn, normally so imperturbable, had come (late) into work that morning, he had been quite unlike himself, agitated and absent-minded. Kayla had wondered at first whether something had happened to one of his children. Then when it became clear it was the business over that tiresome girl that had disturbed his normal equanimity, the worse thought occurred to her that he might have been in love with Floss. When she had asked him if he was all right, if there was anything she could do to help, he had been brusque and dismissive. She was shocked to see the cold fury in his eyes, turned briefly on her. As she left his office, she had suddenly experienced the most dreadful sinking feeling. In two months she would be thirty: she and Quinn had been together for more than three years, and marriage had never once been mentioned.

She had been so certain he was the one, a certainty she had not felt with Jace. Yes, Jace had been great – attractive, nice, good in bed, devoted to her – but she had always believed she could do better, needed more of a challenge. Quinn was something else; though charming, he was exacting, and his occasional piercing, unsmiling stare from beneath lowered brows if she stepped out of line both frightened and excited her. He was like a spirited horse she wasn't sure she could control.

She remembered that time she had taken Jace home for the weekend, because her parents had wanted to meet the new man in her life. He'd been on his best behaviour, a little over-awed by their country house with its grounds, swimming pool and tennis courts; the antique furniture and the Labradors. He and Kayla were given separate bedrooms well apart. Her parents had been very polite, and questioned him, delicately but with persistence, about his background. They hadn't discussed him at all with Kayla, but it had been very clear that they thought he wasn't quite good enough for their daughter. Jace had not been asked back. Her mother had taken to saying, "Are you still seeing Jason?" whenever she called.

The weekend with Quinn was a different matter. She had waited until his divorce came through to mention him to her parents, as they would not have approved of her affair with a married man. When she did take him home, Quinn had been completely at ease as he always was in any milieu, and her parents had fallen instantly under his spell, had become animated and chatty. They hadn't taken exception to the dandified clothes he wore with aplomb, clothes which would normally have raised a disapproving eyebrow. When he charmingly disagreed with them about the recent political scandal, they had striven to see his point of view, had even changed their minds.

Her mother got Kayla on her own within the first half hour and hissed, "Now you're not to let this one get away. *Very* nice. Our sort of person."

On parting her father had told him he was welcome back any time, and invited him to come pheasant shooting when the season began.

Kayla had always accepted that Quinn would not be in a hurry to marry again. She had been sympathetic and understanding, and made every effort to be agreeable when she met his children – not easy, they clearly took their mother's side and were stiff and monosyllabic with her, especially the girl. Though Kayla felt herself established in Quinn's life, she fitted in with him; he made no accommodation for her. For instance, she never saw him on a Thursday evening. This, he told her, was his time for contemplation and planning, an essential oasis of calm in his busy life. Quinn breezed through a packed diary each week that would have felled a lesser man, worked weekends and frequently attended breakfast meetings and business-related evening occasions; he was certainly entitled to one night to himself a week. Still, she had niggling doubts. Perhaps he kept Thursdays clear for a regular-as-clockwork liaison with another woman . . .

The months and years passed. Quinn took her to Glyndebourne, to a garden party at Buckingham Palace, to grand dinners at City livery companies, to the Mediterranean for a week on a chartered yacht. He did not ask her to move into his apartment. Her daydreams of Ansel presenting her with an enormous diamond engagement ring over dinner at an expensive restaurant remained just that; dreams.

Now she wondered if her situation would be the same in five or ten years' time, whether the current arrangement suited Quinn so well he felt no need to change it. He was impervious to hints (showing him pictures of gorgeous houses on the fringes of London – "Oh, Ansel, you must look, this house is to die for!" – telling him about Sarah's baby and how sweet he was) and she did not dare to broach the subject of marriage, let alone give him an ultimatum. Perhaps she should look for someone else while she was still young enough . . . but she didn't want anyone else. She wanted Quinn.

Most likely she only needed to be patient for a little longer. Persistence would win the day.

A knock on the door interrupted her ruminations on their relationship. It must be a neighbour or the janitor, since the bell hadn't rung. Not Quinn, who had his own key. She walked impatiently to the door and flicked the screen switch. Jace stood there, Floss Dryden by his side. Kayla gasped and backed away, got out her phone and speed dialled Quinn's number.

"Kayla. What is it?"

Her voice low, almost a whisper, she said, "Ansel, Jace is outside my door with Floss Dryden."

His tone changed, became intent and authoritative. "Where's your gun?"

"In my jacket."

"Put it in your pocket. Let them in and keep them talking. I'll come straight over."

"Will you ring the police?"

"Leave it with me. He's dangerous, don't try to do anything yourself, just keep them talking. Don't let them go. Put the phone away and open the door. Be very nice to him and wait for me."

"I'll do my best . . . it might be awkward . . ." He had disconnected. Kayla ran to the wardrobe and swapped the phone for her gun. Her dress had no pockets, so she tucked the gun behind a sofa cushion, swiftly checked her appearance in the mirror and went to open the door.

Ignoring Floss for the moment, she cried, "Jace! After all this time! What are you doing here?"

Jace smiled as he took her in from head to toe, a complicated half smile that was both tender and wary. Kayla had time to notice his brand new old-fashioned clothes; he looked older, leaner than before, but otherwise hadn't changed. Quinn had said he was dangerous; he was a wanted criminal; but seeing him now, she could not believe he would ever hurt her.

He said, "Hi to you, too."

"What happened to you for five years?"

"Bad stuff. Good stuff. Life."

Kayla gazed at him, shaking her head. "Same old Jace. You look terrific. You know there's a warrant out for your arrest?"

"Yeah." He gave her the old slow smile. "Are you going to arrest me, then?"

"I ought to."

Kayla became aware of Floss stirring. She wasn't smiling; her expression was guarded. "You'd better come in. Both of you. Tell me what's going on."

They walked into the room and she closed the door. Jace followed her to the sofa where they sat facing each other. Floss perched bolt upright on the edge of a chair opposite them. Having got the sofa to herself and Jace, Kayla rose gracefully to her feet again.

"Let me get you a drink. Coffee? Wine?"

As Floss said, "Nothing, thanks," Jace said, "Wine."

Kayla disappeared briefly into the kitchen, and returned with two champagne flutes and a chilled bottle of Pol Roger, which she handed to Jace to open and pour.

She stared into his eyes. "It's *so* good to see you, Jace. I thought you'd gone forever and I'd never see you again." She lifted her glass. "Here's to you. Now tell me everything that happened, why you disappeared."

"First, I didn't steal the TiTrav."

Kayla's eyes widened. "It never sounded the sort of thing you'd do. So who did?"

"Quinn. That's why he killed McGuire."

"*Quinn?*" There was a pause. "But... Scott killed McGuire."

"No. He got the blame, but it wasn't him. It was Quinn, because he'd taken the TiTrav from McGuire and he didn't want him talking."

Kayla stared at him. Jace had been gone since 2045, and now turned up out of the blue with this extraordinary story. It occurred to her that her ex-boyfriend might be suffering from paranoid delusions – a mental illness could have been responsible for his abandoning home and friends and running away five years ago. She said gently, "Jace, I really don't think that's what happened. What makes you think it did? Everyone knew Scott killed McGuire."

"Scott wouldn't have shot him through the heart by accident. He learned to shoot pistols in the US to competition standard."

"Even so, it was the first raid he'd been on. He was young, he was over-excited, he made a mistake."

"No, Quinn used him as a fall guy. That's why he was there. Remember at the briefing, you didn't want him to come? And Quinn insisted?"

"Yes, but that doesn't mean anything. You could just as

easily say Scott had the TiTrav and killed McGuire to cover it up. Do you have any concrete proof at all of what you're alleging?"

Jace's surface calm began to crack and break up round the edges. His voice became louder, insistent. "Quinn told me himself!"

Kayla looked at him dubiously. "Why would he do that?"

"Because I sussed him. Then he wanted me to join him time travelling. He thought I could be useful. He said he was going to make himself obscenely rich. He offered me money."

Kayla just shook her head. None of this rang true at all. Quinn was Chief of IEMA Intelligence, highly paid to enforce time laws. He had a private fortune made from shrewd investments on the stock market. He didn't need more money, he wasn't a criminal; he was a pillar of society, on friendly terms with the Prime Minister and King William. Jace was living in a fantasy world.

Seeing her expression, Floss pushed up her shirt sleeve, displaying a TiTrav. "Look."

Kayla stared and caught her breath. *So Jace did steal it . . . and for some reason he's given it to her . . .*

Floss said, "D'you know where I found this? Hidden under Quinn's ottoman in the dressing room in his flat."

Kayla didn't ask what Floss had been doing at Quinn's home. If she'd been invited there by Quinn, Kayla didn't want to know. "Why were you searching his apartment? That's quite an odd thing to do."

"To find his TiTrav. I knew he'd got one."

"How did you know?"

Floss hesitated. "I can't tell you that. But I can tell you when Jace wouldn't play ball Quinn tied him up and dumped him in future London and he nearly died. He spent five years there on his own struggling to survive. Quinn's a liar, a killer and a time criminal."

Kayla didn't know what to say in the face of these wild, unsubstantiated accusations. Clearly mistaking her silence for shock, Jace took her hand. "I'm sorry. Floss told me you were . . . seeing him."

"Yes – well, I thought you were gone for good. We've been together for nearly four years." *I don't know what's going on, but Jace is crazy and God knows what that girl's up to. I wish Ansel would hurry up and arrive, he'll know what to do . . .* Jace looked away, as if he didn't want to think about her and Quinn being together for four years. Surreptitiously, she turned her wrist a fraction in order to glance at her watch.

Immediately, Floss jumped to her feet. "Jace, it's time we went."

Jace frowned. "What's the rush?"

"You agreed you'd leave when I said. I'm saying we go now."

"I haven't asked Kayla yet."

"Come *on!*"

"Asked me what?"

He turned back to her. "The moment my chip passes a reader I'll get arrested. That makes life difficult. I wondered if you'd put me up while I get the evidence together to bring down Quinn. You've got access to the department files, too, which would help me work out what he's been up to."

Floss said urgently, "Jace, we're not safe here. I don't trust her. We need to go."

At that moment the door opened and to Kayla's relief, Quinn entered the apartment, gun in hand.

CHAPTER 38

Confrontation

"Hands in the air, Jace. You too, Floss."

Jace's face closed and hardened. He dropped Kayla's hand, but didn't raise his own. Taking his lead, neither did Floss. She cursed herself; she had noticed Kayla's elegant black dress without drawing the obvious conclusion, that her having changed from work clothes meant she was expecting company, and the fact that Kayla hadn't mentioned this was damning. How stupid she had been, not to have worked it out earlier . . .

Quinn said to Jace, "Do as I say, or make no mistake, I will shoot you."

Jace turned to Kayla and said bitterly, "You knew he was coming, didn't you?"

Quick as a flash, Kayla produced a gun from behind a cushion and pointed it at him. "I'm sorry about this, Jace. Best to do as he says."

Quinn lowered his weapon a little and transferred his attention to Floss. His eyes flicked to her left wrist and up again.

Though scared and shaking all over, Floss felt hyped-up, super-aware of every detail, adrenaline racing through her veins. Quinn was looking at her differently, with a new respect in his eyes, she was gratified to see. She stared back with all the insolence she could muster. *I'll give him sweet timidity . . .*

"Aren't you a tiny bit worried about what might come out in the investigation after you arrest us or kill us?"

"Why should I be? An innocent man has nothing to worry about. And I'm not going to kill you. Hand over the TiTrav you have on your wrist."

"What, you mean this one, the one that you stole from McGuire before you killed him?"

Quinn raised his eyebrows. "Did Jace tell you that?" He smiled. "And you believed him?"

"Certainly did. After all, I found the TiTrav in your apartment. Quite a strange thing for a time cop to own. But do tell me your version of how it got there, I'm fascinated."

"I have no idea how it got there – assuming you're telling the truth." He shrugged. "Perhaps Jace planted it in my apartment for you to find. As for why he would do that, I can only speculate."

Kayla said, "I think Jace is delusional – paranoid – he needs psychiatric help."

"No I don't," Jace said. "How about, I'm not mad, your boyfriend's a crook?"

She shook her head sadly. "Jace, please let us help you. We're your friends, we're on your side, we understand you aren't in control of your actions. They won't charge you if you're ill, you have nothing to worry about. We need to get this sorted out."

Quinn was still focused on Floss. "I advise you to give me the TiTrav. Now."

"Else you'll shoot me?"

"No. I won't shoot you. Although it's highly irregular, I'm going to make you an offer. It's not your fault you've somehow got mixed up in this. IEMA should never have brought you here, so I'm prepared to make a concession in your case. Give me the TiTrav and I'll take you straight back to your own time. I'll ensure you are left there in peace, that the Time Police won't come again to fetch you. The whole thing will be over as far as you're concerned. That's what you want, isn't it?"

"Come on, Quinn, what kind of pathetic offer is that? I don't need you to take me. I have my own TiTrav. I can take myself any time I want, *to* any time I want."

"It's up to you, naturally. I thought you might prefer my suggestion to the alternative, which is my arresting both of you and letting the judicial system take its course."

"What you mean is *you'd* prefer it, because you'd get to keep the TiTrav. Plus you know if I was arrested I won't keep quiet. Once they've worked out where you got the TiTrav from, being done for timecrime will be the least of your worries. You might find yourself trying to talk your way out of a murder charge."

"Very well. Have it your own way." His manner became formal. "Florence Dryden, I am arresting you on suspicion of committing timecrime, and being in illegal possession of a TiTrav. You will be given the opportunity to contact a lawyer in due course."

Jace butted in. "Floss, take yourself out of here. I'll be all right."

Floss highly doubted this. She wasn't going to go, leaving him behind, unless there was absolutely no alternative. She'd hoped Jace had been working out a plan while she and Quinn were sparring. A glance towards the sofa told her Kayla was following the conversation, but keeping her eyes fixed on Jace. Her hand holding the gun was steady. If she could only distract her, maybe he could grab the gun. He was near enough. But how? She could always tell Kayla about Quinn's other girlfriends mentioned in his journal, but that seemed kind of low... on the other hand, she couldn't think of anything else that might get them out of this mess. She went for it.

"Hey, Kayla, I bet you didn't know Quinn keeps a journal? A very private one. I took a quick look at it when I picked up the TiTrav. There was loads and loads, he's been writing it for five years, but I could give you edited highlights, just all the stuff he hasn't told you . . ."

Kayla's eyes turned towards Floss. Unbelievably fast, Jace's right arm moved sideways from the elbow and sliced into her arm. She cried out in pain and surprise as the gun smashed into her face and fell from her hand. Jace grabbed it and leaped to his feet. Quinn swung to face him, raising his gun. For a few tense seconds they each watched the other narrowly for any hint of movement that might suggest a finger pulling a trigger. The pause lengthened.

In the end, Floss walked over and stood between them, facing Quinn. "This is silly. If either of you fire, you'll both get hurt, maybe killed, and bleed all over Kayla's nice cream carpet. Now I have a suggestion of my own. If you don't agree to it, I'm going to go back in time to warn us, so we won't be in Kayla's flat when you arrive, but waiting in the hallway up the stairs to jump you. Or shoot you, if Jace thinks that's better."

Quinn said, "You forget you are standing in front of me and I have a gun pointing at you. But leaving that to one side for the moment, what's your suggestion?"

"You both take the ammunition out of your guns and give it to me. You first, because I trust Jace to keep his word, and I'm not so sure about you. Then we'll leave. Jace, will you do it if Quinn does too?"

More seconds trickled by. Jace said, "Okay. But make sure that after he takes out the magazine, he ejects the round still in the gun."

"Quinn?"

"Very well."

Slowly, eyes on Floss, half smiling, he lowered the gun, released the magazine and let it drop into his hand. He pulled the slide on the top of the gun and a bullet popped out. He plucked it from the air with casual ease, put the bullet and the magazine on to Floss's palm and pocketed the gun. She moved a little to one side and watched Jace do the same. As he handed her the ammo, with the tail of her eye she saw Quinn's hands move. He had got the gun out again, and there was a soft click as he slipped something into it. He had a second magazine.

"*Jace!*"

But even as she cried out Jace barrelled past her, knocking her on to all fours. The gun went off, a muted bang, and plaster burst from the ceiling. She scrambled to her feet. The two men were fighting savagely, slamming each other round the room, barging into furniture, thudding and grunting. Quinn rammed Jace into a mirrored console which exploded into fragments. Jace punched him, grabbed his arm and yanked him round fast and hard, and as he hit the wall Quinn's gun spun out of his grasp. They crashed to the carpet grappling, Quinn's hand groping about, shards of mirror crunching beneath them. Floss leaped forward and grabbed just as his fingers touched the gun, and dropped it in her pocket with the magazines. She watched anxiously, not certain who was winning, looking for a way to help . . . she noticed Kayla had retreated to a corner and was on her phone, talking urgently. The men knocked over a flower arrangement which rolled to the floor, water and flowers spilling everywhere unregarded. The elegant living room was a shambles. Jace's arm went round Quinn's neck, straining, and they both became still. Seizing her moment, Floss jumped forward and aimed a kick at Quinn's groin with all her strength. The blow connected. He collapsed doubled up in agony, and after a moment Jace let go of him and stood up, breathing hard. His face was bleeding, but less than Quinn's.

Standing side by side they looked on as Quinn writhed, clutching himself and groaning. The only other sound was a faint glug glug as the champagne bottle lying on the floor emptied its contents. Floss was slightly staggered by the effectiveness of her attack. She had no experience of assaulting people. Blood from the cuts on Quinn's face made red blots on his shirt and the formerly immaculate carpet. Kayla put down her phone and ran and crouched beside him, moving bits of broken mirror away from him, picking them off his skin, careless of cutting her own fingers. Quinn seemed oblivious to anything except his pain. They watched him for a while.

Floss pulled herself together. "Now it really is time to go," she said, seizing Jace's arm. "She's called the police."

"Good." The rage in his eyes had gone icy cold. "I can hand him over to them."

"Don't be crazy! You haven't got any evidence. And it won't matter what you tell them, this looks bad."

A croak came from their feet. "Stay, by all means." Quinn was still curled in a foetal position. "Attempt to incriminate me . . . and the best you can hope for is we'll go down together . . . most likely, you'll go down alone." He shut his eyes again.

"You fucking lying bastard." Jace stepped towards Quinn.

Kayla's eyes were wild. "Don't hurt him!"

Quinn said, "He won't kill me . . . not in cold blood."

"True. Maybe I'll dump you in future London, 2185. See how you get on there."

Quinn went to shrug and winced instead. "You know I wouldn't survive a week."

Kayla cried, "Jace, no! Please!"

Jace turned to her, his expression unreadable. She had smears of blood on her face, and looked distraught. He walked back to Floss and put his arm around her waist.

Floss pressed the two buttons.

Friday, 24th July 2015

Back in her flat, Floss, shaking with relief, put Quinn's gun and the ammunition on the kitchen counter. Then she made Jace, shaking with fury, stand still while she brushed him down to remove the worst of the mirror fragments. She hoovered them up, then got him to sit on a chair in the middle of the room so she could try to pick out any tiny splinters in his skin. "Well, that was fun. Not. Keep still."

"He'll tell the police I materialized with the TiTrav and beat him up. That's the version that will go on record. A blameless citizen set upon by a vicious time criminal. Kayla will say the same, except she'll tell them I'm raving. What a total fiasco."

"We didn't know he was going to turn up."

"Kayla did, though." He paused for a moment. "And he knew I was there, he had his gun out. She must have rung him when she saw it was me. She shopped me to Quinn. How can she . . . *like* a man like that?"

"He's very charming. She must be in love with him. And he's plausible. I thought he was nice myself."

Jace, following his own train of thought, was not listening. "She's a time cop. I can't blame her. I suppose she thought she was shopping me to IEMA, telling Quinn. I wonder if he'd have killed me, if you'd agreed to give him the TiTrav and go home? I should have broken his neck."

"I'm glad you didn't."

"I might have done if you hadn't kicked him in the balls."

He went quiet for a minute. "I didn't mean the gun to hit her face. I hope I didn't hurt her."

She said soothingly, "Her face looked all right to me. That was Quinn's blood on it. She may have cut her hands a bit on the glass, that's all."

"I'll never prove I'm innocent now. Quinn'll keep his job as Chief of Intelligence. He's unassailable. Kayla still believes he's honest. I can never go back. Not unless I get more proof, and I don't see how I can do that."

"At least the meeting with Bill went well."

Her old boss had been delighted to see her, fascinated by her story, and enthusiastic about using her samples to counter the contraceptive virus. She'd left his home confident about his discretion, satisfied she had done all she could to use her father's research to save humanity, and feeling a lot better. Frustrating though it was for Jace that Quinn was still on the loose, at least she had achieved her objective.

There was a silence while Floss worked and Jace brooded. "There, I think that's the lot, unless you can feel some I've missed. Let me just wash the blood off." Floss ran warm water into the sink, got out a clean facecloth and cleaned him up. She stuck Elastoplasts on the deeper cuts that were still bleeding.

She wondered what Jace would do now.

"I don't feel like cooking. Let's go out and have a pizza," she said.

CHAPTER 39

Quinn gets a present, Floss and Jace get a pizza

Quinn stayed on the carpet for a few minutes after they had left until he was reasonably certain he was not going to throw up. Then he allowed Kayla to help him to the sofa where he lay prone, locked in a private world of pain. She wanted to clean his cuts, but he waved her away. After a bit he cautiously sat up and sipped the brandy Kayla brought him. The doorbell rang – the police – and she went to let them in; a uniformed man and woman who surveyed the smashed furniture, the hole in the wall the bullet had made, the broken glass, plaster, flowers, water, wine and blood on the carpet, then looked at Quinn limp and bleeding on the sofa. They exchanged glances.

"Looks like you've had a bit of trouble here, sir. What happened?"

He let her tell them.

Eyes shut, he listened to Kayla's proficient narration of the evening's events. He could not have done it better himself, though he wouldn't have bothered with anxious excuses concerning Jace's sanity. The power of coherent thought slowly began to return, fighting its way through the pain. It had been excruciatingly tantalizing to see his TiTrav so near yet unobtainable on Floss's slender wrist, and worse to watch her depart still wearing it. She seemed to be in league with Jace. How had they met? She'd read his journal, she said . . . so must have come across his name and decided on a mission of mercy. He could imagine her doing that.

Now there was an interesting woman, and how pretty she had looked while deriding him. He remembered the way her eyes had sparkled during their verbal joust, something he had not had leisure to consciously think about at the time. He felt somehow liberated by the fact that she knew the truth about him. A pity she hadn't stuck to a war of words. He had never experienced anything like that kick, and still felt terrible ten minutes later.

He'd have had more options had Kayla not been there, or Jace . . .

The police were getting to their feet, explaining there was nothing they could do at this stage, the suspects' chips being already in the auto report system. "Sorry we missed the fight, but chasing time-travelling perps is more your people's line of business than ours," the senior officer said as they left.

Kayla suggested he should stay the night so she could fuss over him, but Quinn ordered a pod and went home, after telling her to get everything, including the ruined carpet, replaced and send him the bill. He wanted to be alone to think. The spacious calm of his apartment soothed him; the panoramic view, the silence. He showered and changed his clothes, then realized he was hungry. Sitting on his own sofa eating salmon en croute with a white burgundy, aching all over – he suspected a rib was cracked – and uncharacteristically low spirited, he considered the various defeats of the last two days. The one shred of luck had been Floss not disclosing to Kayla what she had gleaned from his journal; she had not had time to spill the beans about his other women. If Kayla broke up with him, he would miss her. She suited him well, was beautiful, intelligent, good company, presentable and prepared to accept him on his own terms. He'd be unlikely to find anyone more fit for purpose.

But that aside, things had gone badly for him. Quinn was not accustomed to losing, and did not like it. Also, it seemed improbable that Jace had gone for good; he was a man with a grudge, a tough, intelligent and dogged man who had nothing to do with his time except work out ways of getting revenge. He was a human sword of Damocles hanging over Quinn's head, a bomb that could go off at any moment and bring his life crashing down. Quinn had thought he was done for earlier that evening, when Jace's arm had been round his neck, slowly forcing his head backwards. He had waited for his spinal column to snap; then came the obliterating pain from Floss's kick, and Jace had let him go. On reflection, that kick might have saved his life.

Quinn finished his meal. Glancing up he noticed something white, a piece of paper, beside his computer. His immediate conviction was that Floss had visited again, and left him a message. This thought was considerably more appealing than all the others jostling in his mind. He crossed the room and picked up the note.

I've brought you a timely present. I wonder if you can work out where it is?

His heartbeat accelerated. The handwriting was his own.

Quinn walked through his bedroom and into the dressing room, crouched by the ottoman and felt underneath for the slit in the canvas. His fingers closed round something smooth and metallic . . . he drew it out. A TiTrav – not his old one, this was silky black, a little lighter in the hand and a different design, with the buttons to one side of a slightly larger screen. It was brand new, still with the temporary password tag attached. As he looked, its ice-blue light pulsed. A warm glow suffused his body, banishing pain and depression. Life felt good; he was back in control of his world. It occurred to him his future self must be doing well, to own more than one TiTrav. Then he thought again – by delivering this, his future self would be wiping his own timeline in favour of a new one. What had happened to him to make that a desirable option?

Unbidden, the notion crossed his mind that he could visit Floss in her own time . . . he dismissed this beguiling idea as frivolous. The first thing he needed to do was remove all threat of Jace returning. He would go back to 4th September 2180, to Bunhill Fields five minutes after he had left him, and put a bullet in his brain.

Floss and Jace walked down Upper Street to Pizza Express. They sat at a small table by the window, eating pizzas, drinking Pinot Grigio and watching people pass by. Jace found he was keeping an eye out for Quinn – ridiculous. The man no longer had his TiTrav, and could only time travel under the austere auspices of IEMA; he was securely stuck in his own time. Floss was attacking her pizza as if taking part in a speed pizza-eating contest. She glanced up and noticed his eyes on her.

"Thinking you might get shot makes you really hungry. Never knew that." Jace was feeling ravenous too, he realized. They both focused on the food for a bit.

When her plate was nearly empty, Floss said, "So what next?"

"Quinn'll send an IEMA team after me. Not that he'll want to, but he doesn't have a lot of choice, what with Kayla being there, and the police called. I'm on the wanted list, I time travelled in the presence of witnesses. Not just any old witnesses, either – he's Chief of Intelligence, she's Head of Timecrime. It would look suspicious if he didn't."

"What about me? Will they come after me?"

"Again, Quinn won't want to. On my own, I'm a wanted criminal telling an unbelievable story, maybe off my head. With you there, my allegations look a bit more solid. Quinn could argue you aren't subject to laws not passed in your own time, and that you're now back in 2015 with no obvious ill effects in 2050, so why not leave you there – but people would wonder what his angle was, why he cared. They'd wonder until they worked it out."

"But he's in charge and good at getting his own way. I might be all right."

Jace shook his head. "It was a big mistake to let them see you had the TiTrav. That'll be their main focus."

Floss thought about this. "Maybe if I don't go back to my flat for a while it'll blow over."

Jace's face expressed his doubts. *It's not going to blow over unless I make it.*

"I could call in sick at work, then take some time off, stay with a friend . . ." She grinned. "I could leave a note on my door saying I'd given the TiTrav to you."

"Be my guest." Jace topped up her glass, then raised his eyes to hers. He had to make her see the danger she was in. "Floss, I'm really sorry. It's not realistic to think you can lie low for a while, then resume your normal life as if nothing has happened. You'll be taking a big chance. I'm not sure I can fix this thing, and if I can't . . . when you go to any of your usual haunts, home, job, friends and family, IEMA could be waiting for you. Then back to 2050, a trial, and fifteen years' jail. Time cops are thorough, and we don't give up."

"They may be thorough, but they're not superhuman. I'll be on the lookout for them. I'll buy a personal alarm, and stay in crowded places whenever possible. The last thing they'll want to do is cause a stir, because that could change the timeline, and the more trips they make, the greater the risk."

She doesn't get it. He tried to explain. "If they're determined to get you, they will. Realistically you need to disguise yourself and get a new identity and a new job. Stay away from friends and family. Start again."

She looked at him, appalled. "I'm not going to do that!" The people on the next table glanced their way, and Jace frowned a warning. Floss leaned forward and lowered her voice. "I'd lose everything; my whole life. Even with a new identity – and God knows how I'm supposed to get that – I couldn't work in the same field because it's quite small, and I'd be recognized. The obvious thing for IEMA to do is check out all female research scientists in my age group. So I'd lose my home, my family and friends, a job I love, and they could *still* find me if they're as relentless as you say!"

"There's no point making it easy for them."

"There's no point living a life that isn't mine."

"You'll feel differently if they arrest you."

"Even if they do, there's always the possibility they might believe what I tell them about Quinn."

"They might, at that. What they'll know for absolute certain, though, because Kayla saw it and you'll admit it, is that you've time travelled. And they don't recognize any mitigating circumstances for timecrime. And they won't send you back to your own time."

Floss said, "Why don't we use the TiTrav to go back and warn ourselves?"

Jace quoted, "Encountering yourself is theorized to be dangerous to the fabric of reality."

Floss rolled her eyes. "I've already encountered my younger self! You're being annoying. You told me all this physics stuff went over your head."

"Some of it stuck."

"What are *you* going to do now? About Quinn?"

"Realistically, there's nothing I can do. The bastard was right. It was always my word against his, but now there's evidence I time travelled, forget it." His eyes narrowed and he gave a bleak smile. "Not that I plan on being realistic. When you take the TiTrav back to Ryker, I'll come with you and stay in 2050. While I'm deciding what to do I might go someplace remote, Scotland maybe. Camp, survive off the land."

"But that would be like being back in 2185!"

"I'm not intending to be there for long. Just till I work out the best way to crack this."

"If they went to future London, they could see you'd lived there. That would prove your story."

"It would prove I'd travelled to the future illegally and stayed, not that Quinn dumped me there."

"I don't know – no one would believe you went there by choice."

They ordered desserts. After the meagre and monotonous diet Jace had survived on for five years, meals were a recurring pleasure. He ate a spoonful of fudge cake and felt an involuntary blissful smile spread over his features as the chocolate melted on his tongue. Floss was looking at him in a funny way. "What?"

"It's nothing – just . . ." She glanced away as she muttered, "For a moment you looked like your old photos."

Their meal finished, coffee drunk, Jace made a last attempt to persuade Floss to take evasive action. She remained adamant.

"Whatever. I'll take my chances. Just like you're doing."

He gave up. "Let's go to the flat and you can pack a bag. We'll have to leave fast if the SWAT team turns up banging on the door."

"Quinn came on his own last time."

"He wasn't arresting you then." He signalled to the waiter for the bill. "Perhaps you should have taken him up on his offer."

She gave him a look. "Yeah. What was I thinking? I could be at home with my feet up now, instead of getting lectures on time paradoxes from tiresome ex-time cops."

The waiter handed Jace the bill, and he realized he couldn't pay it. Floss grinned at his discomfiture and plucked it from his hand. "My treat." She gave the waiter her credit card.

"I said I'd take the TiTrav back straight away, and I think I'd better just in case IEMA catch up with us before I do. I don't want to let Ryker down."

"We'll go as soon as we've collected your stuff." Jace smiled. "Maybe he'll let us borrow it for a bit. Give us time to rob a few banks and buy a couple of private islands, as a fallback."

CHAPTER 40

Expect the unexpected

Full of new energy in spite of his aches and bruises, Quinn got out his second pistol, loaded the ammunition and put it in his concealed waistband holster. He changed the TiTrav's password, then set the date and location for his trip to the future.

When he had taken Jace to 2180 London, he had chosen to leave him at 7.30 pm GMT, while it was still light enough to see, but the sun was setting and darkness about to fall. Now he set the time for 7.35 pm, so he would avoid meeting his former self (a big IEMA no-no) but Jace would not yet have been able to escape his bonds. Another fight with Jace was the last thing he wanted. He set the details of the return journey to his apartment, five minutes from the present time, and switched on the limiter. After checking he had not forgotten anything, he pressed the two buttons with a feeling of anticipation.

The blackness cleared. Quinn gazed around, frowning. The TiTrav had malfunctioned somehow, had moved him in space not time . . . Bunhill Fields looked exactly the same as it did in 2050; well-kept, its grass mown and stone paths clear, apart from a few scattered autumn leaves from the big trees. A wilted posy of flowers lay beside William Blake's grave. The area was deserted, but beyond the murmur of the breeze moving in the branches he could hear faint sounds of people and traffic. He consulted the screen. The last trip pane showed the correct date, just as he had entered it. The fading amber evening light confirmed the time was right – but this was not future London. If the TiTrav was not working properly, it might be better to get a pod home rather than trust it to take him. Ryker could no doubt sort it out . . .

Quinn walked towards the exit to City Road. The gate was closed and locked; of course, the Fields would be shut at this hour. He'd have to climb over, which looked do-able, just about, in spite of the gate's row of gold-painted spear heads. Outside, the pavement was teeming with people, a mixture of workers going home and revellers commencing a night out. Something seemed a little odd about them as he got nearer . . . many were wearing close-fitting dark glasses. He noticed a woman in a long dress with a glowing, rippling pattern running over it, rather like the skin of a cuttlefish, then he saw that quite a few of the clothes had integral lights . . . a man had one muscled arm bare, displaying a luminous tattoo of a dragon.

Quinn was right up to the gate by now. Wesley's Chapel was there across the road – its courtyard occupied by an encampment of scruffily dressed families – and the Georgian townhouse next to it, but the other buildings were . . . entirely different. One's glass façade resembled a huge screen, showing adverts; a flawless woman's face smiled enigmatically, her deep blue eyes enticing. TOUCH YOUR DREAMS . . . WITH ZENSA. Her eyelashes dipped, the image faded. A wholesome young couple at the top of a skyscraper toasting each other in Coca Cola followed, and Quinn returned to the matter in hand. Exercising caution, working out where to place each foot beforehand, he climbed over the gate and dropped to the pavement. He looked about him, oblivious to the covert stares of passers-by at his clothes and the cuts on his face.

The road had strange markings on it and was crammed with nose-to-tail pods, smaller than those he was used to, moving at a crawl, slowed by people dodging between them. Silicon Roundabout was now multi-layered, roads swooping and twisting around it. Skyscrapers shouldered along the City skyline, which more resembled Dubai than the London he knew.

His brand new TiTrav had not malfunctioned after all. Something must have happened to avert the disaster with the contraceptive virus. This, he finally accepted, was future London in the year 2180. The old uninhabited and ruined London was gone forever, as was his best and simplest opportunity to rid himself of Jace.

Why hadn't his future self told him more, given him some useful information? He must have had his reasons. Most likely, it was important his former/present self did not deviate from his current course, even if that involved blunders he would avoid if he knew about them.

There was no point lingering, nothing for him here. A shabby child asked him for spare coins, and Quinn shook his head impatiently. He pressed the buttons to return to his own time.

CHAPTER 41

Parting and meeting

Saturday, 7th May 2050

Jace told Floss she didn't have to come with him, but she wanted to see the TiTrav safely back in Ryker's hands, as she had promised. Not that she didn't trust Jace; but something might go wrong... also, she was worried about him. His determination to get even, coupled with zero idea of how to do it, was likely to end in disaster. Perhaps Ryker would talk some sense into him.

She reminded herself that none of this was any of her business.

Jace thought it safest to arrive in a nearby park and walk to Ryker's railway arch, in case he had a customer in his workshop. Floss wore trousers and jacket from her 2050 wardrobe to blend in, but Jace only had his Primark clothes, so they set the time for 9.30 pm, after dark when they would be less visible. Spinning, blackness; then wind sighing in the trees and the smell of rain and mown grass greeted them. A line of streetlights fifty yards away showed where the road was. They walked to a lamppost by the railings, and Jace linked his fingers to give Floss a leg up. No one was about in the scruffy streets.

They reached Ryker's cul de sac and saw light gleaming

from his windows. All the other buildings were dark. Floss rang the bell; the dog barked and after a moment Ryker opened the door.

He smiled, as if pleased his confidence in her had been warranted. "You brought it back, then. Come in." He nodded at Jace and they went inside. Ryker found them a couple of chairs, then got out three bottles of Tiger Beer, flipped off the caps and passed them round.

Floss took off the TiTrav and handed it to Ryker, who laid it by his computer. He turned to Jace. "Made up your mind what you're going to do?"

"Not as such," Jace said.

"He's going to go to Scotland, live rough and seethe for a bit," Floss interpreted. She told him about the encounter with Quinn at Kayla's, on the principle that being in possession of Quinn's TiTrav, he needed to know. Ryker listened without saying much, though she could tell he appreciated the bit about her kicking Quinn.

Then he said, "I've been thinking. What I want to do is hire this out, but there's two problems with that. One, all my contacts are crooks, and not all of them can be trusted. It won't be long before someone decides not to bring it back. Two, one of them might do something stupid that'll mess up the world. I don't want to wake up one morning and find myself living in a dictatorship or some post-apocalyptic wasteland, and if it was my fault I'd feel bad about it. What I need is someone I can rent out with the TiTrav, who'd keep it on his wrist and stop the punters doing anything too bonkers with it. He'd have to be able to look after himself if things turned nasty." He looked at Jace. "Dunno if you'd be interested . . . ? Gamekeeper turned poacher type of thing. I'd pay you. We'd have to have a trial period, see if it worked, but if it did, we'd be like partners."

Floss could see Jace was torn; on the one hand, it went

against everything he and IEMA stood for; he'd turned down a similar offer from Quinn with contempt. On the other hand, Ryker wasn't going to leave the TiTrav sitting in a drawer, and if Jace agreed he'd have the chance to limit irresponsible time travel. Plus right now he was short on other options.

Ryker said, "I'd want you to keep it, so if I get searched I'm clean. I'd have to work out a way of contacting you. Dead letter box, maybe."

Floss thought this a promising idea. She said to Jace, "That would make it much easier for you to hide from the authorities."

Jace was eyeing Ryker narrowly. "This may sound a dumb question, most people could do with more money, but we have to be talking about millions to hire a TiTrav. You don't strike me as the type to be hankering after a mansion and a yacht. Why are you prepared to risk your freedom for money?"

Ryker's manner became less friendly, his voice cool. "That's my business."

"If we're going to be partners you have to trust me. If someone's blackmailing you I need to know."

"It's not that! Like you said, I could do with more money, who couldn't." He took a swig of beer. Jace waited. After a moment Ryker muttered, "It's for Pete's daughter. Saffy McGuire. I told you five years ago, he was going to use that TiTrav to buy her a little place of her own and pay for university. I thought I could do it instead. Seems only right."

This pleased Floss. She said, "That's nice of you."

Ryker seemed embarrassed by her approval. "I might buy myself a new bigger workshop too," he said defensively. "Instead of renting." He turned back to Jace. "Interested?"

"I'll give it a go. Can you get me a new chip?"

Ryker nodded. "No problem. You can start the job now by taking Floss home, then come back here and we'll sort out the logistics."

Floss got Jace to drop her in a side street near King's Cross. He waited while she rang Zoë in Cambridge and asked if she could crash on her floor for a week. This settled, they each paused before parting forever. Jace said, "Well. It was nice knowing you."

"I hope everything works out. Do be careful."

Jace nodded. "You too." His fingers moved to the buttons. He glanced around to check no one was looking in their direction. Floss added quickly, "If you ever find yourself in London, my time, look me up."

"I will. Good luck," he said, and vanished.

Floss walked inside the station and found the ticket office, waiting in line behind a couple of other travellers. She'd probably never see Jace again, never find out what happened to him. And this was good; her life was back to normal, like she wanted, and she had no reason to feel this almost physical sense of loss. A moment later someone else joined the queue immediately behind her. An absurd conviction that it was Jace standing there waiting to surprise her made her heart beat faster. *Don't be ridiculous.* She turned around.

Quinn smiled at her in a matter-of-fact way as if they had only just parted, having arranged to meet here. The lacerations on his face were nearly healed. In his time it had evidently been a few weeks since the fight. His outfit looked only a little outré; a short black jacket with a military cut over a plain white shirt, black britches and boots. He was clearly trying to blend in.

How did he get here? Has he got the TiTrav off Jace? Oh God, is Jace okay . . .

Floss put her hands behind her in case he was planning to grab her again, though surely he wouldn't with all these people around . . . She scowled to hide her fear. "What do you want?"

Her hostility appeared to amuse him. He said pleasantly, "I want to buy you a drink and talk to you."

"We have nothing to talk about."

His eyebrows went up. "Leaving the manifest untruth of that to one side for the moment, I'm sure you'd like to hear what I have to say. I came to give you a friendly warning."

The people in front of her had moved on, tickets purchased. The clerk said, "Where to?" Floss had no intention of revealing her destination to Quinn. If he knew where she was going, there would be no point going there. And if Jace was in prison or dead she wanted to know.

"Sorry, it's okay," she said to the ticket man, and turned away from the counter. "All right, then," she said grudgingly to Quinn. "Just don't try anything."

Quinn led her across the concourse and into a wine bar, Floss staying a step behind in order to keep an eye on him, her anxiety about Jace growing. He crossed the room to a small table in the corner, his height, assurance, and unusual clothes drawing glances from the other customers. The waiter appeared with a menu, which Quinn scanned rapidly.

"Champagne. A bottle of the Laurent Perrier cuvée rosé."

The waiter left. *What on earth will that cost?* Sidetracked for a moment, she hissed, "I'm not going to pay for this!"

"When I offer to buy a young woman a drink, I do not expect her to pay."

"But –"

Indulgently, he removed an American Express card from his pocket, and showed it to her before putting it back. "I came prepared."

The waiter returned with assorted canapés and the champagne in a misted silver bucket. He peeled off deep pink foil, eased out the cork and poured the wine. Floss started to pick up her glass, saw how much her hand was trembling, and put it down again. She had to know. She turned towards Quinn and took his left hand in her left hand – for a split second he misunderstood and looked surprised and gratified – then pulled up his cuff with her right so she could see his TiTrav. Floss stared at its unfamiliar blackness and newness. She let his hand drop again, breathing deeply, reassured.

Quinn was looking at her shrewdly. "It's not the one Jace had. I see you are relieved." Floss did not answer. She drank some champagne instead, hardly registering how delicious it was. Quinn continued, "We haven't apprehended him yet. Maybe we won't, though knowing him as I do, it would not astonish me if he did something rash and made our job easy. But that's not what I came to discuss. Nor did I come to tell you, though I suspect you will be interested if not altogether surprised, that there's been a swerve in the timeline. Humanity's future is secure, at least for the next couple of centuries. The disastrous mutation of the contraceptive virus has been averted."

Floss was pleased by this news, which meant her plan had worked. Her father's forethought, with her assistance, had saved humanity; it was a sort of lasting memorial to him. She glowed, and wished she could tell Jace. He'd probably find out...

Quinn was watching her. "I note you don't ask me how this happened. Of course, a side effect of this good news is that all traces of the old future London have been wiped."

Quinn paused briefly while she digested the significance of this. The evidence of Jace's five years there had gone. No wonder Quinn was looking smug. He refilled her glass. "Now to the real reason for my visit. I feel responsible for you. I like to think we became ... friends while you were in my time. You're in trouble. I want to help if I can."

"That's really not necessary. I'm fine."

"So you say." He focused intently on her, gazing into her eyes. "On Monday – my time – a team will be coming to pick you up. They'll arrive outside Zoë Parker's flat in Cambridge, at half past midnight tonight."

"How did you know I was going to Zoë's?"

"I made it my business to know."

Creepy. "You came to warn me not to be there?"

"Yes," Quinn said simply.

"Why?"

He sat back in his chair. "Really Floss, you can't be as naïve as all that. Why do you think?"

"Because they might believe what I tell them."

He considered, then nodded as if awarding her half a point. "There's that, too," he said.

CHAPTER 42

The meaning of life

Floss put down her champagne glass and rang Zoë; apologized, thanked her, and told her she'd had a change of plan. As she ended the call, an idea came to her. Raising the phone she took a photo of Quinn. She studied the result, holding it to her left, out of his reach. "Hmm. A nice clear shot of the Chief of IEMA Intelligence sitting in a 2015 bar, drinking champagne and committing timecrime. Might come in handy some day, you never know."

She went to replace the phone in her pocket, and Quinn's hand shot out and grabbed her wrist. His eyes were cold, staring into hers; she hadn't seen them like that since the day she first met him, when he'd picked her up from her own time.

Floss didn't care. She returned his stare. "You're not going to intimidate me, so don't bother trying. And I wouldn't advise attempting to steal my phone in a bar full of people."

After a moment Quinn released her and she put the phone away. "You're right, it wouldn't be wise and it's not necessary either." He leaned back, once more easy and relaxed. "If you think I can't talk my way out of a little thing like that, you don't know me very well."

Floss glanced at her watch. "I must be off. Thanks for the drink."

Without more ado she got up and headed for the door. As she opened it, she turned and saw Quinn still sitting at the table, watching her as he lifted the bottle to pour himself another glass of champagne.

Floss walked towards the Tube entrance, suddenly bone weary. It had been a long day; after a normal day's work there had been the trip to see her old boss, then the disastrous visit to Kayla's and the fight between Jace and Quinn, then a brief break at Pizza Express, then on her way to Cambridge the unwelcome encounter with Quinn. Longing just to get home and go to bed, she walked quickly down the escalator. Someone behind her was in a hurry too, boots tapping on the metal treads, keeping pace with her. Had Quinn followed her after all? Most likely it was some random stranger running late. Still, she was glad to reach the bottom of the escalator and merge with the crowd. She moved fast, slipping between the other passengers making for the platform. A train was waiting, doors open, and she hopped on. The doors clunked shut, the train departed. She got off at the next station, Highbury and Islington. Out of the corner of her eye she saw a tall figure in a flashy black jacket, silver buttons catching the light, emerge from one carriage along. For a moment she thought it was Quinn, but it wasn't. She stood still among the milling crowd.

"Jace! What are you doing here?"

Monday, June 13th 2050

The studio lights were hot, and Quinn's skin felt strange under the foundation and powder the makeup girl had applied. In the darkness beyond the table and chairs, three cameramen stood by their equipment. The huge screen behind the set was showing a clip of Floss, her face pale and unsmiling, surrounded by police who escorted her past the crowd, up the steps and into the Victorian splendour of the Royal Courts of Justice.

The screen changed to a livestream panorama of London, and the presenter turned to him. They'd had a brief word before the interview started, and Nandita Rowe had remained steely, brisk and professional in spite of Quinn's efforts to charm her. He surmised from this she planned to give him a hard time. After all, it was what she was renowned for.

She spoke to camera. "You'll remember that a month ago, the International Event Modification Authority got permission from the World Government to lift Florence Dryden from 2015, for reasons that were not disclosed to the public. She subsequently went missing, and was arrested yesterday in her own time on suspicion of timecrime. With me this evening to discuss this unusual – I may say unprecedented – case is Chief of Intelligence at IEMA, Ansel Quinn. Mr Quinn, first of all, you brought this young woman here. Wasn't it a little careless of you to lose her?"

"In order not to 'lose' her, as you put it, we'd have had to watch her twenty-four seven, or incarcerate her in a TT-proof cell. We chose to treat her like the innocent human being she was."

"But she turned out not to be quite so innocent, didn't she? She's now in prison awaiting trial for timecrime. Are you going to admit you got it wrong?"

Quinn smiled. "Before I deal with that question, Nandita, I'd like to say something about Miss Dryden. She's had an incredibly raw deal, for which I bear much of the responsibility. We at IEMA mistakenly believed her to be the catalyst for impending worldwide disaster, and it turned out we were wrong; we took her from her own time and once we'd done that, abiding by WG rules we were not able to take her back. She lost her home, her family and friends. One can understand that, offered the opportunity to return to her own time, she took it."

Nandita changed tack. "Florence Dryden is making the extraordinary allegation that you yourself possess an illegal TiTrav and are guilty of timecrime."

Quinn nodded. "After what she has been through, you can't blame her for being confused and upset." Nandita leaned forwards, nostrils flaring, but before she could press him, Quinn added, as if in passing, "Let me be clear, there is no truth in those allegations. Miss Dryden is mistaken." He smiled. "My concern is to eliminate timecrime, not participate in it."

"How do you explain Florence Dryden's making such a strange mistake?"

"I can't explain – I can only surmise. As you know, she's been seen in company with Jace Carnady, who is wanted for the theft of a TiTrav five years ago. I'm afraid he has been imposing on her. Let me say again, Miss Dryden is, I am certain, blameless in this matter, and I'm very much hoping for an acquittal should the case come to trial. Meanwhile I'm lobbying for her release without charge."

"There's little doubt she time travelled – you yourself admit to seeing her do it."

"Indeed I did. The Head of Timecrime, Kayla Hartley-Hunter, and I both witnessed her and Jace Carnady using a TiTrav."

"Then it's difficult to see how you can argue –"

"My contention is that the circumstances are exceptional. It's quite unfair to prosecute her for breaking a law which was not in existence in her own time."

The interview continued. Quinn was amused by Nandita's increasingly aggressive attempts to rile him. He enjoyed making the points he had come there to make in spite of her, and watching her mounting frustration as he remained calm and even humorous under fire. He bore her no ill will for trying to trip him. She was only doing her job. Once the interview was over and she thanked him icily, he very nearly asked her out to dinner.

Monday, June 13th 2050, evening

Ryker sat back in his new executive ergonomic leather and chrome swivel chair, adjusted its angle to his precise requirements, put his feet up on the desk and took the lids off the various parts of his Chinese meal. Curtis dozed on the floor beside him. Outside, wind howled and rain beat against the windows. Ryker opened a beer and brought up the BBC to find something to watch. There was Nandita Rowe, done up to the nines, grilling some luckless bugger. He bit into a spring roll and smiled as he remembered that guy on Gentle Arts calling her a Doberdoodle. Then the screen changed to the luckless bugger, and he saw it was Quinn, and he was talking about Floss, and she had been arrested.

Ryker sat up, bits of chicken falling out of his spring roll. He'd helped her steal the TiTrav, and now she was in bad trouble because of it. They'd have to rescue her, and that would be impossible now she was under arrest. When not escorted by police, time criminals were kept in cells with floor-to-ceiling metal rods every three feet, some with random jutting loops of steel. TiTravs were programmed not to time into places where there was insufficient clear space. Sufficient space was defined as 6 by 6 by 8 feet, and no oncoming obstructions such as a person, a drone or a truck. Okay, Ryker could adjust the safety parameters on the TiTrav, but he wouldn't want to chance materializing and finding a metal rod through his body. Better to go back and pick her up before IEMA did.

He made himself go on eating though his appetite had gone – no sense in wasting food – and continued watching. What was Quinn playing at, pretending to be keen to get Floss released? He must be up to something... Nandita Rowe wound up the interview, and the programme changed to an item about humanoid robotics which, under normal circumstances, would have interested Ryker. He turned it off, put the cartons and the rest of the food in the bin, shrugged into his jacket and picked up his keys. Curtis joined him, tail wagging.

"It's your lucky day, Curtis. An extra walk."

They went into the pouring rain to summon Jace.

Almost hidden by dripping shrubbery was a missing bar in the railings, a convenient entrance to the park after hours. No one was out in this dismal weather – not that anyone round here cared what you did, but Ryker was habitually cautious. He ducked unobtrusively through the gap, followed by Curtis. They made their way to an overgrown statue of a dog, a memorial to someone's long-dead pet. Ryker crouched round the back and moved a decaying branch. At the base of the statue's plinth was a deep crack in the stone. Ryker drew out a diary, its covers buckling with the damp, turned to that day's date, and wrote '9.20 pm' on it before replacing the diary and the branch. He made his way back to the workshop, where Jace would now be waiting for him.

Saturday, 7th May 2015

Jace said abruptly, "You have to come with me." He was hardly looking at Floss; he was scanning the faces of the crowd, many of whom were giving him covert glances as they passed. "IEMA's going to take you back to face trial, and I don't know when they'll pick you up."

"Bloody hell." Floss began scanning the sea of faces, too. "Just give me a minute." She reached for her phone. "I'll have to tell my mother I'm going."

"No time." Jace grabbed her hand, pulled her back along the platform, and round a corner to a relatively secluded staircase. "Hold on to me."

As the world went black, Floss realized that in addition to greater problems, she was time travelling without a patch and would shortly be feeling very sick indeed.

CHAPTER 43

Floss's team

Jace took Floss to Ryker's first. The workshop appeared around them to a volley of furious barks from Curtis. Understandably, the dog really hated people materializing into his owner's space. Floss dropped Jace's arm and made a dash for the sink.

"Curtis!" Ryker put his Chinese meal down on the computer desk and swung his feet to the floor. Now Curtis was quiet, horrible noises from Floss in the kitchenette competed with the item on humanoid robotics Ryker had been watching. He turned it off. "What's happening?"

"IEMA arrested Floss. You saw it on the news and sent me to pick her up before they did. I found her with Quinn."

"*Quinn?* How did he get there?"

Jace shrugged. "Must have got his hands on a TiTrav. Perhaps a Department one."

"What was he doing? Arresting her?"

"Don't think so, they were having a drink. Champagne. Seemed more like he was chatting her up. Bastard just can't help himself. I skulked round corners till she came out alone."

Floss was now rinsing her mouth and gulping water. She

joined them, her face pallid and sweaty. "He was doing the same as you. He came to warn me IEMA was going to arrest me."

Jace said, "Then his warning didn't work, or he was up to something. They did arrest you. Ryker saw it on the news today and sent me to get you. By collecting you, I've changed the timeline so that didn't happen, and now he can't remember it."

Ryker grimaced. "I hate that. Makes me feel like I'm losing my marbles. Another time I'll come with you." He turned to Floss. "Have a seat. How are you feeling? Here, I know what you need." He went to a cupboard and got out a bottle and three mismatched glasses, then poured three generous shots and handed them round. "Have some of Jace's brandy."

"Thanks." Floss took the glass with shaky fingers. "I'll feel better in a minute. I must tell you, you know future London with no people?" They nodded. "Quinn told me that doesn't happen now. They defeated the contraceptive virus with my father's samples."

Jace wasn't sure how he felt about this. The place where he'd spent five years of his life now only existed in all its intricate reality in his memory; the magical stuff as well as his grinding struggle to survive. He remembered the infinite stars on a clear night, man's ugly buildings transformed to beauty by the plants which covered them, the tiger who brought her cubs to the pond that first year. He remembered the bitter cold in winter, his desperate stratagems to survive, the absolute loneliness. Quinn, Floss and Ryker had seen that future London, but they had been passing through. It belonged to him alone.

"So you saved the human race?" Ryker grinned at Floss. "Bet the buggers don't thank you."

❖

Saturday, 7th May 2015

Quinn had decided to go himself with the IEMA team detailed to pick up Floss. Normally Kayla would have dealt with it. They could only arrest her after her return from 2050, since she could not be taken into custody for a crime she had not yet committed. After his warning, she was surely bright enough to evade capture – but her arrest would not be disastrous in any case. He was in charge of the investigation, he could remove her phone and delete the photo. And without Jace to confirm her story, a jury was no more likely to believe her than Kayla had been. Another consideration; so far, he'd failed to make any headway with Floss; if she was once more out of her own time, isolated, incarcerated and facing trial, she might be more pleased to see him. Which ever way it went, Quinn was confident he would win.

After the fruitless trip to Cambridge, her home earlier in the evening was the next option. They materialized in a deserted dead end round the back of her building, then Quinn and two of the team went to her front door. A neighbour obligingly pressed the lock release to let them in, reassured by Quinn's manner over the entry phone. At the top of the staircase was the duck-egg blue door to Floss's flat. Quinn knocked, and when there was no answer, Farouk picked the lock.

The place was empty. Quinn looked around with interest; Floss's flat, though small, was decorated and furnished with quirky charm, redolent of her personality. He could see why she'd been less than enthusiastic about the bland windowless apartment in 2050. Next, the team went to the flat a couple of weeks in the future, during the day. To his relief, everything was exactly the same, with the addition of a light film of dust. They enquired discreetly at her workplace; they searched her mother's flat while she was out. They found no trace of Floss. The obvious conclusion was that she had not returned to 2015, and could be absolutely anywhere, any time.

Monday, June 13th 2050, evening

"What happens next?" Now Floss no longer felt queasy, she had leisure to contemplate her situation, and a pretty depressing one it was. She slumped in her seat. "I won't be able to go back, will I – I've lost . . . everything. My job. My flat. My whole life." Her eyes filled. Oh God, she was going to cry with self-pity. *Pull yourself together.* A tear spilled on to her cheek, and she brushed it away. Her lip trembled and she couldn't stop it. Both men were looking apprehensively at her, which didn't help.

"I can set you up with a chip," Ryker volunteered. "If you want, you can work for me. Just for now. Go with Jace and keep an eye on him when I rent out the TiTrav."

After a moment when it seemed he might protest, Jace said, "Great idea. I could do with someone to delegate stuff to. Be nice to have my own team again. I've got a spare room you can use – I'm renting a cottage on the Isle of Harris, in the Outer Hebrides. You'll be safe there. Remote doesn't get much remoter. Grass, sheep, boulders, sea, weather, and a bus once a day to the post office/café if you want a bit of excitement."

Floss felt more dejected than ever. She didn't want to go to the Outer Hebrides. Then she remembered Jace had already been through what she was experiencing now. He had not moaned. She hadn't been sympathetic enough, she realized – and they had offered her somewhere to live and a job, of sorts, which was really nice of them. She gulped some brandy and forced a smile. "Thank you, that would be awesome."

"Look on it like you're taking a year out."

"That's right," Ryker said. "Lots of things can happen in a year. You may get your old life back. You may find a new one you like better. We've got a time machine. That gives us options. There might come a time when you can go right back to where you left off, you never know."

Jace said, "Yeah. Sometimes you've just got to go with the flow."

Suddenly Floss felt happier. It could just be the brandy hitting her empty stomach, but things could be worse – much worse. She could be in jail. Maybe everything would work out. She smiled, a genuine smile, at the men's attempts to rally her, and then smiled again at their look of relief. Raising her glass, she said, "To the future."

Jace raised his. "And the past. And to possibilities. We're like gods playing a game of chess, where any piece can be moved to any square, and any move taken back."

Ryker grinned. "Here's to making the most of it."

Sunday, 8th May 2015

Emma was washing up when she heard a noise coming from the living room. She paused, plate in hand, then Floss's voice said, "Mum! Where are you?"

"Coming." She wiped her hands and went into the living room. Floss was standing there grinning, wearing combat trousers and a vest top Emma hadn't seen before, her hair in a plait down her back. Floss's hair was blonder, her skin slightly golden from the sun; she looked well, bright-eyed and excited. She rushed up and gave her mother a quick hug.

"Where did you spring from?"

"2050. I've come to tell you some really important stuff, and to ask a favour."

"Better sit down, then. Can I get you anything?"

"No thanks." Floss sat on the sofa next to Emma. "First, now I'm in the future, here it'll be like I've gone missing. I'm sorry, it's going to be grim for you, with everyone sympathizing and the police investigating and everything. But you mustn't worry, because I'm fine, alive and well, just thirty-five years ahead. And maybe the gone missing thing won't even have to happen, because we might be able to sort things out so I can come back to the same time. But even if I can't, I'll still come and see you now and then, so you'll know I'm all right."

This was unwelcome news; a bit as if Floss was moving to Australia, but without email or telephones. Emma liked having her daughter living in the same city. But if it was to keep her safe . . .

Floss fished in her pocket and got out photos and bits of paper. She handed the photos over. Emma looked. The first showed a solidly-built man in his thirties sitting in a bar, astute blue eyes staring into the camera. At the top of the photo Floss had written: ANSEL QUINN – baddie. Floss handed her a second photo, of a dark-haired man wearing a piratical jacket and shirt: JACE CARNADY – goodie. Emma raised her eyebrows.

"Just in case either of them come calling. It's really important not to trust Quinn, though he's very persuasive and you'd probably like him."

Emma nodded. "Who's Jace?"

"He's the guy I work with now."

"He's very good-looking. What's the favour you wanted?"

Floss handed a piece of paper to Emma. On it was written next Wednesday's date, and a string of numbers. Below that was a list of account details and passwords.

"Do the lottery with those numbers. You'll win about one and a half million. Then you can pay off my mortgage for me."

Emma nodded. "Okay."

Floss screwed up her eyes. "It might be more complicated than that – I'm not too sure if they'll let you do it or not. But you've got my keys, and can get into my laptop and use those passwords. If you can't pay off the mortgage, then pay a chunk into my bank account so at least the monthly payments get made."

"Leave it with me. Creditors generally don't care who pays off a bill, and with that sort of money, if I have a problem I can get advice."

"I knew you'd be able to sort it out. Keep an eye on the flat for me, won't you?"

"Of course." Emma looked fondly at her daughter. "What are you doing in your new life? Have you got friends, somewhere to live?"

Floss grinned. "I've got a team. At the moment I'm living in the Outer Hebrides with Jace." She dug in her pocket, got out a handful of small cowrie shells in delicate shades of yellow and pink still trickling sand, and handed them to her mother. "I picked these up on the beach. We're right next to it." Out of another pocket she produced a new-fangled phone and brought up a photo of her and Jace and a lot of empty scenery.

Emma wondered if Floss was going out with this Jace . . .

Floss read her mind. "*Mu-um!* We just work together. He's still got a thing going on about his ex. There's Ryker too, you know, you met him. I've got a new job that I thought I wouldn't like, so I put off coming to see you, but actually it's great, sort of demanding, but interesting. Lots of time travelling. Jace is teaching me Krav Maga and how to shoot. Quite different from my proper job. I hope to come home eventually, but I'm looking on this as a sabbatical."

"As long as you're happy . . ."

"I am." Floss beamed. "It's brilliant."

ABOUT THE AUTHOR

Lexi Revellian lives and works in London – in Islington and Hoxton, where her novels are set – making jewellery and silver under her real name, Lexi Dick. She has made pieces for 10 Downing Street, Her Majesty the Queen and Lady Thatcher.

Lexi started writing in 2006, and has been unable to stop.

❖

To be notified when Lexi Revellian publishes a new novel (no spam will be sent, ever) email: lexi14@hotmail.com

❖

www.lexirevellian.com

OTHER NOVELS BY LEXI REVELLIAN

REMIX

Caz Tallis restores rocking horses in her London workshop. When shabby but charismatic Joe and his dog turn up on her roof terrace, she is reluctantly drawn into investigating a rock star's murder from three years before - an unsolved case the police have closed. Which, as her best friend James says, is rather like poking a furnace with a short stick . . .

REPLICA

Accidentally duplicated, homeless, penniless and pursued by MI5, Beth's replica must learn how to survive on icy London streets. Unaware of what has happened, the original Beth falls for the agent hunting her double. As the replica proves hard to catch and the stakes get higher, he has to decide whose side he is on.

ICE DIARIES

It's 2018 and Tori's managing. Okay, so London is under twenty metres of snow, almost everybody has died in a pandemic or been airlifted south, and the only animals around are rats – but she's doing fine. Really. The problem is that eventually provisions will run out. Tori needs to make the two-thousand-mile journey south to a warm climate and start again.

One day she comes across an exhausted and wounded stranger face-down in the snow. Morgan is a cage fighter from a tougher, meaner world where it's a mistake to trust people. He's on the run from the leader of the gang he used to work with. He's disturbingly hot. And he has a snowmobile.

WOLF BY THE EARS

21 year-old Tyger Rebel Thomson, desperate to escape from her New Age traveller upbringing, works as a waitress and cleaner while studying in her spare time for a degree that will lead to a career in the City. Her goal is to save enough to buy a tiny flat of her own. She has no time for boyfriends; she's working too hard.

Her agency sends her to clean for a billionaire Russian oligarch. Grisha Markovic is a man with enemies, many of whom would like him dead. When Grisha notices how bright Tyger is, he makes her his PA and takes a fatherly interest in her. But she begins to suspect that the fatal crash his last PA died in may not have been an accident...

Tyger could be on her way to the life of her dreams – assuming, that is, she lives long enough to get there.

TORBREK...and the Dragon Variation

An adventure story with daring deeds, dragons, friends, foes and romance – and no darned elves.

When Tor saves the Princess from the terrifying, fire-breathing dragon and delivers her to the handsome knight she is destined to marry, nothing is quite as it seems; the dragon is overweight and hasn't breathed fire for years; the Princess and her supposed suitor don't hit it off; and Tor shouldn't be in the rebel cavalry at all because she's a woman disguised as a man. Which doesn't help when she is attracted to a fellow soldier...

TIME CHILD and other stories

Eight short stories about life, death, romance, time travel, angels and publishing.

TRAV ZANDER, sequel to TORBREK

Trav Zander is a freelance solver of problems. His latest job, for a fee of fifty thousand ducats, is to locate the dragon in the mountains, and bring it to Carl of Thrales, recent inheritor of the kingdom of Ser. Carl wants the ultimate weapon; a warrior dragon. And if he puts Zander in the dungeons instead of paying him, it won't cost him a penny.

    Meanwhile, Torbrek disguises herself as a maid to work in Carl's palace and discover why he wants a fighting dragon . . .

❖

www.lexirevellian.com

Printed in Great Britain
by Amazon